Mario Puzo was born in New York and, following military service in World War II, attended New York's New School for Social Research and Columbia University. His best-selling novel, *The Godfather,* was preceded by two critically acclaimed novels, *The Dark Arena* (1952) and *The Fortunate Pilgrim* (1965). In 1978, he published *Fools Die,* followed by *The Sicilian* (1984), *The Fourth K* (1991), and the second installment in his Mafia trilogy, *The Last Don* (1996), which became an international best-seller and the highest-rated TV miniseries of 1997. In 2000, William Heinemann published posthumously the novel *Omertà*; and *The Family*, the last novel he wrote before his death, was published by Arrow Books in 2003. Mario Puzo also wrote many screenplays, including *Earthquake, Superman* and all three *Godfather* movies, for which he received two Academy Awards. He died in July 1999 at his home in Long Island, New York, at the age of seventy-eight.

# MARIO PUZO

# The Dark Arena

arrow books

This edition first published in the United Kingdom in 1992
by Mandarin Paperbacks

13 15 17 19 20 18 16 14 12

Copyright © Mario Puzo 1953, 1955

Mario Puzo has asserted his right under the Copyright, Designs and
Patents Act, 1988 to be identified as the author of this work

First published in Great Britain in 1973 by
William Heinemann

Arrow Books
Random House, 20 Vauxhall Bridge Road,
London SW1V 2SA

www.rbooks.co.uk

Addresses for companies within The Random House Group Limited
can be found at: www.randomhouse.co.uk/offices.htm

The Random House Group Limited Reg. No. 954009

A CIP catalogue record for this book
is available from the British Library

ISBN 9780099418023

The Random House Group Limited supports The Forest
Stewardship Council (FSC), the leading international forest
certification organisation. All our titles that are printed on
Greenpeace approved FSC certified paper carry the FSC logo.
Our paper procurement policy can be found at:
www.rbooks.co.uk/environment

Printed in the UK by CPI Bookmarque, Croydon, CR0 4TD

For Erika

"*Fathers and teachers, I ponder 'What is hell?' I maintain that it is the suffering of being unable to love.*"

"*Oh, there are some who remain proud and fierce even in hell, in spite of their certain knowledge and contemplation of the absolute truth; there are some fearful ones who have given themselves over to Satan and his proud spirit entirely. For such, hell is voluntary and ever consuming; they are tortured by their own choice. For they have cursed themselves, cursing God and life. They live upon their vindictive pride like a starving man in the desert sucking blood out of his own body. But they are never satisfied, and they refuse forgiveness, they curse God Who calls them. They cannot behold the living God without hatred, and they cry out that the God of life should be annihilated, that God should destroy Himself and His own creation. And they will burn in the fire of their own wrath forever and yearn for death and annihilation. But they will not attain to death . . .*"

THE BROTHERS KARAMAZOV

# THE DARK ARENA

# 1

WALTER MOSCA felt a sense of excitement and the last overwhelming loneliness before a homecoming. The few ruins outside of Paris were remembered and familiar landmarks, and now on the last leg of his journey he could hardly wait to come to his final destination, the heart of the ruined continent, the destroyed city that he had never thought he would see again. The landmarks leading into Germany were more familiar to him than the approaches to his own land, his own city.

The train rocked with speed. It was a troop train with replacements for the Frankfort garrison, but half the car was taken by civilian employees recruited from the States. Mosca touched his silk tie and smiled. It felt strange to him. He would feel more at home with the G.I.'s at the other end, and, he thought, so would most of the twenty or so civilians with him.

There were two dim lights, one at each end of the car. The windows were boarded up, as if the car had been built so that its occupants would not be able to see the vast ruins through which they would travel. The seats were long wooden benches, leaving only one very narrow aisle along one side.

Mosca stretched out on his bench and put the blue gym bag under his head for a pillow. In the bad light he could hardly recognize the other civilians.

They had all traveled on the same Army ship together, and like himself, they all seemed excited and eager to reach Frankfort. They talked loudly to be heard over the roar of the train, and Mosca could hear Mr. Gerald's voice dominating the rest. Mr. Gerald was the highest ranking civilian in the shipment. He had with him a set of golf clubs, and on board the ship had let everyone know that his civilian grade was equal to the rank of Colonel. Mr. Gerald was happy and cheerful, and Mosca had a vision of him playing golf over the ruins of a city, the long drive above flattened and level streets, the approach to a rounded heap of rubble, and putting carefully into the top of a decaying skull.

The speed of the train slackened as it moved into a small deserted station. Outside it was night, and in the blind railroad car it was very dark. Mosca dozed, hearing only vaguely the voices of the others. But as the train picked up speed leaving the station it shook him fully awake.

The civilians were talking more quietly now, and Mosca sat up to watch the soldiers at the other end of the car. Some were sleeping on the long benches, but there were three circles of light surrounding three card games, giving their end of the car a friendly glow. He felt a faint nostalgia for the life he had led so long and left just a few months ago. By the light of their candles he could see them drinking from their canteens, not water he felt sure, and breaking out K-rations to munch chocolate bars. A G.I. was always prepared, Mosca thought with a grin. Blankets on his back, candles in his pack, water or something better in his canteen, and a rubber in his wallet at all times. Ready for good luck or bad.

Mosca stretched out again on the bench and tried to sleep. But his body was as stiff and unyielding as the hard wood beneath it. The train had picked up speed and was going very fast now. He looked at his watch. It was nearly midnight, and it was still a good eight hours to Frankfort. He sat up, took a bottle from the small, blue gym bag and, resting his head against the boarded window, kept drinking until his body relaxed. He must have fallen asleep, for when he looked down again to the soldiers' end of the car, there was only one circle of candlelight; but in the darkness behind him he could still hear the voices of Mr. Gerald and a few other civilians. They must have been drinking for Mr. Gerald's voice was patronizing, condescending, and he was boasting of his coming power, how he would put his paper empire on an efficient basis.

Two candles detached themselves from the circle at the other end of the car, their flares wavering unevenly down the aisle. As they passed him, Mosca was startled out of his drowsiness. The G.I. carrying the candles had on his face a look of malevolent and stupid hatred. The bright, yellow glow of the candles dyed the already drink-flushed face a dark red and gave the sullen eyes a dangerous, senseless look.

"Hey, soldier," the voice of Mr. Gerald called out, "how about leaving us a light?"

The candle obediently came to rest near Mr. Gerald and his group of civilians and the sound of their voices rose, as if they had taken courage from the flickering light. They tried to include the G.I. in their conversation, but he, his candles resting on the bench, his own face in darkness, refused to answer. They forgot about the soldier and spoke of other things; only once Mr. Gerald, leaning into the candlelight as if to show himself with absolute trust, said condescendingly but with real kindness to the G.I., "We were all of us in the Army too, you know." And then with a laugh to the others. "Thank God that's over."

One of the other civilians said, "Don't be too sure, we still have the Russians."

They forgot about the G.I. again until suddenly over and above their voices, above the noise of the train running so blindly across the continent, the silent G.I. shouted loudly and in drunken arrogance, yet as if in some panic, "Shut up, shut up, don't talk so much, shut your goddamn mouths."

There was a moment of surprised, embarrassed silence, and then Mr. Gerald leaned his head into the candlelight again and said to the G.I. quietly, "You had better get to your end of the car, son." There was no answer from the G.I., and Mr. Gerald continued to speak, picking up where he had been interrupted.

Suddenly he was standing up, fully lit by the flaring candles, his voice cut off. And then he said quietly, without alarm but with almost terrified disbelief, "My God, I've been hurt. That soldier did something to me."

Mosca sat up straight and other dark figures rose from the benches, one of them knocking out a candlelight as he brushed it to the floor. Mr. Gerald, still standing but not so brightly lit, said in a quiet horrified voice, "That soldier stabbed me," and fell out of the light into the darkness of his bench.

Two men from the G.I. end of the car hurried down the aisle. By the light of the candles they carried, Mosca could see the glint of officer bars.

Mr. Gerald was saying over and over again, "I've been stabbed, that soldier stabbed me." In his voice the terror was gone, it was surprised, incredulous. Mosca could see him sitting upright on the bench and then, lit up by the full power of the three candles, could see the rent in the trouser leg, high up on the thigh, the dark stain flowing over and around it. The Lieutenant bent over, holding his candle close and gave an order to the soldier with him. The soldier ran down to the other end of the car and returned with blankets and a first-aid kit. They spread the blankets on the floor and made Mr. Gerald lie down. The soldier started to cut off the trouser leg, but Mr. Gerald said, "No, roll it up; I can get it mended." The Lieutenant looked at the wound.

"It's nothing much," the Lieutenant said. "Wrap him in a blanket." There was no sympathy in his young, blank face or in his voice, only an impersonal kindness. "We'll have an ambulance waiting in Frankfort, just in case. I'll wire at the next stop." Then he turned to the others and asked, "Where is he?"

The drunken G.I. had disappeared; Mosca, peering into the darkness, saw a form huddled in the corner of the bench before him. He said nothing.

The Lieutenant went to his end of the car and returned wearing his pistol belt. He threw the beam of his flashlight around the car until he saw the huddled form. He prodded it with his flashlight, at the same time drawing his pistol and hiding it behind him. The G.I. didn't move.

The Lieutenant poked him roughly. "Get up, Mulrooney." The G.I. opened his eyes, and when Mosca saw the dumb, sullen animal glare, he felt a sudden pity.

The Lieutenant kept the beam of his flashlight in the soldier's eyes, blinding him. He made Mulrooney stand up. When he saw that his hands were empty, he slipped his pistol back into its holster. Then he turned the G.I. around with a rough shove and searched him. He didn't find anything, so he threw the light of his flash on the bench. Mosca saw the bloodstained knife. The Lieutenant picked it up and pushed the G.I. ahead of him to the other end of the car.

The train began to slow down and gradually came to a halt. Mosca walked to the end of the car, opened the door and looked out. He saw the Lieutenant going to the station to wire ahead for the ambulance; otherwise there was no one. The French town behind the station was dark and still.

Mosca went back to his bench. Mr. Gerald's friends were bending over him, reassuring him, and Mr. Gerald was saying impatiently, "I know it's a scratch, but why did he do it, why did he do such a crazy thing?" And when the Lieutenant came back into the car and told them the ambulance would be waiting at Frankfort, Mr. Gerald said to him, "Believe me, Lieutenant, I did nothing to provoke him. Ask any of my friends. I did nothing, nothing, to make him do such a thing."

"He's just crazy, that's all," the Lieutenant said. And then added, "You're lucky, sir, if I know Mulrooney he was aiming at your balls."

For some reason this seemed to cheer them up, as if the seriousness of intent made the event more interesting, made the scratch on Mr. Gerald's thigh important. The Lieutenant brought his bed roll back and fixed Mr. Gerald on it. "In a way you did me a favor. I've been trying to get rid of Mulrooney since the first day he came into the platoon. He'll be safe for a couple of years now."

Mosca couldn't sleep. The train had begun to move, and he walked down to the door again, rested against it and looked at the black, shadowy countryside pass by. He remembered the same, nearly the same, land going by so slowly, from the back of trucks, tanks, on foot, crawling on the ground. He had believed he would never see this country again, and he wondered now why everything had turned out so badly. He had dreamed for so long about going home, and now he had left again. In the darkened train, he remembered his first night at home.

The large square sticker on the door had read "Welcome Home Walter," and Mosca noticed that similar stickers with different names were pasted on two of the other apartment doors. The first thing he saw when he entered the apartment was the picture of himself taken just before he went overseas. Then his mother and Gloria swarmed over him, and Alf was shaking his hand.

They all stood away from each other, and there was just one moment of awkward silence.

"You've gotten older," his mother said, and they all laughed. "No, I mean more than three years older."

"He hasn't changed," Gloria said. "He hasn't changed a bit."

"The conquering hero returns," Alf said. "Look at all those ribbons. Did you do something brave, Walter?"

"Standard," Mosca said, "most of the WACs got the same set." He pulled off his combat jacket and his mother took it from him. Alf went into the kitchen and came out with a tray of drinks.

"Christ," Mosca said, startled, "I thought you lost a leg." He had completely forgotten his mother writing about Alf. But his brother had obviously been waiting for this moment. He drew up his trouser leg.

"Very pretty," Mosca said. "Tough luck, Alf."

"Hell," Alf said, "I wish I had two of 'em. No athlete's foot, no ingrown toenails—you know."

"Sure," Mosca said. He touched his brother's shoulder and smiled.

"He put it on especially for you, Walter," his mother said. "He doesn't usually wear it around the house even though he knows I hate to see him without it."

Alf raised his drink. "To the conquering hero," he said, and then with a smile, turning to Gloria. "To the girl who waited for him."

"To our family," Gloria said.

"To all my children," his mother said affectionately. Her glance included Gloria. They all looked at Mosca expectantly.

"Let me drink this one, and then I can think of something."

They all laughed and drank.

"And now for supper," his mother said. "Help me set the table, Alf." The two of them went into the kitchen.

Mosca sat down in one of the armchairs. "A long, long trip," he said.

Gloria went over to the mantel and picked up the framed photo of Mosca. With her back to him she said, "Every week I'd come here and look at the picture. I'd help your mother get supper, we'd eat together and then sit here in this room, looking at this picture and talking about you. Every week, for three years, like people visiting a cemetery, and now that you're back it doesn't look a bit like you."

Mosca got up and went over to Gloria. Putting his arm on her shoulder he looked at the picture, wondering why it irritated him.

The head was thrown back in a laugh, and he had obviously stood so that the black and white diagonal stripes of his division would show clearly. The face was youthful and full of an innocent good nature. The uniform was nattily fitted. Standing there in the heat of the southern sun he had been a typical G.I. getting himself photoed for an adoring family.

"What a jerky grin," Mosca said.

"Don't make fun of it. That was all we had for a long time." She was silent for a moment. "Ah, Walter," she said, "how we cried over it sometimes, when you didn't write, whenever we heard rumors about a troop ship being sunk or a big battle being fought. On D Day we didn't go to church. Your mother sat on the couch, and I sat here by the radio. We just sat here all day. I didn't go to work. I kept turning the radio to different stations; as soon as one news bulletin was finished I'd try to get another station, even though it would say the same thing. Your mother just sat there with a handkerchief in her hand, but she didn't cry. I slept here that night, in your room, in your bed, and I took the picture with me. I put it on the dresser and said good night to it, and then I dreamed that I would never see you again. And now here you are, Walter Mosca, in the flesh, and you don't look a bit like the picture." She tried to laugh, but she was crying.

Mosca was embarrassed. He kissed Gloria gently. "Three years is a long time," he said. And he thought: On D Day I was in an English town getting drunk. I was giving a little blonde what she claimed was her first drink of whiskey and her first lay. I was celebrating D Day but even more celebrating that I wasn't in it. He had a strong desire to tell Gloria the exact truth, that he hadn't thought of them that day, or of any thing that they had thought of, but all he said was, "I don't like the picture . . . And besides when I came in you said I hadn't changed a bit."

"Isn't it funny," Gloria said, "when you came in the door you looked exactly like your picture. But when I kept looking at you it seemed as if your whole face had changed."

His mother called from the kitchen, "It's ready," and they went into the dining room.

All his favorite foods were on the table, the rare roast beef with the small roasted potatoes, a green salad and a slab of yellow cheese. The tablecloth was snowy white, and when he was finished he noticed the napkin untouched beside his plate. It had been good but not as good as he had dreamed it would be.

"Ah," Alf said, "a big difference from G.I. chow, hey, Walter?"

"Yeah," Mosca said. He took from his shirt pocket a short, fat, dark cigar and was about to light it when he noticed they were all looking at him with amusement, Alf, Gloria and his mother.

He grinned and said, "I'm a big boy now," and lit the cigar, exaggerating his pleasure. They all four of them burst out laughing. It seemed as if the last awkwardness, the strangeness of his coming home so different in face and manner, had been swept away. Their surprise, and then amusement at their surprise when he had taken out the cigar had broken down the barrier between them. They went into the living room, the two women with their arms around Mosca's waist, Alf carrying the tray with the whiskey and ginger ale. The women sat close to Mosca on the sofa, and Alf handed them all drinks and then sat down opposite them in one of the soft armchairs. The floor lamp sent a gentle yellow glow over the room and Alf said in the benign and half-joking tone he had used all evening, "The story of Walter Mosca will now be told."

Mosca drank. "First, the presents," he said. He went to his blue gym bag still lying by the door, took out three small boxes wrapped in brown paper and handed one to each of them. While they were opening the packages he took another drink.

"Christ," Alf said, "what the hell are these?" He held up four enormous silver cylinders.

Mosca laughed. "Four of the best cigars in the world. Specially made for Hermann Goering."

Gloria opened her package and then gasped. In a black velvet box was a ring. Small diamonds were set around a square, dark green emerald. She got up and flung her arms around Mosca and then turned to show the ring to his mother.

But his mother was fascinated by roll after roll of tightly packed wine-red silk falling to the floor in large folds. His mother held it up.

It was an enormous, square flag, and in the middle, superimposed on a white, circular background, rested the spider-black swastika. They were all silent. In the quiet of this room they had seen for the first time the symbol of the enemy.

"Hell," Mosca said, breaking the silence, "it was just a gag. You were supposed to see this." He picked up the small box lying on the floor. His mother opened it, and seeing the blue-white diamonds she raised her eyes and thanked him. She folded the huge flag into a tight little square, then rose and picked up Mosca's blue gym bag, saying, "I'll unpack this."

"They are lovely presents," Gloria said, "where did you get them?"

Mosca grinned and said, "Loot," emphasizing the word comically so that they would laugh.

His mother came back into the room with a large bundle of photos in her hand.

"These were in your bag, Walter. Why didn't you show

them to us?" She sat on the sofa and started looking at the photos one by one. She passed them on to Gloria and Alf. Mosca helped himself to a drink as they exclaimed over the different pictures and asked questions about where they had been snapped. Then he saw his mother turn pale, staring hard at one of the photos. For a moment Mosca had a feeling of panic, wondering if the really obscene pictures he had picked up were still there. But he was sure he had sold them all on the boat. He saw his mother pass the photos on to Alf, and he was angry with himself that he had felt any kind of fear.

"Well, well," Alf said, "what's this?" Gloria went over and looked at the picture. He saw the three pairs of eyes turned to him, waiting.

Mosca leaned toward Alf and when he saw what it was, he felt a surge of relief. He remembered now. He had been riding on the back of a tank when it happened.

In the photo was the huddled figure of a German bazooka man lying crumpled in the snow, a dark line running black from his body to the end of the print. Over the body stood himself, Mosca, staring straight into the camera, his M–1 slung over his shoulder. He, Mosca, looked curiously misshapen in his winter combat clothing. The blanket, in which he had cut holes for his head and arms, hung like a skirt beneath his combat jacket. He seemed to stand there like a successful hunter, ready to carry home the fallen game.

And not in the picture were the burning tanks on the covered plain. Not in the picture were the charred bodies sprinkled across the whitened field like rubbish. The German had been a good bazooka man.

"My buddy took that picture with a Leica the kraut

had." Mosca turned to his drink and turning back saw them still waiting.

"My first victim," he said, trying to make it sound like a joke. And yet it was if he had said the Eiffel Tower or the Pyramids, explaining a background against which he had been standing.

His mother was studying the other photos. "Where was this taken?" she asked. Mosca sat down beside her and said. "That was in Paris on my first leave." He put his arm around his mother's waist.

"And this?" his mother asked.

"That was in Vitry."

"And this?"

"That was in Aachen."

And this? And this? And this? He named the towns and told funny little stories. The drinks had put him into a good mood, but he thought: This was in Nancy where I waited two hours on line to get laid, this was in Dombasle where I found the dead naked German with his balls swollen big as melons. The placard on the door had said, "Dead German Inside." And it hadn't lied. He wondered even now why someone had troubled to write it, even as a joke. And this was in Hamm, where he got his first piece in three months and his first dose. And this and this and this were the countless towns where the Germans, men, women and children rested in their shapeless, rubbled tombs and gave out an overpowering stench.

And in all these the background against which he stood was like a man being photographed on a desert. He, the conqueror, stood on the flattened, pulverized remains of factories, homes, human bones—the ruins stretching away like rolling sand dunes.

Mosca sat back on the sofa. He puffed on his cigar. "How about some coffee?" he asked. "I'll make it." He went into the kitchen, Gloria following him, and together they set out the cups, cut the whipped-cream cake she took from the frigidaire. And while the coffee boiled on the stove, she clung to him and said, "Darling, I love you, I love you."

They brought the coffee into the living room, and it was their turn to tell Mosca stories. How Gloria had never gone out on a date in three years, how Alf had lost his leg in a truck crash in a southern Army camp, and how his mother had gone to work again, clerking in a large department store. They had all had their adventures, but thank God the war was over, the Moscas had come through safely, a leg lost, but as Alf said, with modern transportation what did legs mean, and now here they all were, safe in this little room.

The enemy so far away, so utterly crushed, could no longer give them fear. The enemy was surrounded, occupied, starving and melting away with disease, with no physical and moral strength ever to threaten them again. And when Mosca fell asleep in his chair, they, who all loved him, watched for a few minutes with a quiet, and almost tearful pleasure, almost not believing that he had traveled so far in time and place, and by some miracle had returned, found his way back to safety unharmed.

It was the third night before Mosca could get Gloria alone. The second night had been spent at her house where his mother and Alf had settled details for the wedding with Gloria's sister and father, not really out of meddlesomeness but because of their joy and enthusiasm that everything had come out right. They had all decided that the wedding would be as soon as possible but that it must wait until Walter had a steady job. Mosca had gone along more than willingly with the idea. And Alf had surprised Mosca. The timid Alf had grown into a confident, assured, sensible man and played the family head to perfection.

On that third night his mother and Alf had gone out and Alf had grinned and said, "Watch the clock, we'll be home at eleven." His mother had pushed Alf out of the door and said, "If you go out with Gloria don't forget to lock the door."

Mosca had been amused at the note of doubt in her voice, as if the thought of leaving him and Gloria alone in the house was against her better judgment. Good Christ, he thought, and he stretched out on the sofa.

He tried to relax but was too tense and had to get up and pour himself a drink. He stood at the window and smiled, wondering how it would be. He and Gloria had spent evenings together in a small hotel room the few weeks before he had gone overseas, but he could hardly remember now. He went to the radio and turned it on and then went into the kitchen to look at the clock. It was nearly eight-thirty. The bitch was a half-hour late. He went to the window again but it was too dark now to see anything. As he turned away there was a knock on the door, and Gloria came into the apartment.

"Hello, Walter," she said, and Mosca noticed that her voice trembled slightly. She took off her coat. She had on a blouse with just a few large buttons, and with this a wide pleated skirt.

"Alone at last," he said with a grin and stretched back on the sofa. "Fix a couple of drinks." Gloria sat on the sofa and leaned over to kiss him. He put his hands on her breast, and they kissed for a long time. "Drinks coming up," she said, and pulled away from him.

They drank. The radio was playing softly and a floor lamp cast its soft yellow glow over the room. He lit two cigarettes and gave her one. They smoked and when he stubbed out his cigarette he saw that she still held on to hers. He took it away from her and carefully crushed it in the ash tray.

Mosca pulled Gloria down so that she lay across his body. He unbuttoned her blouse so that he could slip his hand inside her brassiere and then kissed her. He moved his hand down under her skirt.

Gloria sat up and pushed away from him. Mosca was surprised and instantly alert.

"I don't want to go all the way," Gloria said. The girlish phrase irritated him and he reached for her impatiently. She stood up and away from him.

"No, I really mean it," she said.

"What the hell," Mosca said, "the two weeks before I went overseas were fine. What's wrong now?"

"I know," Gloria smiled at him tenderly, and he felt a quick anger. "But then it was different. You were going away and I loved you. If I did it now it would only make you think less of me. Don't be mad, Walter, but I've talked with Emmy about it. You were so different when you came back that I had to talk to somebody. And we both thought it would be best."

Mosca lit a cigarette. "Your sister's stupid."

"Please don't say things like that, Walter. I won't do what you want because I really love you."

Mosca choked on his drink and tried hard not to laugh. "Look," he said, "if we hadn't slept together that last two weeks I wouldn't have remembered you or written. You wouldn't have meant anything to me."

He saw her face get red. She went over to the armchair facing him and sat down.

"I loved you before that," she said. He saw that her mouth was quivering, and he tossed her the pack of cigarettes, then sipped his drink and tried to reason everything out.

His desire was gone, and he actually felt a sense of relief. Why, he didn't know. There was no doubt in his mind that he could talk or threaten Gloria into doing what he wished. He knew that if he said, "This is the way it has to be or else," she would yield. He knew that he had been too abrupt and that with some patience and a little finesse the evening would end pleasantly. But he found with surprise that the effort was too much trouble for him to take. He was completely without desire.

"It's O.K. Come over here."

She came obediently. "You're not angry?" she asked in a low voice.

He kissed her and smiled. "No, it doesn't matter," he said, and it was true.

Gloria put her head on his shoulder. "Let's just stay here like this tonight and talk. We've never really had a chance to talk together since you've come back."

Mosca pulled away and went to get her coat. "We're going to the movies," he said.

"I want to stay here."

Mosca said with a deliberate, brutal carelessness. "It's either go to the movies or get laid."

She stood up and looked at him steadily. "And you don't care which."

"That's right."

He expected her to put on her coat and walk out of the apartment. But she waited submissively until he had combed his hair and knotted his tie. They went to the movies.

It was nearly noon, a month later, that Mosca, coming into the apartment, found Alf, his mother, and Gloria's sister, Emmy, drinking coffee in the kitchen.

"Do you want some coffee?" his mother asked.

"Yeah, just let me wash up a bit." Mosca went into the bathroom and smiled grimly as he wiped his face dry before going back to the kitchen.

They all sipped coffee, and then Emmy opened the attack.

"You're not treating Gloria right. She waited three years for you, she never had a date and she missed a lot of chances."

"A lot of chances for what?" Mosca asked. Then he laughed. "We're getting along O.K., it takes time."

Emmy said, "You had a date with her last night, you didn't show up. You get home now. It isn't right what you're doing."

His mother saw that Mosca was getting angry and said placatingly, "Gloria waited here until two in the morning; you should have called up."

"And we all know what you're doing," Emmy said. "You leave a girl who waited for you three years to go out with the neighborhood chippie, a girl who's had three abortions and God knows what else."

Mosca shrugged. "I can't see your sister every night."

"No, you're too important for that." He saw with surprise that she really hated him.

"It was everybody's idea that we wait until I get a steady job," Mosca reminded her.

"I didn't know what a bastard you'd turn out to be. If you don't want to get married, tell Gloria. Don't worry, she can find somebody else."

Alf spoke up. "That's silly. Of course Walter wants to marry her. Let's be sensible about this. He's finding things a bit strange, he'll get over it. The thing for us to do is help him."

Emmy said sarcastically, "If Gloria slept with him everything would be fine. You'd be readjusted, wouldn't you, Walter?"

"This is getting stupid," Alf said. "Let's get down to fundamentals. You're angry because Walter is having an affair and isn't bothering to hide it, which is the least he could do. All right. Gloria is too crazy about Walter to give him the air. I think the best thing to do is to set a marriage date."

"And my sister keeps working while he runs around with all the little whores like he did in Germany?"

Mosca looked at his mother coldly, and she dropped her eyes away from his. There was a silence. "Yes," Emmy said quietly, "your mother told Gloria about the letters you get from that girl in Germany. You should be ashamed, Walter, honestly you should."

"Those letters don't mean a thing," Mosca said. And he could see the look of relieved belief on their faces.

"He'll get a job," his mother said, "and they can live here until they find an apartment."

Mosca sipped his coffee. He had been angry for a moment but now he was impatient to be out of this room, away from them. All this crap had gone far enough.

"But he'll have to quit running around with these little chippies," Emmy said.

Mosca broke in gently. "There's only one goddamn thing wrong. I'm not ready to set a date."

They all looked at him with surprise. "I'm not sure I want to get married," he added with a grin.

"What," Emmy was screaming incoherently, "what?" She was so angry she couldn't speak any further.

"And don't give me the three-year crap. What the hell difference does it make to me that she didn't get screwed for three years? Do you think that kept me awake nights worrying? What the hell, did it grow gold because she didn't use it? I had other things to worry about."

"Please, Walter," his mother said.

"Ah, shit," Mosca said. His mother left the table and went to the stove, and he knew she was crying. They were all suddenly standing and Alf, supporting himself against the table, shouted with anger, "All right, Walter, this readjusted crap can be overdone."

"And I think you've been babied too damn much since you've been home," Emmy said with contempt.

There was nothing to say to all this except to tell them exactly how he felt. "You can kiss my ass," he said, and although he spoke to Emmy, his glance included them all. He rose to leave but Alf, holding on to the table, moved in front of him and shouted with rage. "Goddamn you, that's going too far. Apologize, do you hear, apologize."

Mosca pushed him out of the way and saw too late that Alf's false leg was not there. Alf toppled over and his head struck against the floor. Both women screamed. Mosca bent over quickly to lift Alf. "Are you O.K.?" he asked. Alf nodded but kept his face covered with his hands and remained sitting on the floor. Mosca left the apartment.

He always remembered his mother standing by the stove, crying, wringing her hands.

The last time he entered the apartment Mosca found his mother waiting for him—she had not gone out at all that day.

"Gloria called you up," she said.

Mosca nodded in acknowledgment.

"Are you going to pack now?" his mother asked timidly.

"Yeah," Mosca said.

"Do you want me to help?"

"No," he said.

He went into his bedroom and took out the two new suitcases he had bought. He stuck a cigarette in his mouth and looked through his pockets for a match and then went into the kitchen for one.

His mother was still sitting in the chair. She had a handkerchief covering her face and was weeping silently.

He took the matches and started to leave the kitchen.

"Why do you treat me like this?" his mother said. "What have I done?"

He had no pity and the tears stirred no emotion, but he didn't want hysterics. He tried to talk quietly, to keep the irritation out of his voice.

"You haven't done anything, I'm just leaving, it's nothing to do with you."

"Why do you always talk to me like that as if I were a stranger?"

The words touched him, but he could make no gesture of affection. "I'm just nervous," he said. "If you're not going out, help me pack."

She went into the bedroom with him and carefully folded his clothes before he put them into the suitcases.

"Do you need any cigarettes?" his mother asked.

"No, I'll get them on the ship."

"I'll just run down and get some, you never can tell."

"They're only a nickel a pack on the ship," he said. He didn't want her to give him anything.

"You can always use extra cigarettes," his mother said and left the apartment.

Mosca sat on his bed and stared at the picture of Gloria that hung on the wall. He felt no emotion. It hasn't worked out, he thought. It's too bad. And he wondered at their patience, realizing how hard they had tried and what little effort he had made. He searched in his mind for something he could say to his mother, to show her there was nothing she could do to help, that his actions had sprung from another root which neither he nor she could control.

In the living room the phone began to ring, and he went to it. Gloria's voice, impersonal, yet friendly, answered him.

"I hear you're leaving tomorrow. Should I come over tonight to say good-bye or just say it now over the phone."

"Suit yourself," Mosca said, "but I have to go out around nine."

"I'll come before then," she said. "Don't worry, it's just to say good-bye." And he knew that it was true, that she no longer cared for him, that he was no longer what she had loved, and she wished to say good-bye with a friendliness that was really curiosity.

When his mother came back he had made up his mind. "Mom," he said, "I'm leaving now. Gloria called. She's coming over tonight and I don't want to see her."

"You mean now. This minute?"

"Yes," Mosca said.

"But at least you can spend your last night home," she

said. "Alf will be home soon, you could at least wait to say good-bye to your brother."

"So long, Mom," he said. He leaned over and kissed her cheek.

"Wait," his mother said, "you've forgotten your gym bag." And, as she had so many times before when he had left the house to play basketball and finally when he had left for the Army, she took the small, blue gym bag and began to fill it with what he would need. Only again now, instead of the satin-covered shorts, the leather kneeguards and sneakers, she put in his shaving kit, a fresh change of underwear, towel and soap. Then taking a piece of string from one of the bureau drawers she tied the gym bag to the handle of a suitcase.

"Ah," she said, "I don't know what all the people will say. They'll think it's my fault, that I haven't made you happy. And at least after the way you treated Gloria, you could see her tonight, see her and say good-bye and be nice to her so she won't feel so badly."

"It's a tough world for everybody," Mosca said. He kissed her again, but before he could walk out of the apartment she held on to him.

"Are you going back to Germany because of that girl?" And Mosca realized that if he said yes, his mother's vanity would be soothed, that she would know then it was not her fault that he left. But he couldn't lie.

"I don't think so," he said. "She probably has another G.I. by now." And saying it out loud, in all sincerity, he was surprised that it should sound so false, as if the truth he told were a lie to hurt his mother.

She kissed him and let him go. In the street he looked up and saw her at the closed window, the white spot of a handkerchief to her face. He set the suitcases on the ground and waved to her and saw that she had left the window. Afraid that she would come down to make a scene in the street, he picked up his suitcases and walked quickly to the main avenue where he could catch a taxi.

But his mother was sitting on the sofa, weeping, with shame, grief, humiliation. Deep inside her knowing that if her son had died on an unknown beach, buried in a foreign land, the white cross over his body mingled with thousands of others, her grief would have been perhaps greater. But there would have been no shame, and she would have been, in a later time, reconciled, in some measure, proud.

There would not have been this festering sorrow, this knowledge that he was irrevocably gone, that if he died, she could never weep over his body, bury him, bring flowers to his grave.

On the train taking him back to the land of the enemy, Mosca, dozing, swayed from side to side with the movement of the car. Sleepily he walked back to his bench and stretched out on it. But lying there he heard the moans of the wounded man, the chattering of teeth, the sleeping body only now protesting against the insane rage of the world. Mosca rose and walked down to the G.I. half of the car. Most of the soldiers were asleep, and there was only a small halo of light, the flaring of three closely grouped candles. Mulrooney, crumpled up on a bench, was snoring, and two G.I.'s, their carbines lying beside them, were playing rummy and drinking from a small bottle.

Mosca asked in a low voice, "Can one of you guys lend me a blanket, that guy's cold."

One of the G.I.'s threw him a blanket. "Thanks," Mosca said.

The G.I. shrugged. "I have to stay up and guard this joker anyway."

Mosca glanced at the sleeping Mulrooney. The face was blank. The eyes opened slowly, stared at him like a dumb animal, and in that moment, before the eyes closed, Mosca felt a sense of recognition and thought, "You poor stupid bastard."

He walked back down the car, threw the blanket over Mr. Gerald and stretched out again on his bench. This time he fell asleep easily and quickly. He slept dreamlessly until the train reached Frankfort and somebody shook him awake.

# 2

THE MORNING SUN of early June lit every corner
of the roofless terminal, turning it into a vast outdoor
stadium, and as Mosca stepped off the train he drew a
great breath of spring air, smelling already a faint, acrid
dust that rose from the debris and ruins of the city beyond.
Along the length of the train he could see groups of O.D.-
clad soldiers forming into platoons. With the other civilians,
he followed a guide to the bus waiting outside.

They moved through the crowd like conquerors, as in an
earlier time the rich passed through the poor, looking
neither to right nor left, knowing that a path would appear
before them. The conquered, their clothes worn, their
bodies and faces thin, looked like masses of men and women
accustomed to living in flophouses, eating in the soup
kitchens of charity, and they made way sullenly, obediently,
staring with envious eyes at the well-clad, well-fed Americans.

They came out of the station into a large square. Opposite them was the Red Cross club, G.I.'s in olive drab
already lounging on the steps. Walling the square stood
rebuilt hotels that housed the occupation troops and ad-
ministrators. Streetcars crisscrossed each other, and military
buses and taxis filled the wide streets. Even this early, G.I.'s
were sitting on the benches around the station, and each
had beside him a *Fräulein* with her inevitable little suit-

case. It was all the same, Mosca thought, it hasn't changed. The G.I.'s met the incoming trains as suburban wives meet their commuting husbands, picked out a pretty girl and made their propositions with varying degrees of crudity. To spend a night in a cold, dirty station sleeping on a bench, waiting for a morning train; or a good dinner, liquor, cigarettes, a warm bed. He might give her a good deal of pleasure, at worst, if one were careful, a few moments of annoyance during the night. Usually the sensible choice was made.

On all the streets bounding the square stood the sharpers, the black-market operators, the children laying their trap for wary G.I.'s, who emerged from the PX with cartons full of candy, cigarettes, soap, and with eyes watchful as old prospectors carrying sacks of gold dust.

Mosca, waiting to enter the bus, felt a hand on his shoulder. Turning, he saw a dark, bony face topped by the cap of the Wehrmacht that was the standard headgear for German men.

The young man said in a low, urgent voice. "You have American dollars?" Mosca shook his head, turned away and again felt the hand on his shoulder.

"Any cigarettes?"

Mosca started to enter the bus. The hand grasped his shoulder more urgently. "Anything, you have anything you wish to sell?"

Mosca said curtly in German, "Get your hands away quick."

The man stepped back, startled, and then into his eyes came a look of proud contempt, hatred. Mosca went into the bus and sat down. He saw the man looking at him through the window, at his gray gabardine suit, the white richness of his shirt, the streak of color that was his tie.

And feeling the man's look of contempt, he wished for a moment that he was again in the olive drab of his uniform.

The bus moved slowly away from the railroad station and took one of the many exits out of the square. It moved them through another world. Outside that central square which stood like a fortress in a wilderness, the ruins stretched away as far as the eye could see, with only a flora of building remnants, a still-standing wall, a door leading into the open air behind it, a steel skeleton reaching to the sky with pieces of brick, mortar and glass clinging to it like fragments of torn flesh.

The bus unloaded most of the civilians on the outskirts of Frankfort, then continued with Mosca and a few officers to the Wiesbaden airfield. Mosca was the only one of the civilians, beside Mr. Gerald, who had been given his permanent assignment in the States. The others had to wait in Frankfort for definite orders.

When, finally, his documents were checked at the airfield, he had to wait until after lunch for the plane to Bremen. And when the plane left the field he had no feeling of rising from the earth, no sense that the plane could run off the edges of the continent, or even that it was possible to fall. He watched the earth tilt, slanting toward him so that it seemed to be coming up to form a wall of green and brown before his eyes and then as the plane banked away the continent was an endless and depthless valley. And then all the mystery was gone as the plane flew level, and they looked down as from a balcony to the flat, checkered, tableclothed fields.

Now that he was so near his final destination, that this return was so nearly completed, he thought about his few months at home and felt an uncomfortable, vague guilt at the patience his family had shown. But there was no desire to see any of them again, and feeling now a mounting impatience with the plane's slowness, its seeming suspension in the boundless spring-clear sky, he realized that the truth he had told his mother had been a lie, that he was going back because of that German girl, as his mother had said, but going back with no expectation of finding her, with no real hope of their lives coming together after these months of separation, but because he had to return to this continent in any case. He no more expected to find her waiting for him than if he had left her in a trackless jungle, disabled, with no means of sustenance, weaponless against the wild beasts. And thinking so he felt a sickness inside him, a poison of shame and sorrow flowing into his blood and mouth. He saw clearly her body, her face, the color of her hair, thought of her fully in his mind, consciously, for the first time in the months he had left her, and finally, clearly and concretely, as if he had spoken it aloud, he thought of her name.

The police presidio had blown up just a little before noon that hot summer morning nearly a year ago and Mosca, sitting in his jeep in the Hoch Allee, felt the earth shake. The officer he had been waiting for, a young Lieutenant fresh from the States, came out a few minutes later and they drove back to Military Government headquarters on the Contrescarpe. Someone shouted the news and they drove to the police building. The military police had already sealed off the area, their jeeps and white helmets blocking streets leading to the square. The Lieutenant with Mosca showed his identification, and they passed through.

The massive, dark-green building stood on a small rise of ground at the top of the Am Wald Strasse. It was large and square, with an inner courtyard for vehicle parking. German civilians were still streaming out of the main entrance, their faces and clothing covered with dust. Some of the women were weeping hysterically with shock. A crowd was being pushed away from the building, but the building itself seemed silent, untouched.

Mosca followed the Lieutenant to one of the small side entrances. It was an archway packed almost to the ceiling with debris. They crawled through to the inner courtyard.

The great inner square was filled now with a mountain of rubble. Vehicle tops, jeeps and trucks, could be seen sticking above it in some spots like masts of sunken ships in shallow water. The walls to a height three stories high had been hacked away by the explosion, and naked to their view were the desks, chairs and wall clocks of the offices above them.

Mosca heard a sound he had never heard before, a sound which had become a commonplace in the great cities of that continent. For a moment it seemed to come from all sides, a low, steady, monotonous animal scream, not recognizable as human. He located it, and half-walking, half-crawling over the rubble made his way to the right side of the square; saw the fat, red neck encircled by the green collar of the German police uniform. The neck and head in their rigidity were lifeless, the scream came from beneath the body. Mosca and the Lieutenant tried to clear away the brick but rubble kept sliding down over the dead man. The Lieutenant crawled back through the archway to get help.

And now from the many archways and descending the rubbled walls, rescuers began to fill the courtyard. Army doctors from the base hospitals, still in their dress pinks;

G.I.'s; German litter bearers and laborers to dig the bodies out. Mosca crawled back through the archway.

In the street the air was pure. Ambulances were drawn up in a long line, and opposite them the German fire engines stood in readiness. Laborers were already clearing the entrances leading into the courtyard, the rubble being loaded onto waiting trucks. On the sidewalk opposite the building a table had been set up as a command post and he saw his Colonel standing there waiting patiently, a group of his junior officers around him. Mosca noticed with amusement that they were all wearing steel helmets. One of the officers beckoned to him.

"Go up and guard our Intelligence office," he said. He handed Mosca his pistol belt. "If there's another explosion get out of there as quick as you can."

Mosca went in the building through the main entrance. The stairway was a hill of ruins and he climbed it slowly, gingerly. He walked down the corridor with one eye on the ceiling, taking care not to pass under places where it sagged.

The Intelligence office was halfway down the corridor and opening the door he saw that now it was only half a room, the other half part of the rubble in the courtyard. There was nothing left to guard, only one locked file cabinet. But he had a fine view of the drama being played beneath him.

Settling comfortably in a chair, he pulled a cigar from his pocket and lit it. His foot struck something on the floor and looking down he saw with surprise two bottles of beer lying on their sides. He picked one up, it was crusted with mortar and bits of brick. Mosca opened the bottle on the door lock and settled in his chair again.

Below him in the courtyard the scene was static, and in the dust-laden air, almost dreamlike. Beside the body he had found, the German laborers were now picking away bricks carefully in slow motion. Looming above them an American officer stood patiently still, his pink trousers and green blouse turning white with dust. By his side stood a Sergeant, holding in his hands before him the round cylinder containing blood plasma. And this scene had been copied all over the courtyard, as if from a master print. Over them all the dust from the pulverized concrete hung in the sunlit air, then fell gently to dye their hair and clothing white.

Mosca drank his beer and smoked his cigar. He heard someone stumbling along the corridor and went out of the room.

Down the long hall which ended and disappeared where floor and ceiling almost met, staggering out of the dark, inner recesses of the building, came a small file of German men and women. They went past him, not seeing him, blind and weak with shock and terror. The last one in the file was a slight girl in khaki ski pants and woolen blouse. She stumbled and fell and when none of the others turned to help her, Mosca stepped from the room and raised her to her feet. She would have gone on but Mosca stretched out his arm, the bottle of beer at the end of it, and stopped her.

She lifted her head and Mosca saw that her face, her neck, were dead white and her eyes dilated with shock. She said in German, tearfully, "Please let me get out, please." Mosca let his arm fall and she went past him down the corridor. But she went only a few steps and crumpled against the wall.

Mosca bent over and saw that her eyes were open. Not

knowing what else to do he put the bottle of beer to her mouth but she pushed it away.

"No," she said in German, "I'm just too scared to walk." He heard the note of shame, just barely understanding. He lit a cigarette and stuck it between her lips, then lifted the thin body and carried her to a chair in the room.

Mosca opened the other bottle of beer and this time she drank a little. Below them the scene had increased its tempo. The doctors bent over, their hands busy; the men holding the plasma containers knelt on the rubble. Litter bearers made their way slowly over the ruins; the corpses, flattened, dust-covered bodies, making their exits through the many archways.

The girl moved from her chair. "I can walk now." She started to leave but Mosca blocked the door.

In his awkward German he said, "Wait for me outside." She shook her head. "You need a drink," he said, "schnapps, real schnapps, warm." She shook her head again. "No monkey business," he said in English, "honest, cross my heart." And he mockingly held the bottle of beer over his breast. She smiled and brushed past him. He watched her thin figure going slowly but steadily down the corridor to the rubbled staircase.

That was how it began; the dead, conqueror and enemy alike, being carried away below them, the brick dust settling on their eyelids, and he, Mosca, moved to pity and a strange tenderness by her fragile body and thin face. At night in his room they listened to the small radio, finished off a bottle of peppermint liqueur, and when she tried to leave he had kept her there with one pretext or another until it was after curfew and she had to stay. She hadn't let him kiss her the whole evening.

She undressed underneath the bed covers, and he, smoking a last cigarette and drinking the last of the liqueur, had finally joined her. She turned to him with a passionate intensity that surprised and delighted him. Months later she told him that she hadn't been with a man for nearly a year, and he had laughed, and she had said with a rueful smile, "If a man says that everyone pities him; they laugh at a woman."

But he had understood that first night and understood more. That she had been afraid of him, he the enemy, but the radio's soft music, the warm liqueur, the precious and nerve-soothing cigarettes, the fat sandwiches he had bought from the Mess Sergeant . . . these luxuries she had not known for so long, had all combined with her bodily desire, and they had played a game, spinning out time until they knew it would be too late for her to leave. It had all been impersonal, and understanding this hadn't spoiled it, perhaps because physically they were suited to each other, and the night became a long darkness of sensual pleasure, and in the gray morning before the real dawn, she sleeping, he smoking, Mosca thought, "I'll have to keep this steady," and thought with pity, tenderness and some shame how he had punished her fragile body and met there an unexpected, tensile strength.

When Hella woke later in the morning she was frightened, not remembering for a moment where she was, and then she was ashamed that she had surrendered so easily, so casually, and to the enemy. But her legs tangled with Mosca's in the narrow bed filled her whole body with a warm sensuousness. She rose on one elbow, to look at Mosca's face, realizing with recurring shame that she did not really have a clear image of him in her mind, did not know what he really looked like.

The mouth of the enemy was thin and almost ascetic,

the face narrow and strong, not relaxed in sleep. He slept stiffly, his body rigid on the narrow bed, and he slept so silently, scarcely breathing, that she wondered if he were shamming, watching her watch him.

Hella left the bed as quietly as she could and dressed. She was hungry and seeing Mosca's cigarettes on the table she took one and lit it. It tasted very good. Looking out the window, hearing no sound in the street below, she realized it was still early. She wanted to leave but was hoping that he had a tin of food in the room and would offer it to her if he ever woke up. She thought, with rueful shame and pleasure, that she had certainly earned it.

She glanced at the bed and was startled to see that the American's eyes were open and he was studying her quietly. She stood up, felt a ridiculous shyness, and stretched out her hand to say good-bye. He laughed, reached out and pulled her down to the bed. He said mockingly, in English, "We're too good friends for that."

She didn't understand but she knew he was making fun of her and she was angry. She said, in German, "I have to leave." But he didn't let her hand go.

"Cigarette," he said. She lit one for him. He sat up in bed to smoke, the covers falling away from his body, and she saw the white jagged scar running from his groin to the nipple of his breast. She asked in German. "The war?"

He laughed, pointed to her and said, "You." It seemed to Hella for a moment that he was accusing her personally, and she turned her head so that she could not see.

He tried his bad German. "Are you hungry?" he asked. She nodded. He jumped out of bed, naked. With a modesty that seemed to Mosca very funny, she averted her eyes while he dressed.

Ready to leave, he kissed her gently and then said in

German, "Go back to bed." She made no sign that she understood but he knew that she had and for some reason would not do so. He shrugged and left, running down the stairs and out to the motor pool. He drove to the mess hall, picked up a canteen of coffee and some fried egg sandwiches. Back in the room he found her sitting by the window, still dressed. He gave her the food, and they both drank from the canteen. She held out one of the sandwiches to him, but he shook his head. He noticed with amusement that after a hesitant gesture she did not offer it a second time.

"You'll come tonight?" he asked in German.

She shook her head. They looked at each other, he with no trace of emotion on his face. She saw that he would not ask again, that he was ready to erase her from his mind and memory, make the night they had spent together completely nothing. And because her vanity was aroused and he had been a considerate lover, she said, "Tomorrow," and smiled. She took one last drink of coffee, leaned over to kiss him, and left.

She had told him all this in the time after. Had it been three months, four months? A long time of contentment, ease, physical pleasure and comfort. And one day, coming into the room, he had found her in the classical, wifely pose, mending a great, twisted bundle of socks.

"Ah," he said in German, "the good *Hausfrau*."

Hella smiled shyly and looked at him as if she were trying to penetrate into his mind, trying to see what impression the scene had made. That had been the beginning of the campaign to make him not want to leave her, to stay in the land of the enemy with her, also the enemy, and yet though he understood, it was not offensive to him.

And then later, the tried and tested frontal assault, the

lethal weapon of pregnancy, but he had felt no contempt, no pity; just annoyance.

"Get rid of it," he said. "We'll go see a good doctor."

Hella shook her head. "No," she said, "I want to have it."

Mosca shrugged. "I'm going home, nothing can stop me."

"All right," she said. She made no entreaties. She gave herself to him completely in every thing and in every way until one day, though he knew he lied he couldn't help saying, "I'll come back." She watched him intently, knew that he lied and he saw that she knew. And that had been the mistake, starting it. Because in the time that followed he kept repeating the lie, sometimes with drunken fervor, so that they had finally both come to believe in it, she with an inborn, stubborn faith, a stubbornness she had in many things.

The final day he came back to his room and found she had already packed his duffel bag. It stood upright near the window, like a stuffed green dummy. It was after lunch, and the cold lemon-colored sunlight of October filled the room. The truck for the embarkation area would leave after supper.

He dreaded the time he would have to spend with her and said, "Let's go for a walk." She shook her head.

She motioned him to her, and they both undressed. He saw the slight bulge of the coming child. He had no desire but forced himself onward until desire came and was ashamed at her urgent passion. When it was time for supper he dressed and helped her dress.

"I want you to leave now," he said. "I don't want you to wait for the truck."

"All right," she said submissively, and she gathered her clothes together into a bundle and put them into her small suitcase. Before she left he gave her all the cigarettes and German money he had and they left the building together. On the street he said, "Good-bye," and kissed her. He saw she couldn't speak, that the tears were running down her face, but she walked straight down the street, down the Contrescarpe to the Am Wald Strasse, not seeing anything, not turning around.

He watched her until she was out of sight, believing it was the last time he would ever see her, feeling a vague relief that it was all over, and so easily, with no fuss. And then he remembered what she had told him a few nights before and it had been impossible to doubt her sincerity. "Don't worry about me or the baby," she had said. "Don't feel guilty about it, if you don't come back, the baby will keep me happy, will always make me think how happy we were together. And don't come back for me, if you don't want to."

He was angered by what he thought was the false nobility of her speech but then she went on. "I'll wait for you at least a year, maybe two years. But if you don't come I'll be happy. I'll find another man and make my life, that's the way people are. And I'm not afraid, not afraid of having the baby or taking care of it alone. Do you understand that I'm not afraid?" And he had understood. That she was not afraid of any pain or sorrow he might give her, or the cruelty and lack of tenderness that was now part of him, but most of all what she did not understand herself he envied most, that she had no fear of her own inner being, that she accepted the cruelty and rage of the world around her and kept her belief in the giving of love, and that she felt more sorrow for him than for herself.

A brown-green wall tilted before his eyes, blocking off his vision, and as if on a level before him but lying on their sides, were groups of buildings and small oblongs that were people. The plane leveled off and Mosca could see the neat outlines of the airfield, the small groups of buildings that were aircraft hangars and the long, low administration building, gleaming white in the sun. Far away he could see a ragged outline formed by the few tall buildings that were still standing in Bremen. He felt the wheels meet the earth, gingerly, distrustfully, and there swept over him an impatient eagerness to be out of the plane, to stand waiting for Hella outside a door. At that moment, when he was ready to leave the plane, he was sure he would find her waiting for him.

# 3

MOSCA LET a German porter carry his suitcases out of the plane, and he saw Eddie Cassin coming down the ramp of the airfield to meet him. They shook hands, and Eddie Cassin said in the quiet, carefully modulated voice, vibrant with a sincerity that he always used when he felt unnatural, "It's good to see you again, Walter."

"Thanks for fixing up the job and the papers to come here," Mosca said.

"That was nothing," Eddie Cassin said. "It's worth it to me to have one of the old gang back. We had some great times together, Walter." He picked up one of Mosca's suitcases, and Mosca took the other and the blue gym bag and they walked up the ramp, off the flying area.

"We'll go to my office and have a drink and meet some of the guys," Eddie Cassin said. He put his free arm across Mosca's shoulder for a moment and said in a natural voice, "You old bastard, I'm really glad to see you, you know that?" And Mosca felt what he had not felt in his previous homecoming, a sense of true arrival, of reaching a final destination.

They followed a wire fence to a small brick building that stood some distance away from the other installations of the base. "Here I'm lord and master," Eddie said. "Civilian Personnel Office, and I'm the Assistant to the Civilian Personnel Officer who spends all his time flying. Five hundred krauts think I'm God and a hundred and fifty of them are women. How about that for living, Walter?"

The building was a one-story affair. There was a large outer office filled with German clerks scurrying to and fro, a patient horde of other Germans waiting to be interviewed for jobs as mechanics in the motor pool, kitchen help in the mess halls, PX attendants. There were rough-looking men, old women, young men and a great many young girls, some very pretty. Their eyes followed Eddie as he went by.

Eddie opened the door to the inner office. Here there were two desks face to face, so that their occupants could look each other in the eye. One desk was absolutely bare except for a lettered green-and-white shingle which read, "Lt. A. Forte, CPO," and a small neat bundle of papers waiting for signature. On the other desk there were two double-decked baskets overflowing with paper. Almost swamped by other papers scattered over the desk was a small shingle which read "Mr. E. Cassin, Asst. CPO." In the corner of the room was a desk at which a tall and very ugly girl was typing, stopping in her work long enough to say, "Good afternoon, Mr. Cassin. The Colonel called, he wants you to call him back."

Eddie winked at Mosca and picked up the telephone. While he was speaking, Mosca lit a cigarette and tried to relax. He made himself not think of Hella and looked at Eddie. Eddie hadn't changed, he thought. There was the gray, wavy hair framing the delicate, yet strong features. The mouth was as sensitive as a girl's yet the nose was long and imperial, the set of his jaw determined. The eyes were hooded as if with sensuality and the grayness of his abundant hair seemed to have tinged his skin. Yet the impression was one of youthfulness, a frank warmth of expression that was almost naïve. But Mosca knew that when Eddie

Cassin was drunk the sensitive and delicately cut mouth twisted into an ugly line, the whole face grayed and went old and vicious. And since that viciousness had no real strength behind it and because men would laugh at it as Mosca often had, the viciousness, in words and physical action, was vented on the woman who was his companion or mistress of the moment. He had one set opinion of Eddie Cassin, a crazy bastard about women and a lousy drunk, but otherwise a really nice guy who would do anything for a friend. And Eddie had been smart enough never to make a pass at Hella. He wanted to ask Eddie now whether he had seen Hella or knew what had happened to her but he could not bring himself to do so.

Eddie Cassin put down the phone and opened a drawer of his desk. He took out a bottle of gin and a tin of grapefruit juice. Turning to the typist he said, "Ingeborg, go wash the glasses." She took some glasses, empty containers of cheese spread, and left the office. Eddie Cassin went to a door that led to a smaller office behind them. "Come on, Walter, I want you to meet a couple of friends of mine."

In the next office a short, stout, pasty-faced man in the same olive green Eddie wore was standing by his desk, his foot on the rung of a chair and his body bent over so that his paunch rested on his thigh. He held in his hand a *Fragebogen* or questionnaire and was studying it. Before him, standing stiffly at attention, was a short squat German, the inevitable gray-green Wehrmacht cap under his arm. By the window sat a long-looking American civilian with the long jaw and square small mouth of a weatherbeaten American farmer, and with his air of self-centered strength.

"Wolf," Eddie said to the pudgy man, "this is an old buddy of mine, Walter Mosca. Walter, Wolf here is our security man. He clears the krauts before they can get a job on the base."

After they had shaken hands, Eddie went on. "That guy by the window is Gordon Middleton. He's the man without a job, so he's detailed to help out down here. The Colonel is trying to get rid of him, that's why he hasn't anything special to do." Middleton didn't get up from his chair to shake hands, so Mosca nodded, and the other waved a long scarecrow arm in acknowledgment.

Wolf jerked his thumb at the door and told the German, still standing at attention, to wait outside. The German clicked his heels, bowed, and left hurriedly. Wolf laughed, threw the *Fragebogen* on the desk with a contemptuous gesture.

"Never in the Party, never in the SA, never in the Hitler Youth. Christ, I'm dying to meet a Nazi."

They all laughed. Eddie shook his head wisely. "They all say the same thing. Walter here is a guy after your own heart, Wolf. A rough character with krauts when we were in Mil Gov together."

"Is that so?" Wolf raised a sandy eyebrow. "That's the only way to be."

"Yeah," Eddie said, "we had a big problem in Mil Gov. The krauts would make the coal deliveries to all the German installations, but when it came time to deliver to those Jewish refugee camps up at Grohn on Saturday either the trucks would break down or the kraut coal administrator would say there was no coal left. My boy solved the problem."

"This I'd like to hear," Wolf said. He had an easy, ingratiating way of speaking that was almost oily and had a trick of nodding his head up and down to assure the speaker of his complete comprehension.

Ingeborg brought in the glasses, the bottle and the fruit juice. Eddie fixed four drinks but one without gin. He gave this to Gordon Middleton. "The only guy in the occupation who doesn't gamble, drink or chase women. That's why the Colonel wants to get rid of him. He gives the krauts a bad impression."

"Let's hear the story," Gordon said. His low, drawling voice was a reproach but a gentle one; patient.

"Well,". Eddie said, "it got so that Mosca would have to ride way the hell out to the camp every Saturday to make sure the coal got there. One Saturday he was in a crap game and let the trucks go alone. No coal. He really got chewed out. I'll never forget. I drove him out to where the trucks had broken down and he gave the drivers a little speech."

Mosca rested against the desk, lit a cigar and puffed on it nervously. He remembered the incident and knew the kind of story Eddie would make out of it. Build him up to be a real hard guy and it hadn't been that way at all. He had told the drivers that if they did not wish to drive he would see to their release without prejudice. But if they wanted to stay on the job they had better get the coal to the DP camp even if they had to carry it on their backs. One driver had quit, and Mosca had taken his name and passed cigarettes all around. Eddie was making it sound as if he had knocked the hell out of six of them in a free-for-all.

"Then he went to the coal administrator's house and had a little talk in English that I understood. That kraut was really shitting when he got through. After that he shot crap Saturday afternoon and the coal got to the camp. A real executive." Eddie shook his head admiringly.

Wolf kept nodding his head up and down with understanding and approbation. "That's the kind of stuff we need around here," he said. "These krauts get away with murder."

"You couldn't do that now, Walter," Eddie said.

"Yeah, we're teaching the krauts democracy," Wolf said, so wryly that Mosca and Eddie laughed, and even Middleton smiled.

They sipped their drinks, and then Eddie got up to look out the window at a woman passing by on her way to the exit gate. "There's some nice gash," he said, "how would you like to cut a piece of that?"

"That's a question for the *Fragebogen,*" Wolf said, and as he was about to add something else, the door leading to the corridor was flung open and a tall, blond boy was shoved into the room. His wrists were handcuffed and he was crying. Behind him were two short men in dark sack suits. One of the men stepped forward.

"Herr Dolman," he said, "we have the person who has been stealing the soap." Wolf burst out laughing.

"The soap bandit," he explained to Eddie and Mosca. "We've been missing a lot of Red Cross soap bars we were supposed to give the German kids. These men are detectives from the city."

One of the two men started to unlock the handcuffs. He held his forefinger under the boy's nose, the gesture almost fatherly, and said, "No dumb tricks, eh?" The boy nodded his head.

"Leave them on," Wolf said sharply. The detective stepped back.

Wolf walked close to the boy and shoved the blond head up with his hand. "Did you know this soap was for German children?"

The boy let his head fall and didn't answer.

"You worked here, you were trusted. You'll never work for the Americans again. However, if you'll sign a paper admitting what you've done, we will not prosecute. Do you agree to that?"

The boy nodded his head.

"Ingeborg," Wolf called. The German typist came in. Wolf nodded to the two men. "Take him in there to the other office, the girl knows what to do." He turned to Eddie and Mosca. "Too easy," and smiled his friendly smile. "But it saves everybody a lot of trouble and the kid will get his six months."

Mosca, not really caring, said, "Hell, you promised to let him off."

Wolf shrugged. "Right, but the German cops get him for making a black market. The Chief of Police in Bremen is an old friend of mine, and we co-operate."

"Justice at work," Eddie murmured. "So what if the kid stole some soap, give him a break."

Wolf said briskly, "Can't do it, they'd steal us blind." He put on his cap. "Well, I've got a busy night ahead of me. Have to make a full-scale search on all the kitchen workers before they leave the base. There's something." He grinned at them. "We get a woman cop from Bremen to search the female workers and she comes out with a big pair of rubber gloves and a bar of G.I. soap. You should see where those women hide a stick of butter. Phew." He spit. "I hope I never get that hungry."

When Wolf had left Gordon Middleton stood up and said in his deep, laconic voice. "The Colonel likes him." He smiled at Mosca, good-naturedly, as if it were something that amused him and which he did not resent. Before he left the office he said to Eddie, "I think I'll catch an early bus home," and to Mosca, simply and in a friendly tone, "See you around, Walter."

It was the end of the working day. Through the windows Mosca could see the German laborers massing at the exit gate, waiting to be searched and checked by the military police before they could leave the air base. Eddie went to the window and stood beside him.

"I guess you want to get to town and look for your girl," Eddie said and smiled, a smile almost womanly in its sweetness, in the hesitancy of the delicately cut mouth. "That's the reason I took all the trouble to fix a job here when you wrote. I figured it had to be the girl. Right?"

"I don't know," Mosca said. "Partly, I guess."

"Do you want to fix up about your billet in town first and then look her up? Or go see her now?"

"Let's fix up the billet first," Mosca said.

Eddie laughed outright. "If you go now you'll catch her home. By the time the billet is arranged you won't get to her until at least eight. Maybe she'll be out by then." He watched Mosca carefully when he said this.

"My tough luck," Mosca said.

They each picked up a suitcase and went out of the building to where Eddie had parked his jeep. Before Eddie started the motor he turned to Mosca and said. "You won't ask, but I'll tell you anyway. I've never seen her around the officer or enlisted-men clubs or with any G.I.'s. I've never even seen her." After a pause he added slyly, "And I didn't think you'd want me to look her up."

# 4

AS THEY PASSED through the Neustadt, then over the bridge into Bremen proper, Mosca saw his first remembered landmark. It was a church steeple and tower, the body like a face eaten away by disease, a slim thread of stone and plaster holding the spire toward the sky. Then they were going by the massive police presidio, the white scars of the explosion still showing on its dark, green walls. They traveled on the Schwachhauser Heer Strasse to the other side of Bremen, in what had once been the fashionable suburbs, the houses almost untouched and now used as billets and homes for the occupation forces.

Mosca was thinking about the man beside him. Eddie Cassin wasn't a romantic guy. As far as Mosca knew he was the opposite. He remembered when they had been G.I.'s, Eddie had found in the city a very young, very developed Belgian girl, pretty as a Dresden doll. He had established her in a small, windowless room in the billet and thrown a party. The girl had serviced the thirty-odd G.I.'s in the billet, not leaving the room for three days. The men played cards in the anteroom, a kitchen, waiting their turn. The girl was so pretty and good-natured that the men had pampered her as husbands pamper pregnant wives. They scrounged eggs, bacon and ham and took turns preparing her breakfast tray. They brought packages of food from the mess hall for her lunch and supper. She laughed and joked as she sat up naked in bed to eat from the tray. There was always someone in her room at any hour of the day and she seemed to have a real affection for everyone. She was difficult about only one thing. Eddie Cassin had to visit her once a day for at least an hour. She always called him Daddy.

"She was just too pretty to keep to myself," Eddie had said. But Mosca always remembered a note of mean satisfaction in his voice.

They turned from the Kurfürsten Allee into the Metzer Strasse and drove in late-afternoon shade cast by the long rows of wide and leafy trees. Eddie parked in front of a four-story, new-looking brick building that had a small lawn. "This is it," he said, "the best bachelor billet for Americans in Bremen."

The summer sun dyed the brick a dark red, and the street fell into deep shadows. Mosca took both suitcases and the gym bag, and Eddie Cassin went before him up the walk. They were met at the door by the German housekeeper.

"This is Frau Meyer," Eddie Cassin said and put his arm around her waist. Frau Meyer was a woman of nearly forty, an almost platinum blonde. She had a superb figure molded by years of service as swimming teacher in the *Bunddeutscher Maedel*. Her face had a friendly but dissipated look accentuated by large, very white buck teeth.

Mosca nodded and she said, "I'm very pleased to see you, Mr. Mosca. Eddie has told me so much about you."

They went up the stairs to the third floor, and Frau Meyer unlocked the door to one of the rooms and gave the key to Mosca. It was a very large room. In the corner was a narrow bed and in another corner a huge, white, painted wardrobe. Two large windows let in the dying sun and the first beginnings of the long summer twilight. The rest of the room was bare.

Mosca put the two suitcases on the floor and Eddie sat on the bed. Eddie said to Frau Meyer, "Call Yergen."

Frau Meyer said, "I'll get the sheets and blankets, too." They could hear her going up the stairs.

"It doesn't look so good," Mosca said.

Eddie Cassin smiled. "We have a magician in the house. This guy Yergen. He'll fix everything." And while they waited, Eddie told Mosca about the billet. Frau Meyer was a good housekeeper, saw to it there was aways hot water, that the eight maids were thorough in their cleaning, and (by special arrangement with Frau Meyer) the laundry perfectly done. She lived herself in two comfortably furnished rooms in the attic. "I spend most of my time up there," Eddie went on, "but I think she screws Yergen on the side. My room is on the floor below this one so we can't keep a real close check on one another, thank God."

Mosca, becoming more and more impatient as the twilight deepened, listened to Eddie go on about the billet as if he owned it. Yergen was indispensable, Eddie said, to the Americans billeted in the Metzer Strasse. He could fix the house water pump so that even people on the top floor could take baths. He made up boxes for the chinaware Americans sent home, and packed so skillfully that the grateful relatives in America never complained of breakage. They made a good team, Yergen and Frau Meyer. Only Eddie knew that during the day they would carefully loot the rooms. From one it would be a pair of shorts, another a pair of socks, here a few towels or some handkerchiefs. The Americans were careless and kept no close check on their possessions. From the room of those extraordinarily careless it would be a pack or half-filled pack of cigarettes. All this was done with discretion. The maids who cleaned the rooms were kept honest by strict discipline.

"For Christ sake," Mosca said, "you know I want to get out of here. Get those krauts on the ball."

Eddie went to the door and yelled, "Hey, Meyer, snap it up." And then to Mosca. "She probably knocked off a quickie with Yergen. She loves it." They could hear her coming down the stairs.

She came in with an armful of bedclothing and behind her came Yergen. In his hand was a hammer and in his mouth some nails. He was a short, slender German of vigorous middle age, dressed in overalls and an American Army khaki shirt. There was an air of quiet competence and dignity about him that would have inspired trust and confidence if it had not been for the bunched and wrinkled skin beneath his eyes which gave him an air of shrewd cunning.

He shook hands with Eddie Cassin and then extended to Mosca the same greeting. Mosca shook hands to be polite. The occupation was getting real friendly, he thought.

"I am the 'jack of all trades' here," Yergen said. He brought out the phrase with a stilted relish. "Times you want anything fixed just call on me."

"I'll need a bigger bed," Mosca said, "some furniture, a radio, some other stuff I'll think of later."

Yergen unbuttoned the pocket of his khaki shirt and took out a pencil. "Of course," he said briskly, "they furnish these rooms very badly. Regulations. But I have helped other of your comrades. A small or large radio?"

"How much?" Mosca asked.

"Five to ten cartons."

"Money," Mosca said. "I have no cigarettes."

"American dollars or scrip?"

"Money orders."

"I tell you," Yergen said slowly, "I think you need here a radio, some table lamps, four or five chairs, a couch and a large bed. I get you all these things, we talk about the price later. If you have no cigarettes now, I can wait. I'm a businessman, I know when to give credit. And besides you are a friend of Mr. Cassin."

"That's fine," Mosca said. He stripped to the waist and opened the blue gym bag for a soap and towel.

"And if you want someone to do your laundry, please let me know. I'll give the order to the maid." Frau Meyer smiled at him. She liked his long torso with its white ornamental scar that she guessed ran to his groin.

"What does it cost?" Mosca asked. He had opened a suitcase and was laying out a fresh change of clothing.

"Oh, please, no payment. Give me a few bars of chocolate a week, and I'll see to it that the maids are happy."

"O.K., O.K.," Mosca said impatiently. And then to Yergen. "See if you can get that stuff in here tomorrow."

After the two Germans left, Eddie Cassin shook his head sadly in mock reproof. "Times have changed, Walter," he said. "The occupation has entered into a new phase. We treat people like Frau Meyer and Yergen with respect, shake their hands and always, always, give them a cigarette to smoke when we talk business to them. They can do us favors, Walter."

"Screw 'em," Mosca said. "Where's the washroom?"

Eddie Cassin led him down the hall. The bathroom was an enormous one, with three sinks, the biggest bathtub Mosca had ever seen, and a toilet bowl beside which stood a small table littered with magazines and Stateside news-papers.

"Real class," Mosca said. He began to wash and Eddie sat on the toilet bowl to keep him company.

"You going to move your girl friend in here?" Eddie asked.

"If I find her and she wants to come back," Mosca said.

"You going out to see her tonight?"

Mosca wiped himself dry and fixed a blade in the razor. "Yeah," he said and glanced at the partly open window. The last light of evening was melting away. "I'll try it to-night."

Eddie got up and went to the door. "If it doesn't click, come up to Frau Meyer's rooms when you get back and have a drink." He gave Mosca a pat. "If everything works out, then I'll see you tomorrow morning at the air base." He went out and down the hall.

Alone, Mosca felt an overpowering urge not to finish shaving, to go back to his room and go to bed, or go up to Frau Meyer's and spend the evening drinking with Eddie. He felt a strange reluctance to leave this building to go and find Hella, thinking of her name again now, con-sciously, but he made himself finish shaving and then he combed his hair. He walked over to the bathroom window and opened it wide; the side street was nearly empty. But down along the ruins he saw a woman in black, a dark mass in the failing light, pulling out the grass that grew here and there in the rubble. She had a great armful of it. And nearer to him, almost underneath his window, he saw a family of four, a man, his wife and two small boys, build-ing a wall that was as yet no more than a foot high. The boys carried from a small handcart the broken bricks they had salvaged from the rubbled city and the man and woman hacked and scraped until the bricks fitted into the wall. The skeleton of the house framed them and etched them into Mosca's mind. The last light of the day vanished, and the whole street and the people were now just dark masses moving through a deeper and more massive darkness. Mosca went back to his room.

He took a bottle out of his suitcase and had a long drink. He was careful about dressing, thinking, "It's the first time she'll see me without my uniform." He put on a light gray suit and a white open shirt. He left everything as it was in the room—the suitcases open but unpacked, the soiled clothing on the floor, the shaving kit thrown carelessly on the bed. He had one last long drink, then ran downstairs and went out into the warm and heavy summer night.

He caught a streetcar, and the ticket taker asked for a cigarette, spotting him for an American immediately. Mosca gave it to him and then kept a watchful eye on each streetcar going by in the opposite direction, thinking that perhaps she had already left her room to go some place for the evening. Every so often he became tense and nervous, thinking he had seen her, that the back or profile of some girl looked like hers, but he could never be sure.

When he left the trolley and walked down the remembered street, he wasn't sure of the house and had to check the list of names that was posted on the door of each building. He made only one mistake, for the second list he read did have her name. He knocked, waited a few minutes and knocked again.

The door opened, and in the dim light of the hallway he recognized the old woman who owned the house. Her gray hair neatly pinned around her head, the old black dress, the threadbare shawl, all gave her the universal look of sorrow of aged women everywhere.

"Yes," she asked, "what is it?"

"Is Fräulein Hella at home?" Mosca was surprised at the ease and fluency of his German.

The old woman did not recognize him or realize that he was not a German. "Please come in," she said, and he followed her down the dimly lit hall to the room. The old woman knocked and said, "Fräulein Hella, you have a visitor, a man."

Finally he heard her real voice, quietly, but on a note of surprise. "A man?" And then "Wait one moment, please." Mosca opened the door and went into the room.

She was sitting with her back to him, hastily pushing clips into her just washed hair. On the table beside her stood a gray loaf of bread. Against the wall was a narrow bed, a night table beside it.

As he watched, Hella finished pinning the hair around her head and snatched up the loaf and slice of bread to take them to the wardrobe. Then she turned; her eyes met Mosca standing by the door.

Mosca saw the white, bone-ridged, almost skeletal face, the body even more fragile than he had remembered it. Her hands emptied as the gray bread fell to the wooden, buckled floor. Her face showed no surprise, and for a moment he thought the look was one of annoyance and slight displeasure. Then the face dissolved into a mask of sorrow and grief. He walked over to her, and her face seemed to crumple and fold, the tears following the many creases down to where his hand held the pointed chin. She let her head fall and pressed it against his shoulder.

"Let me see you," Mosca said, "let me look at you." He tried to lift her face, but she kept it against him. "It's all right," he said, "I wanted to surprise you." She kept sobbing, and all he could do was wait, looking around the room, the narrow bed, the old-fashioned wardrobe, and on the dresser, enlarged, framed, the photos he had given her. The light from the single table lamp was dim, a depressing, weak yellow, the walls and ceiling sagged inward from the weight of the ruins above them.

Hella lifted her face—she was half-laughing, half-crying. "Ah, you, you," she said. "Why didn't you write? Why didn't you let me know?"

"I wanted to surprise you," he said again. He kissed her gently, and lying against him, she said in a weak, incoherent voice, "When I saw you I thought you were dead or I was dreaming or crazy, I don't know, and I look so terrible, I just washed my hair." She looked down at the shapeless, faded housedress and then lifted her face to him again.

He saw now the dark circles under her eyes, as if the pigment from the rest of her face had been drained and held there to stain the skin almost black. The hair under his hand was lifeless, still wet, her body against him hard and angular.

She smiled and he saw the gap along the side of her mouth. He caressed her cheek and asked, "And this?"

Hella looked embarrassed. "The baby," she said, "I lost two teeth." She smiled at him, asked like a child, "Do I look very ugly?"

Mosca shook his head slowly. "No," he said, "no." And then remembering. "What about the baby, did you get rid of it?"

"No," Hella said, "it was born too soon, it only lived a few hours. I just left the hospital a month ago."

And then, because she knew his disbelief, his lack of

faith, she went to the dresser and pulled out a bundle of papers tied together with old string. She leafed through it and gave him four official documents.

"Read them," she said, not hurt or angry, knowing that in the world and time in which they lived, she had to give proof, that there was no absolute trust.

The official stamps and seals of the different bureaus dispelled his doubt. Almost regretfully he accepted the fact that she had not lied.

Hella went to the wardrobe and took out a pile of clothing. She held each one up, the little undershirts, blouses, the small trousers. Some of the materials and colors were familiar to Mosca. And then he understood that because there was nothing else to be had, she had cut up her dresses, even her underclothing, and sewed them together to fit a smaller body.

"I knew it would be a boy," she said. And then suddenly Mosca was very angry. He was angry that she had given the color from her face, the flesh along her hips and shoulders, the teeth, the clothing so cleverly cut and fitted together and that she had received nothing in return. And he knew that what had brought him back was his own need and not hers.

"That was silly," he said, "that was goddamn silly."

Mosca sat on the bed and Hella sat beside him. For a moment they were both embarrassed and stared at the bare table, the only chair, the indented walls and sagging ceiling, and then moving slowly, as if taking part in an ancient tribal ritual, like heathens cementing their relationship with a vague and fearful god, not knowing if the ceremony would bring disaster or good fortune, they stretched out on the narrow bed and came together, he finally with a passion inspired by drink, guilt, remorse, and she with love, tenderness and an absolute faith that this consummation was good, that it would bring happiness to them both. And she accepted the pain given to her not-yet-healed body, the cruelty of his passion, his lack of faith in her and in himself and in all things, knowing the final truth that, of all the human beings that he had known, he had need of her, her faith, her body, her belief and love for him.

# 5

THAT SECOND SUMMER of peace went by quickly for Mosca. The work at the air base was so light, it seemed as if he were there only to keep Eddie Cassin company, listen to his stories and cover up for him when he was too drunk to come in and work. Eddie Cassin didn't have much to do. Lieutenant Forte came in for a few minutes each morning to sign papers and then went up to the Operations Office to sweat out a flight and pass the day talking to his fellow pilots. After work Mosca had supper with Wolf and Eddie and sometimes Gordon at the Rathskellar, the official mess for American officers and civilians in Bremen.

Evenings he and Hella kept to their room, lying together on the couch reading, the radio tuned to a German station that played soft music. When the last of the warm summer twilight died away they would look at each other and smile and go to bed. They would let the radio play until very late.

The floor on which they lived was quiet, but on the floors below parties went on night after night. In the summer evenings the sound of radios filled the Metzer Strasse, and jeeps loaded with Americans in their olive-green civilian uniforms, pretty, barelegged German girls on their laps, stopped in front of the building with a screaming of brakes and shrilling cries of the young women. The laughter and clinking of glasses carried out to passersby who turned their heads curiously and cautiously as they went on down the street. Later they might hear Eddie Cassin cursing drunkenly as he fought with one of his girl friends outside the building. Sometimes the parties would break up early, and a late summer night breeze, its freshness tainted with the smell of rubble, would rustle leaves and branches of the trees that lined the street below.

On Sundays Hella and Frau Meyer prepared dinner in Meyer's attic apartment, usually a rabbit or duck that Eddie and Mosca drove out to a nearby farm to trade for, and with it garden vegetables from the same farm. Then gray German bread topped off with PX coffee and ice cream. When they had finished eating, Hella and Mosca would leave Eddie and Frau Meyer to their drinking and go for a long walk through the city, and beyond it to the flat, green countryside.

Mosca smoking his cigar, Hella wearing one of his starched, white shirts, sleeves rolled neatly up above the elbow, they would go up past the police building, its massive, green-colored concrete showing gray scars chipped out by the explosion and past the Glocke Building, a little farther on, which now housed the American Red Cross Club. In the square before it, children waited and begged for cigarettes and chocolate. Stubble-cheeked men in Wehrmacht caps and torn, dyed Army jackets picked up the butts as soon as one of the olive-drab G.I.'s leaning against the building flicked it away. The G.I.'s lounged easily, eyeing the women, picking out the *Fräuleins* who passed by slowly as if walking on a treadmill, and who a short time later, circling the building, passed by again, and then again and again until it was like watching someone known riding a merry-go-round, the familiar face appearing inevitably before the watchful, expectant and amused onlookers. In the warm summer afternoon the square was like a gay, thriving market place, making the day seem not like Sunday, taking away the Sunday atmosphere of quiet and suspended motion.

Great olive-drab Army buses and mud-covered trucks poured into the square every few minutes, bringing occupation troops from the hamlets surrounding Bremen and some from as far away as Bremerhaven. The G.I.'s were natty in pressed olive drabs, the trouser legs tucked neatly into polished, mahogany-colored combat boots. There were English troops sweltering in their heavy woolens and beretlike headgear. American merchant mariners, wild looking in raggedy trousers and dirty sweaters and occasionally with bushy, full-grown beards, waited sullenly for MP's to check their papers before they could enter the building.

Sporadically the German police in their dyed, soldierlike uniforms cleared the square, shooing the child beggars down the many side streets, pushing the haggard-looking butt snipers to the far corner of the square and then letting them rest on the steps of the German Communications Building. The *Fräuleins* on their merry-go-round speeded up the tempo slightly but were never molested.

Mosca would pick up sandwiches in the Red Cross, and they would go on, mingling with the stream of people on their way to Burger Park.

The enemy on Sunday still took their traditional afternoon strolls. The German men walked with the dignity of family chiefs, some with unfilled pipes in their mouths. Their wives pushed baby carriages and children gamboled sedately and somewhat tiredly before them. The summer sun caught the loose dirt raised by the light afternoon breeze that swept through the ruins, imprisoned it, flooded it, so that over the whole city hung an almost imperceptible veil of golden dust.

And then, finally, after they had crossed a great, reddish prairie of ruins, an earth of leveled homes, a soil of crushed brick and dust and iron, they would come out into the countryside, and walking until they were tired, would come to rest in a green and heavily grown field. They would rest and sleep and eat the sandwiches they had brought, and if the spot were secluded enough, make love peacefully in the empty world which seemed to surround them.

When the sun faced them across the sky, they walked back into the city. Over the prairie of ruins dusk would fall, and coming into the square they could see the G.I.'s leaving the Red Cross Building. The victors had had their fill of sandwiches, ice cream, Cokes, ping-pong and the professional, sterilized friendliness of the hostesses. In the street the soldiers would lounge just as if they were on the street corners back home. The lines of *Fräuleins* passing up and down would thin out, enemy and conqueror disappearing together down the rubble-filled side streets to half-destroyed rooms in shattered buildings, or if time pressed, to cavelike cellars. In the square, black and almost still, there were only a few hopeful beggars, a child, tired and now stationary girls. As from a dying carnival, the blurring music would filter out of the building and wash gently over the silent figures in the darkened square, sift through the ruins down to the Weser, as if following them to the quiet river, and as Mosca and Hella walked along the bank, they left the music behind and gazed across the water to the moonlit skeletal city on the other side.

In the Metzer Strasse Frau Meyer and Eddie Cassin

would have tea and cookies waiting for them; sometimes Eddie would be in a drunken stupor on the couch but come alive when he heard their voices. They would drink their tea and talk quietly, feeling the new raw peace of the gentle summer night and the slow, rising drowsiness that would lead to safe and dreamless sleep.

# 6

IN THE BILLET, the room next to Mosca's was occupied by a short, heavy-framed civilian wearing the usual olive-green uniform. But on it was a blue-and-white patch stitched with the letters "AJDC." They saw him rarely, and no one in the billet knew him, but late at night he could be heard moving around his room, the radio playing softly. One evening he gave Mosca a lift in his jeep. They were both going to the Rathskellar for supper. His name was Leo, and he worked for the American Joint Distribution Committee, a Jewish relief organization. The initials were also painted on his jeep in great white letters.

As they were driving through the streets, Leo asked Mosca in a high voice with an English accent, "Have I met you some place, you look familiar to me?"

"I used to be with Mil Gov right after the war," Mosca said. He was sure they had never met.

"Ah, ah," Leo said, "you came up to Grohn with the coal trucks, eh?"

"That's right," Mosca said surprised.

"I was an inmate there, a DP," Leo grinned. "You didn't do such a good job. Many a week end we went without hot water."

"We had trouble for a while," Mosca said. "It got straightened out."

"Yes, I know," Leo smiled. "A fascist method but perhaps necessary."

They had supper together. Leo in ordinary times would have been fat. He had a hawk-nosed, big-boned face, the left side of which twitched spasmodically. He moved nervously and quickly but with the awkwardness and lack of co-ordination of one who had never participated in any kind of athletics. He was ignorant of almost all sports.

Over their coffee Mosca asked, "What do you people do?"

"It is UNRRA work," Leo said. "Distribute supplies to the Jews who are in the camps waiting to leave Germany. I was myself eight years in Buchenwald."

A long time ago, a time that was no longer real, Mosca thought, that was one of the big reasons he had enlisted, to fight against concentration camps, but that hadn't been him, that was the guy in the photo, the one Gloria and his mother and Alf cared so much about. But remembering this aroused a strange emotion in him, of embarrassment and shyness because he no longer gave a damn.

"Yes," Leo said. "I went in when I was thirteen." He rolled up his sleeve and on his arm as if printed there with purple ink was a six-digit number with a smeared letter before it. "My father was there with me. He died a few years before the camp was liberated."

"You speak English pretty well," Mosca said. "Nobody'd think you were German."

Leo looked at him with a smile and said in his quick, nervous voice, "No, no, I am not a German. I am a Jew." He was silent for a moment. "I was a German, of course, but Jews cannot any longer be Germans."

"How come you haven't left?" Mosca asked.

"I have a very good job here. I have all the privileges Americans have and I earn good money. And then I must make up my mind whether to go to Palestine or the United States. It is very difficult to decide."

They talked for a long time, Mosca drinking whiskey and Leo coffee. At one point Mosca found himself trying to explain different sports to Leo, really trying to tell how it felt because the other had spent his childhood and his youth in the concentration camp, had it stolen, irretrievably lost.

Mosca tried to explain how it felt to go up for a shot in basketball, the thrill of faking a guard out of position and rising easily in the air to float the ball through the basket, the quick whirling and running on the warm wooden floor of the gym, the soaking, sweaty tiredness and the magical refreshment of the warm shower afterward. Then walking down the street, his whole body relaxed, carrying the blue gym bag, and the girls waiting for them in the ice-cream parlor. Later the peaceful and complete oblivion of perfect sleep.

Riding back to the billet, Leo said, "I am always on the ways, my job makes me travel a great deal. But with the cold weather coming I will spend more time in Bremen. We'll get to know each other better, eh?"

"I'll show you how to play baseball," Mosca said with a smile, "get you ready for the States. And don't say 'on the ways.' That's German. Say 'on the road,' or 'traveling.' "

After that he would come to their room some nights and drink tea and coffee, and Mosca taught him how to play cards—poker, casino and rummy. Leo never talked about the time he had spent in the camps and never seemed depressed, but he never had the patience to stay in one place long and their quiet life was not appealing to him. They became good friends, Leo and Hella, and he claimed that she was the only girl who had been able to teach him how to dance properly.

And then when autumn came and the trees dropped their leaves on the bicycle paths and laid a speckled brown-and-green carpet along the shaded streets, the freshened air stirred Mosca's blood and lifted him out of his summer lethargy. He became restless, ate more often at the Rath-skellar, went drinking at the Officers' Club—all places where Hella was not allowed to enter because she was the enemy. Returning late to the billet, a little drunk, he would eat the thick, canned soup Hella warmed up for him on the electric plate and then sleep fitfully through the night. On many mornings he would wake at dawn and watch the gray clouds being swept across the sky by the early October wind. He watched the German workers walking briskly to the corner where they could catch a *Strassenbahn* to the heart of the city.

One morning as he stood by the window, Hella rose and stood by him. She was in the undershirt she used for bedclothing. She put her arm around him, and they both looked down at the street below.

"Can't you sleep?" she murmured drowsily. "You're always up so early."

"I guess we'll have to start getting out more. This home life is too much for me."

Mosca watched the russet blanket of leaves being rolled up Metzer Strasse, covering the dirt bicycle path underneath the trees.

Hella leaned against him. "We need a baby, a wonderful baby," she said softly.

"Christ," Mosca said, "the *Führer* really drummed that crap into your heads."

"Children were loved before that." She was angry that he could laugh at what she wanted so much. "I know it's thought stupid to want children. In the *Flak* the Berlin girls used to laugh at us farmers because we cared about babies and talked about them." She pushed away from him. "All right, go to work," she said.

Mosca tried to reason with her. "You know we can't get married until they lift the ban. Everything we do here is illegal, especially your being here in the billet. When the kid comes we'll have to move to German quarters and that's illegal for me. There's a million things I'd have to do that they could ship me back to the States for and no way to take you with me."

She smiled at him and there was a trace of sadness in it. "I know you won't leave me here again." Mosca was surprised and shocked that she should know this. He had already decided to go underground with false papers if some trouble should come.

"Ah, Walter," she said, "I don't want to be like the people downstairs; drink, dance at the club, go to bed and never have anything to keep us together except ourselves. The way we live, that's not enough." She stood there, the undershirt reaching just over her hipbone and navel, without dignity and without shame. He wanted to smile.

"It's no good," he said.

"Listen to me. When you went away I was happy I was going to have a baby. I thought I had such very good luck. Because even if you didn't come back there would be another human being in the world I could love. Do you understand that? From my whole family I only have one sister left, and she is far away. Then you came and you left and I had no one. In all the world there was no one that it would be pleasure for me to bring pleasure to, no one that was part of my life. There's nothing more terrible."

Below them some Americans came out of the building into the cold street, unlocked the security chains on their jeeps and warmed up the motors, the rising and falling throb coming faintly through the closed windows.

Mosca put his arm around her. "You're not well enough." He looked down at the thin, naked body. "I don't want anything to happen to you." And as he said the words a wave of fear swept over him that she would leave for some reason, and that in the gray winter mornings he would stand alone at the window, the room empty behind him, and that the fault in some unforeseen way would be his. Turning to her suddenly, he said in a gentle voice. "Don't be mad at me. Wait a bit."

She rested in his arms and then quietly she said, "You're afraid really of yourself. I think you know that. I see how you are with other people and how you are with me. Everyone thinks you're so unfriendly, so"—she searched for a word that would not make him angry—"so rough. I know you're not that way, not really. I could never want a better man, in everything. Sometimes Frau Meyer and Yergen, when I say something nice about you, they look at each other. Oh, I know what they think." Her voice was bitter, the bitterness of all women speaking in defense of their own against a world that does not comprehend the reason for their love. "They don't understand."

He picked her up, put her on the bed and drew the blanket over her. "You'll catch a cold," he said. He leaned over to kiss her before he left for work. "You can have anything you want," he said, then smiled. "Especially something that easy. And don't worry about them ever making me leave, no matter what."

"I won't," she said laughing. "I'll be waiting for you tonight."

# 7

A BAND was playing fast dance music when they entered the German night club. It was a long rectangular room bare of ornament and bleak with white, unshaded light. The walls were roughly calcimined and the high, domed ceiling gave it a vast cathedral-like air. It had been a school auditorium, but the rest of the building had been blown away.

The chairs were of the hard, folding variety, the tables were equally bare and stern. There were no decorations. The room was full, people jammed together, so that the waiters in many instances could not serve a table directly and had to ask intervening couples to pass the drinks on. Wolf was known here, and they followed his portly figure to a table near the wall.

Wolf offered his cigarettes all around and said to the waiter, "Six schnapps." At the same time he slipped the rest of the cigarettes in the pack into the waiter's hand. "The clear stuff." The waiter bowed and hurried off.

Frau Meyer turned her blonde head to look at the room. "It's not very nice here," she said.

Eddie patted her hand. "Baby, this is for people who lost the war."

Mosca smiled at Hella. "Not too bad is it?" She shook her head. "It's a change," she said. "I should see how my fellow Germans enjoy themselves." Mosca missed the slight guilt in her voice, but Eddie understood and his delicate mouth curved into a smile. One weapon found, he thought, and felt a sudden elation, a sudden passion.

"There's a good story about this place," Wolf said. They had to bribe the Education Officer at Mil Gov to certify it as unfit for any school activities and then bribe the Fine Arts Officer as O.K. for entertainment purposes. Nobody knows whether it's really safe." He added, "Not that it matters, it'll be closed up in a couple of days anyway."

"Oh, why?" Hella asked.

"Wait and see," Wolf said, smiling with a knowing air.

Leo said with his usual good humor, "Look at them," he gestured around the room. "I never saw sadder looking people in my life. And they are paying to have such a bad time?" They all laughed. The waiter brought their drinks.

Eddie raised his glass. His handsome face settled into a mock seriousness. "Happiness to our two friends, a perfectly matched couple. Look at them. One, a princess so sweet and fair. The other, a scowling brute. She will mend his socks and have his slippers ready each evening and for a reward she will receive some well-chosen hard words and a blow. My friends, this marriage will be perfect. It will last a hundred years if he doesn't kill her first." They drank, Mosca and Hella smiling at each other as if they possessed an answer, a secret no one at the table could guess.

The two couples went out to dance on the small floor before the raised stage at the other end of the room. Wolf and Leo were left alone. Wolf looked around with a practiced eye.

Cigarette smoke rose over the mass of people to the high, domed ceiling. The patrons were a curious mixture, old couples who had perhaps sold a piece of good furniture and decided on one night out to relieve the dull monotony of their lives; young black-market operators, good friends of American mess sergeants and PX officers, sat at tables with young girls who wore nylon stockings and smelled of perfume; older men who trafficked in diamonds and furs, automobiles and other valuables, sat with girls not richly dressed, sedate mistresses of long standing, a salaried relationship.

The densely packed room was not noisy, the general conversation not loud in volume. The drinks were ordered at long intervals, and there was no food of any kind in sight. The band tried its best to play American tunes jazz style, the drummer's square head shaking from side to side in a strained but reserved imitation of American performers helpless with inner rhythm.

Wolf nodded to some people at other tables, black-market operators he had done business with for cigarettes. They had been spotted for Americans as soon as they came in, he thought, and curiously enough more because of the ties they wore than anything else. The other people here were just as well dressed but for some reason the black market could not supply ties, the people here wore dull, ragged pieces of cloth for neckwear. Wolf stored this away in his mind. Another way to make an easy dollar.

The music ended, and everyone went back to the tables. Eddie, flushed with dancing and the contact with Frau Meyer's body, watched Hella intently as she sat down and then leaned over on Mosca's chair, her hand resting on his shoulder. In his mind he saw the hard, white body on a brown Army blanket, spreading, spreading, his face close to her neat and passive head. In a moment he felt sure of his success—how it would happen he did not know—and then the image shattered as from the rose-colored circle of light under which the band played, the only friendly color in the room, came three short, commanding blasts of a trumpet.

The small hum quieted, the white bright lights dimmed, and the room became cavernous, the high, domed ceiling invisible in the darkness above them.

On the auditorium stage a line of girls came out dancing so badly that when they exited there was not even a polite smattering of applause. They were followed by a juggler and then by acrobats. And then a girl singer with a robust figure and a high, weak voice.

"Christ," Mosca said, "let's get the hell out."

Wolf shook his head. "Wait a bit."

The audience was still attentive, still expectant. The trumpet gave out another flourish, and the lights dimmed almost to darkness; the stage at the end of the room became a luminous, yellow square, and into it, strolling nonchalantly from the outside darkness of the wings, came a small, dapper man with the full, round, rubberlike face of the born comedian. He was greeted with a storm of applause.

He began to talk to the audience conversationally, as if there were no barrier between them.

"I must apologize that part of my famous act cannot be performed tonight. My dog, Frederick, is not to be found anywhere." He paused, his face sorrowful, and then in simulated anger: "It's a shame, really a shame. Ten dogs I have trained and always they disappear. In Berlin—gone. In Düsseldorf—gone, and now here. Always the same." A girl came rushing out on the stage. She whispered in his ear. The comedian nodded his head and turned briskly to the audience. "My friends, the management has asked me to announce that meat sandwiches will be available right after this performance." He winked. "No ration card necessary but at an exorbitant price of course. Now as I was saying—" He stopped. On his face a look so comical in its wonder, dismay and then complete understanding shattered the audience into a great wave of laughter. "Frederick, my Frederick," he shrieked, and rushed off the stage. He came strolling back into the light munching a sandwich. As the laughter subsided he said sadly, "Too late. But he is a good friend to the last. A truly tasty sandwich." And with an enormous bite he made most of it disappear.

Waiting for the applause to die, he wiped his mouth and then took a piece of paper from his pocket.

Raising a hand for silence he began, "Today everyone worries about calories. I read here that we need 1300 calories to stay alive and that we get 1550 calories in the ration established by Military Government. No criticism of the authorities intended, but I wish to point out tonight how careful we must be with our extra two hundred calories. Now, a few simple rules."

He told all the old jokes about calories but so expertly that one ripple of laughter followed another. He was interrupted by a scantily clad girl who came dancing on the stage and whirled around him. He watched her with a greedy and appraising eye and then from his pockets drew out a carrot, a small head of lettuce and a handful of green beans. He counted on his fingers and shook his head. Then shrugged and said, "She will take a thousand calories at least."

The girl pushed against him. He explained to her in pantomime what the trouble was. She reached between her breasts and drew out a small bunch of grapes. He pantomimed; not enough. She started to reach into her shorts, but he, with a look of noble abnegation said loudly: "Please, I couldn't." As the girl exited sadly from the stage he thrust out with his arm and said, "If I had only a hot beefsteak." The laughter rose to the high-domed ceiling.

On the stage the comedian's rubbery face was exalted and flushed with the power he held over them. Exuberantly he did quick imitations: Rudolph Hess, drooling, raving insanely, escaping in a plane to England; Goebbels explaining a night out to his wife with the most ridiculous and outrageous lies; Goering promising that no bombs would ever fall on Berlin as he dived underneath a table to escape the falling debris. When the comedian made his exit there was a tremendous applause. It continued until he reappeared. The audience gasped and was still.

His hair was combed over his eyes and there was a smudge on his upper lip that could be a short, small mustache. He had screwed up his rubbery face into a startling Hitlerian mask. He stood near the wings, the look on his face half-parody, half-earnest. He radiated power and magnetism. He held the audience with his glance and in a loud voice that rang to the high-domed ceiling asked: "Do you want me back?"

There was a moment of shocked silence and as he stood there, slowly on that white-floured face appeared the deadly smile of a successful anti-Christ. The audience understood.

The room exploded. Some men leaped onto chairs and tables and shouted, "Yah, Yah." The women clapped furiously. Some stomped on the floor with their feet, and others banged tables with their fists. The din filled the room, crashed against the walls and reverberated against the ceiling.

Wolf was on his feet looking across the crowd at the stage with a grim smile on his face. Mosca had understood and leaned back in his chair sipping his drink. Frau Meyer was looking down at the table trying to restrain a smile of pleasure. Eddie was asking her, "What goes on, what the hell goes on?" Frau Meyer said, "Nothing, nothing."

Hella looked at Leo across the table. His face was rigid, but the tic on the left side was out of control. She flushed and unconsciously shook her head from side to side as if to disclaim any responsibility, any share in what was going on. But Leo turned his eyes away from her and stared again at the stage.

The comedian's rubbery face was normal now and he had brushed his hair back as he bowed. The illusion was gone, and he accepted the applause as if it were his due, given for the pleasure his art afforded.

The band struck up a tune. Wolf sat down nodding his head as if he understood many things. People moved out to dance. There were many glances at their table. Two young men seated nearby had the girls with them almost hysterical with their murmured wit.

Leo stared down at the table, feeling his face twitching. He was angry, with a hurt and helpless despair. He hoped one of the others would suggest leaving.

Mosca, watching him, understood and said to Wolf and the others, "Let's get out." As he stood up he saw that one of the young men had turned his chair so that he faced their table and could stare at Leo with an amused grin. The front of his head was bald, his face heavy, the features thick and forceful.

Mosca said to Wolf with a nod of his head, "Let's take that guy with us."

Wolf studied Mosca as if he saw something he had guessed and hoped for. "O.K. I'll use my Intelligence card to get him outside. You got a weapon, just in case?"

"One of those small Hungarian things," Mosca said.

Leo raised his head. "No, I don't want to do anything like that. Let us just leave."

Hella took Mosca's arm. "Yes, let's leave," she said. The others rose. Wolf was shaking his head up and down again as if he understood something. He glanced at Leo with a look of pity and contempt. He saw that Mosca had frowned and shrugged and was on his way out. As Wolf went past the other table he leaned over and put his face close to the young German's and looked into his eyes. "A loud laugh can be very unhealthy, do you understand me?" He flashed his Intelligence card, knowing the German would be able to read it. As he followed the others, he smiled, and no laughter followed their retreat.

They drove back to Mosca's room for a drink. Hella began to prepare bacon sandwiches on the electric plate which stood on a footlocker.

They all sat around the large, square table, except Eddie who stretched out in the stuffed chair in one corner of the room. Mosca unlocked the white painted wardrobe and took out liquor and cigarettes.

Eddie from his chair asked, "How do the bastards get away with it?"

"They won't," Wolf said. "He's pulled some raw stuff, but tonight he went too far. How do you like the reception he got, though?" Wolf shook his white, heavy face up and down in amused wonder. "These krauts never learn. You'd think that if they just took a walk down the street they'd never want to fight again. But they're rarin' to go. Just in their blood."

Mosca said jokingly to Leo, "Looks like you'd better make up your mind where you're going, Palestine or the States."

Leo shrugged and sipped his coffee.

Wolf asked, "Can you go to the States?"

"Oh, yes," Leo said. "I can go there."

"Then go." Wolf studied him. "If tonight's any indication, you're too soft for that pioneer stuff."

Leo put his hand up to the left side of his face.

"Leave it lay," Mosca said.

"No. Don't misunderstand me, Leo, when I say the trouble with your race has always been that they never fight back. Some people think they're cowards. I think it's a matter of being too civilized. They don't believe in force. Like tonight. If we'd taken that guy outside and knocked him around, it would have helped, in a small way. If you people ever get a country of your own, thank your terrorist organizations. Terror and force are great weapons. Organizations in every country use them and never underestimate their power. I'm surprised you don't know that after what you've been through."

Leo said slowly, "I'm not afraid to go to Palestine, and in some ways I know it is my duty. But I think, too, how it will be a hard time. I want now—pleasure. That is the only way I can think of it. And yet I am ashamed that I think this way. But I will go away."

"Don't put it off too long," Wolf said. "These krauts will never change. It's in their blood. You can see it every day."

Leo went on as if he had not heard. "As for terror and force, I don't believe. My father was in camp with me, he was a German, by the way, my mother was a Jew. My father was a political prisoner, he went before me."

The tic on Leo's face went into motion again and he put up his hand to hold it still. "He died there but taught me before he died. He told me that one day I would be free and that the most terrible thing that could happen to me was to become like the people who kept us there. I believe him still. It is a little hard, but I believe him still."

Wolf shook his head. "I know. I know people like your father." His voice was expressionless.

Hella and Frau Meyer passed hot bacon sandwiches around. Leo refused his. "I'm going to bed," he said. He left and they could hear him in the next room, his radio tuned to a German station playing soft string music.

Frau Meyer went over to Eddie and pushed him playfully. "Stop dreaming," she said.

Eddie smiled, his handsome, delicate face soft with a sleepy tenderness. As Hella knelt by the electric plate, he watched her over his glass and thought, "It will be in this room," and every piece of furniture stood out clearly as if there were no people there. He was always doing this, his mind always creating scenes with women he had not even approached.

Wolf munched on his bacon sandwich. "It's funny the ideas people get." His voice lowered. "The men who ran Leo's camp were probably ordinary guys like you and me. Just following orders. During the war when I was in counter-intelligence, we'd get some prisoners, and the Major would look at his watch and say, 'I want such and such information by two o'clock.' We got it." Wolf accepted a cigar from Mosca and puffed on it. "I got back to the States for a leave before I started on this job and saw some of those war movies. You know, the hero gets tortured but dies of pain before he gives in and talks." Wolf waved his cigar in exasperation at the memory. "Of course, they can't even hint what's really done." He paused and looked at Mosca intently. "They're ashamed to admit it. A man can't control himself if the right things are done to him. Not one goddamn one."

Mosca filled the glasses, everybody was sleepy except Wolf. Frau Meyer sat curled in Eddie's lap, and Hella had stretched out on the couch against the wall opposite the bed.

Wolf smiled. "I had a special technique. I'd never ask a question until I gave them a little punishment first. Like that old gag about the newly married couple. The husband raps her in the mouth as soon as they're alone and says 'That's for nothing, watch what you do.' Same idea." He grinned disarmingly, his dead-white face filled with cheerful good humor. "I know what you think, here's a no-good son of a bitch. But somebody has always had to do that kind of work. You can't win wars without it. Believe me, I don't get any of this sadistic kind of pleasure like in the movies. But it's necessary. Hell, I even got a decoration out of it." He added hastily and sincerely, "But of course we never were as rough as the Germans."

Eddie yawned. "All very interesting, but I think I'll go down to my room."

Wolf laughed defensively. "I guess it *is* too late for a lecture." He let Eddie and Frau Meyer leave before him. He finished his drink and said to Mosca, "Come on downstairs, I want a talk with you." They went down to the street and sat in Wolf's jeep.

"All that Eddie thinks of is gash," Wolf said in an angry, contemptuous voice.

"He was just sleepy," Mosca said.

"How come you carry a weapon?" Wolf asked.

Mosca shrugged. "Used to having one, I guess. And the war isn't over long."

Wolf nodded. "I don't like to be out at night without one either."

There was another moment of silence, and Mosca moved restlessly.

Wolf puffed on his cigar. "I wanted to get you alone, because I have an idea about making ourselves a pile of dough. I guess everybody in the occupation has a little hunk of gravy. Now I got a lot of contacts, diamonds for cigarettes, all that kind of stuff. I can fix you up."

"Hell," Mosca said impatiently, "I can't get my hands on that many cigarettes."

Wolf hesitated and then went on. "You know, some day you may need a lot of dough. For instance, if they catch Hella in your room it'll be your ass, you'll get sent back to the States." He held up his hand. "I know, you'll go underground, a lot of guys have done it. But you'll need money. Or, say it came to a pinch, and you had to take her out of Germany. You can get phony papers, but they cost an arm and a leg. And wherever you go, Scandinavia, France, any other place, living comes high. Ever think of it?"

"No, I haven't," Mosca said slowly.

"Well, I got an idea. I need help and that's why I'm asking you. I'm no philanthropist. You interested?"

"Go ahead," Mosca said.

Wolf paused again, puffing on his cigar. "You know the money we use, the Army scrip? The black-market operators break their necks to get it. Then they trade it back to G.I.'s for money orders. But they have to make it pretty slow. We can change all the scrip we can get our hands on into money orders, something we couldn't do with the old occupation marks."

"So?" Mosca said.

"Now here's the thing. The last couple of weeks the

German operators seem to have a hell of a lot of scrip. I'm making a nice bit of change turning it into money orders for them. I'll cut you in on that, by the way. Now here's the angle. I got curious and started snooping around, and I heard a terrific story. When the scrip money was shipped from the States the boat docked in Bremerhaven. And even though everything was top-secret, something slipped and a case of scrip, over a million bucks, disappeared. The Army keeps quiet because it makes them look stupid as hell. How do you like that?" In telling the story Wolf became excited. "A million bucks," he repeated.

Mosca grinned at the pure hunger in Wolf's voice. "A lot of money," he said.

"Now here's my idea. The money is probably split up all over the country, but there must be a gang here with a big chunk. If we could only find them, that's the thing. It's a long shot."

Mosca said, "How do we find it and how do we take it?"

"Finding the money is my job," Wolf said, "but you help. It's not as hard as it sounds and remember, I'm a trained man. I have a lot of contacts. I'll take you around and introduce you as a big Post Exchange wheel who's looking to dump cigarettes at three or four bucks a carton. They'll jump at the price. We'll get rid of twenty or thirty cartons that way. I can get the butts. The word'll get around. Then we'll say we have to get rid of five thousand cartons in one lump. A big deal. We'll make up a story. If everything works out somebody'll come to us, and we'll close the deal. They show up with twenty thousand bucks worth of scrip. We take it. They can't go to the police, theirs or ours. They're screwed." Wolf stopped, took a last nervous puff and threw his cigar into the street. Then he said quietly, "It'll be hard work, tramping around town a couple of nights a week. And the final business takes guts."

"Real cops and robbers," Mosca said and Wolf smiled. Mosca looked out into the dark street and over the ruins. Far away, as if separated from them by a lake or prairie, he could see a lone streetcar with its yellow light moving slowly through the blackness of the city.

Wolf said slowly, seriously. "We have to prepare for our future. Sometimes I feel that my life before now was just a dream, nothing serious, maybe you feel the same. Now we have to get ready for our real life, and it's going to be tough, real tough. This is our last chance to fix ourselves up."

"O.K.," Mosca said, "but it sounds complicated as hell."

Wolf shook his head. "It may not work out. But meanwhile I'll throw you some of this exchange business. You'll make a good few hundred anyway, no matter what happens. If we're lucky, just a little lucky, we'll split fifteen or twenty thousand. Maybe more."

Mosca got out of the jeep as Wolf raced the motor, then watched him drive away. Looking up he saw Hella's dark head in the pane of light that was his window. He waved to her and then entered the building and ran up the stairs.

# 8

MOSCA SLOUCHED DOWN in the parked jeep, trying to escape the cold October wind of late afternoon. The frozen metal of the floor chilled his whole body.

Farther on up the street was an important intersection, streetcars swinging to the right and left, and military vehicles pausing momentarily for drivers to read the long row of white shingles that directed them to different headquarters in the city. Ruins stretched away on four sides like rough pasture land, and beyond the crossroads, where little houses began to stand, a small German movie theatre opened its doors, and a long waiting line moved slowly inside.

Mosca was hungry and impatient. He watched three covered trucks filled with German prisoners of war go by and stop at the intersection. Probably war criminals, he thought. A jeep with two armed guards followed dutifully behind. Leo appeared in the door of the tailor shop and Mosca straightened up in his seat.

They both saw the woman across the street start to run before she screamed. She left the sidewalk and ran awkwardly, wildly toward the intersection. She waved one arm frantically and screamed continuously a name that her emotion made unintelligible. From the last truck of prisoners a figure waved to the woman in return. The truck picked up speed, the jeep at its heels like a shepherd dog.

The woman saw there was no hope and stopped. She fell to her knees and then collapsed her full length on the street, blocking traffic.

Leo climbed into the jeep. The roaring and shaking of the motor gave them an illusion of warmth. They waited until the woman had been carried to the sidewalk, then Leo put the jeep in motion. They didn't say anything about what they had seen. It was none of their concern, but far back in Mosca's mind a vague, familiar image began to stir and form and shape itself.

Just before the war's end he had been in Paris and found himself caught in an immense throng. Trying to escape from it had been like a nightmare, and against his will he had been carried to the center, the focal point. There, inching slowly through the crowd which filled the streets, the sidewalks, the cafés, were a string of open trucks filled with Frenchmen; freed prisoners of war, slave laborers, men given up for dead. The cheering and shouting from the crowd drowned the jubilant cries of the men in the trucks. But they jumped up and down and leaned out over the sides of their trucks to be kissed, to accept the white flowers offered and thrown to them. Suddenly one of the men had flung himself from the truck, slithered off the heads of people he landed on and fell to the ground. A woman fought her way to the man and caught him to her in a fierce, possessive embrace. From the truck someone flung a crutch and shouted obscene congratulations that at any other time would make a woman blush. But she had laughed with the rest of the crowd.

The pain, the shock, the guilt Mosca had felt then he felt now.

When Leo stopped the jeep in front of the Rathskellar

Mosca got out. "I don't feel like eating," he said. "I'll see you at the house later."

Leo, busy putting the padlock on the jeep's security chain, lifted his head in surprise. "What's wrong?" he asked.

"Just a headache, I'll walk it off."

He felt cold and lit a cigar; the heavy tobacco smoke warmed his face. He took the small, quiet side streets, impassable to vehicles because of the rubble which had overflowed the ruins and sidewalks, picking his way over the loose stones and bricks, careful in the gathering dusk not to fall.

When he entered his room he felt really ill, his face hot and feverish. Without turning on the light he undressed and flung his clothes over on the couch and went to bed. Under the covers he was still cold and could smell the stale cigar butt he had left lying on the table edge. He huddled and curved his body together for warmth but the chill shook him continuously. His mouth was dry, and the pounding in his head became a slow monotonous beat, barely painful.

He heard a key turn in the door and Hella moving into the room. The light flashed on. She came to the bed and sat on it.

"Aren't you well?" she asked with concern. It gave her a queer shock to see him so.

"Just a chill," Mosca said. "Get me some aspirin and throw that cigar out."

She went to the bathroom for a glass of water and when she gave it to him she brushed her hand over his head and murmured, "It's funny to see you ill. Shall I sleep on the couch?"

"No," Mosca said. "I'm cold as hell. Come in here with me."

She put out the light and came to the bed to undress. Dimly in the blackness of the room he could see her hanging her clothes over the back of a chair. He felt his body burning with fever and desire, and when she came into bed he pressed against her. Her breasts and thighs and mouth were cool, her cheeks cold, and he held her as tightly as he could.

When he rested back against the pillow he could feel the sweat between his thighs and rolling down his back. The headache was gone but his very bones seemed to hurt. He reached over her body to the night table for water.

Hella ran her hand over his burning face. "Darling, I hope that didn't make you worse."

"No, I feel better," Mosca said.

"Do you want me to sleep on the couch now?"

"No, stay here."

He reached over for a cigarette but after a few puffs crushed it against the wall and watched the red shower of sparks fall on the blanket.

"Try to sleep," she said.

"I can't sleep. Anything special happen today?"

"No, I was just having supper with Frau Meyer. Yergen saw you come into the building and came up to tell me. He said you didn't look well, and he thought I might want to come right down. He's a very kind man."

"I saw something funny today," Mosca said and told her about the woman.

In the blackness of the room he could feel the silence. Hella was thinking, If I had been in the jeep surely I would have taken her and followed, set her mind at rest about what she had seen. Men were harder, she thought, there was less pity in them.

But she said nothing. Slowly, as in other dark nights, she ran her fingertips over his body, over the scar that cut down the whole trunk of his frame. She ran her fingers over the bumpy seam as a child runs a toy back and forth over a welt in the sidewalk, the slight rise and fall almost hypnotic.

Mosca sat up straight so that his shoulders rested against the wooden headrest of the bed. He folded his hands behind his neck as a cushion and said quietly, "I was lucky I got that where nobody sees it."

"I see it," Hella said.

"You know what I mean. It would be different if it were on my face."

She kept her fingers moving over the scar. "Not to me," she said.

The fever in his body made Mosca uncomfortable. The fingers moved soothingly over him, and he knew she would accept what he had done.

"Don't fall asleep," he said. "I always meant to tell you something but I never thought it important enough." Mockingly he gave his voice the singsong inflection of one about to tell a fairy tale to a child. "I'll tell you a little story," he said. He groped for a cigarette on the night table.

The ammunition dump stretched for miles and miles, the shells stacked in clusters like black cordwood. He, Mosca, sat in the cab of the bullet-shaped truck and watched the prisoners load the vehicles in front of him. The prisoners wore green twill fatigues and on their heads floppy hats of the same material. They would have blended easily into the forest around them if it had not been for the large, white letter "P" painted heavily on their backs and on each trouser leg.

From somewhere in the forest three blasts of a whistle sounded recall. Mosca jumped out of the cab of the truck and yelled, "Hey Fritz, c'mere."

The prisoner he had made straw boss over his three truckloads of workers came to him.

"We got time to finish this load before we start back?"

The German, a small man of forty, with a curiously wrinkled, old-young face, stood before Mosca without obsequiousness, shrugged his shoulders and said in broken English, "We be late for chow."

They grinned at each other. Any of the other prisoners would have assured Mosca that the load could be finished, merely to remain in favor.

"O.K., dump what you got," Mosca said. "We'll let the bastards squawk." He gave the German a cigarette and the German shoved it into the pocket of his green twill jacket. It was against regulations to smoke in the dump area though, of course, Mosca and the other G.I. guards did so.

"Get the rest of the Fritzes loaded and give me a count." The German left him and the prisoners began to pile into the trucks.

They moved slowly over the dirt road through the forest. Where other roads intersected more vehicles joined the procession, until, finally, the long line of open trucks, in single file, left the shade of the forest and entered the open countryside, the lemon-colored sunlight of very early spring. For guards and prisoners alike the war was very far away. They were safe, between them the issue had been settled. They moved in quiet and seeming content from the forest land of the ammunition dump to the barracks enclosed in barbed wire.

The G.I. guards, men who had been wounded too badly to be returned for line duty, had had enough of war. The prisoners regretted their fate only in the evening when they saw their guards pile into jeeps for a trip to the nearby town. The prisoners' faces behind their barbed wire had the wistful envy of children watching parents prepare to leave their homes for an evening out.

Then, in the very early morning light, they would ride out together to the forest. During the morning breaks, the prisoners would scatter around on the grass munching pieces of bread they had saved from breakfast. Mosca gave his crew more time than was usual. Fritz sat with him on a pile of shells.

"Not too bad a life, eh, Fritz?" Mosca asked.

"It could be worse," the German said, "it's peaceful here." Mosca nodded. He liked the German though he never took the trouble to remember his real name. They were friendly, but it was impossible to forget the relationship of the conqueror and conquered. Even now Mosca held his carbine in his hand as a symbol. There was never a bullet in the chamber and sometimes he forgot to put a magazine in its slot.

The German was in one of his depressed moods. Suddenly he began to pour out a flooding speech in his native tongue which Mosca understood imperfectly.

"Isn't it queer that you stand here, seeing that we do not move as we wish? What a duty for human beings. And how we kill each other and hurt each other. And for what? Tell me, if Germany had kept Africa and France, would I personally have earned another penny thereby? Me, myself, do I help myself if Germany conquers the world? Even if we win, I win only a uniform for the rest of my life. When we were children how it used to thrill us to read of our country's golden age, how France or Germany or Spain ruled Europe and the world. They build statues to men who give death to millions of their fellows. How is this? We hate each other, we kill each other. I could understand if we gained something. If afterward they said: Here, here is an extra piece of land we took from the French, everyone gets a little piece of cake. And you, we already know you are the winners. And do you think you will win anything?"

In the warm sun the other prisoners rolled on their backs, slept in the cool grass. Mosca listened only half understanding, vaguely displeased, not reached. The German spoke as one of the vanquished, without authority. He had walked the streets of Paris and Prague, the cities of Scandinavia, with cheerful pride; a sense of justice came only behind barbed wire.

For the first time the German put his hand on Mosca's arm. "My friend," he said, "people like you and me meet face to face and kill each other. Our enemies are behind us." He let his hand fall. "Our enemies are behind us," he repeated bitterly, "and commit the crimes for which we die."

But most of the time the German was cheerful. He had shown Mosca a picture of his wife and two children, and a picture of himself taken with comrades outside the factory in which they had worked. And he would talk about women.

"Aha," the German would say with an almost wistful zest. "When I was in Italy," or "When I was in France, the women they were wonderful. I must admit it, I like them better than German women, let the *Führer* say what he likes. Women never let politics interfere with more important things. It's been that way through the centuries."

His blue eyes twinkled in the lined, old-young face. "I'm always sorry we did not get to America. Those beautiful girls with the long legs, like marzipan the color. Really unbelievable. I remember them from your movies and magazines. Yes it is too bad."

And Mosca playing the game would say, "They wouldn't even look at you krautheads."

The German would shake his head slowly but with decision. "Women are hardheaded," he would say. "Do you think they starve because they should not use their bodies with the enemy. In these things women think clearly. They have more fundamental values. Ah, yes, occupation duty in New York would have been wonderful."

Mosca and the German would grin at each other and then Mosca would say, "Get the rest of the Fritzes to work."

On the final evening, when the recall whistle blew, the prisoners milled together quickly from all over the clearing in which they were working, and the trucks were loaded in a few minutes. The drivers started their motors.

Mosca almost fell for the ruse. Mechanically his eyes looked for Fritz. Still unsuspecting, he took a few steps toward the nearest of the three vehicles and then seeing the strained look on some of the prisoners' faces sensed immediately what had happened.

He ran to the beginning of the dirt road and signaled the drivers out of the cabs of their trucks. As he ran he worked the bolt of the carbine, throwing a cartridge into the chamber. Then taking from his pocket the whistle he had never used, he blew six short blasts. He waited a moment and blew six more.

While he waited he made all the prisoners dismount

from the trucks and sit in a close-packed circle on the grass. He stood a distance away, watching them, though he knew none would try to escape.

The security jeep came directly through the woods, and he could hear it crashing through the underbrush before it entered the clearing. The Sergeant in it had long, handlebar mustaches in the English style and was very big and heavy. When he saw the orderly scene he left the jeep slowly and walked over to Mosca. The other two G.I.'s sauntered to opposite sides of the clearing. The driver took his submachine gun from its jeep scabbard and sat behind the wheel, one foot dangling out of the vehicle and touching the ground.

The Sergeant stood before Mosca, waiting. Mosca said, "There's one guy missing that I know about. My straw boss. I didn't make a count."

The Sergeant was in natty O.D.'s and wore a pistol and webbed cartridge belt around his broad middle. He moved among the prisoners and ordered them to form in ranks of ten. There were five ranks and two men for an incomplete sixth. The two men who formed their own rank had an air of guilt, as if they were to blame for the missing men.

"What does that make it?" the Sergeant asked Mosca.

"Four missing, altogether," Mosca said.

The Sergeant looked down on him. "A nice trick your ass-hole buddy pulled." And for the first time since he had learned of the escape Mosca felt a sense of shame and some fear. But he could not feel angry.

The Sergeant sighed. "Well it was a good racket while it lasted. There'll be a hell of a shakeup, the chicken shit will really fly." He said to Mosca in a gentler voice, "Your ass'll be back up in the line, you know that?" They both stood there thinking of the easy life they had led, no reveille, no formation, no inspections, no fear—almost civilian.

The Sergeant straightened angrily. "Let's see what we can do with these bastards. *Achtung,*" he shouted, and walked up and down in front of the Germans standing rigidly at attention. He said nothing for a few minutes and then began to speak to them quietly in English.

"All right. We know where we stand. The honeymoon is over. You men were all treated well. You were given good food, a good place to sleep. Did we ever work you too hard? You didn't feel well we let you stay in barracks. Who has a complaint? Step forward any man." The Sergeant paused as if one of them might really do so, then went on. "O.K., let's see if you appreciate it. Some of you know when these men left and where they went. Speak up. We'll remember it. We'll appreciate it." The Sergeant stopped walking up and down and faced them. He waited as they murmured among themselves, some explaining to the others what the Sergeant had said. But after they were still, none of the green-twilled prisoners stepped forward.

The Sergeant said in a different tone, "All right, you bastards." He turned to the jeep and said to the driver, "Go back to the barracks and draw twenty picks and twenty shovels. Get four men and another jeep. If no officer hears about this we might get through. And if that jerky Supply Sergeant squawks about the shovels tell him I'll come in and break his goddamn head." He motioned the driver on his way.

Then he signaled the prisoners to sit on the grass.

When the jeeps returned with the extra men and a trailer loaded with tools the Sergeant lined up the prisoners in two ranks facing each other. He issued the tools and since there were not enough to go around he made the extra men go to the other side of the clearing and lie in the grass on their faces.

No one spoke. The prisoners worked steadily digging the long trench. The rank with picks would hack at the earth, then rest. The men with shovels lifted the loose dirt away. They worked very slowly. The guards around the clearing leaned against the trees, seemingly indifferent and unalert.

The Sergeant winked at Mosca and said in a low voice, "A good bluff always works. Watch this."

He let them dig for a short time more, then he called a halt. "Does anyone here wish to speak?" He gave them a grim smile.

No one answered.

"O.K." The Sergeant waved an arm. "Keep digging."

One of the Germans let his shovel fall. He was young and rosy cheeked. "Please," he said. "I wish to tell you something." He walked away from his fellow prisoners into the open space that separated him from the guards.

"Spit it out," the Sergeant said.

The German stood there wordless. He looked back uneasily at his fellow prisoners. The Sergeant understood. He took the German by the arm and led him over to the jeep. They stood there talking earnestly in low voices, watched by prisoners and guards alike. The Sergeant listened with his head thrust forward intently, his great body bent over, one arm thrown familiarly over the prisoner's shoulder. Then he nodded. He motioned the informer into the jeep.

The prisoners were loaded onto the three trucks and the caravan moved through the now-deserted forest, the other roads crossing theirs empty of life. In the jeep bringing up the rear the Sergeant drove, his long mustaches waving in the breeze. They left the forest, and as they entered the open countryside it was strange to see the familiar land bathed in a different light, the riper and reddish sun of late afternoon.

Turning his head for a moment the Sergeant spoke to Mosca. "Your buddy planned this for a long time. But he's out of luck."

"Where is he?" Mosca asked.

"In town. I know the house."

The caravan entered the camp, and then the two jeeps swung in a wide arc away from the trucks and raced toward the town. Then close together, as if coupled, they went down the main street, and on the corner on which stood the church, turned right. They halted by a small stone house. Mosca and the Sergeant went to the front door. Two of the men in the other jeep moved slowly to the rear of the house. The other men stayed in the jeeps.

The door was opened before they could knock. Fritz stood there before them. He wore old, crumpled blue serge trousers, a white collarless shirt and a dark jacket. He gave them an uncertain smile. "The rest are upstairs," he said. "They are afraid to come down."

"Call them," the Sergeant said. "Go up and tell them they won't be hurt."

Fritz went to the foot of the stairs and called up in German. "All is in order. Come down. Don't be afraid."

They heard a door open above them, and the three other prisoners came slowly down the stairs. They were dressed in ragged civilian clothes. On their faces was a sheepish, almost guilty look.

"Go out to the jeeps," the Sergeant said. Then he asked Fritz, "Whose house is this?"

The German raised his eyes. For the first time he looked at Mosca. "A woman I used to know. Let her go, she did it for—you know—she was lonely. It has nothing to do with the war."

"Get out there," the Sergeant said.

They all left. The Sergeant whistled for the two men behind the house. As the jeeps pulled away, a woman came down the street carrying a large bundle in brown wrapping paper. She saw the prisoners in the jeep, turned, and walked back in the direction from which she had come. The Sergeant gave Mosca a sour grin. "Goddamn women," he said.

On a lonely stretch of road nearly halfway back to camp the Sergeant's lead jeep pulled to the side and stopped. The other jeep halted close behind. On one side of the road was a rough stony pasture leading into the dark line of the forest two hundred yards away.

"Get those men out of the jeeps," the Sergeant said. They all dismounted and stood awkwardly, ill at ease in the deserted road. The Sergeant stood for some moments, deep in thought. He felt his mustaches and said, "A couple of you guys can bring these krauts back to camp. Empty the tools out of that trailer and bring it back." He pointed to Fritz. "You stay here."

"I'll go back," Mosca said quickly.

The Sergeant looked him up and down, slowly, with insolent contempt. "Listen, you son of a bitch, you're staying here. If it wasn't for me your ass'd be up in the line. By Christ, I'm not going to chase krauts all over the country whenever they get a bug up their ass. You stay here."

Two of the guards moved off silently with the three prisoners. They got into the jeep and disappeared down the road. Fritz turned his head to watch them go.

The four men in their olive drab stood facing the lone German and the stony pasture beyond him. The Sergeant stroked his mustache. The German's face was gray, but he stood stiffly, as if at attention.

"Start running," the Sergeant said. He pointed across the pasture to the forest.

The German did not move. The Sergeant gave him a shove. "Run," he said, "we'll give you a good start." He pushed the German onto the pasture grass, spinning him so that he faced the forest. The sun was gone, and there was no color on the earth, only the grayness of falling twilight. The forest was a long dark wall, far away.

The German turned, facing them again. His hand went to his collarless shirt as if searching for some dignity. He looked at Mosca, then at the others. He took a step toward them, off the grass and stone. His legs trembled, and his body wavered for a moment, but his voice was steady. He said, "Herr Mosca, *Ich hab' eine Frau und Kinder.*"

On the Sergeant's face came a look of rage and hatred. "Run, you bastard, run." He rushed to the German and struck him in the face. As the German began to fall he lifted him and shoved him toward the pasture. "Run, you kraut bastard." He shouted it three or four times.

The German fell and rose and turned to face them again, and again he said, not pleading this time but as if in explanation, "*Ich hab' eine Frau und Kinder.*" One of the guards stepped forward quickly and struck him in the groin with the butt of his carbine and then, letting the weapon dangle in one hand, smashed the German's face with the other.

The lines in the wrinkled face sprang leaks of blood. And then, before he began to walk across the stony pasture toward the dark wall of the forest he gave them one last look. It was a look of lost hope and more than fear of death. It was a look of horror, as if he had seen some terrible and shameful thing in which he had never believed.

They watched him walk slowly across the pasture. They waited for him to run, but he walked very slowly. Every few steps he turned his body around to watch them, as if it were some game, breeding a childish distrust. They could see the white of his collarless shirt.

Mosca saw that every time the German turned to watch them and then turned back again his course veered a little to the right. He saw the slight, rocky rise of ground that led to the forest. The trick was obvious. The men knelt on the dirt road and raised the carbines to their shoulders. Mosca let his hang barrel downward to the dirt road.

As the German made his sudden dash for the gully the Sergeant fired and the body had begun its fall as the other shots rang out. The fall carried his body over the slight ridge, but the legs remained in view.

In the silence that followed the sharp, scattered reports of the carbines, under the gray wisps of smoke that spiraled above their heads, the living men froze in the positions from which they had fired. The acrid smell of powder floated away on the evening air.

"Go in," Mosca said. "I'll wait for the trailer. You guys go in." No one had noticed his not firing. He turned from them and walked a few steps down the road.

He could hear the roar of the jeep as it moved away, and he leaned against a tree, staring across the stony pasture, and over the danglings legs to the black, impenetrable wall of the forest. In the coming night, it seemed very near. He lit a cigarette. He felt no emotion, only a slight physical nausea and internal looseness. He waited, hoping the trailer would arrive before it became really dark.

In the now complete blackness of the room Mosca reached over Hella's body for the glass of water on the night table. He drank and leaned back.

He wanted to be completely honest. "It doesn't bother me," he said. "It's just when I see something like today, that woman chasing the truck. I remember what he said, he said it twice. 'I have a wife and children.' It didn't mean anything then. I can't explain it, but it's like the way we spent all our money whenever we could, because saving it didn't mean anything." He waited for Hella to speak.

He went on. "I tried to figure it out after, you know. I was afraid of going back into combat, and I guess I was afraid of that Sergeant. And he was a German, and Germans had done a hell of a lot worse. But the main thing was, I didn't feel any pity, when he was hurt, when he begged, when he was killed. Afterward, I was ashamed and surprised, but I never felt pity and I know that's bad."

Mosca reached down toward Hella's face and tracing along the cheek felt the wetness in the hollows beneath her eyes. For a moment he felt the nausea, and then the fever in his body burned it out. He wanted to tell her how it was, how it was like nothing else ever known, how it was like a dream, like magic, the fear all around. In the strange, deserted towns the dead people lay, the fighting went on over their rubbled graves, black flowers of smoke grew through skull-like homes, and then later the white tape lay everywhere, around the charred enemy tank, to show that it had not been demined, outside the doors of houses as in a child's game, a chalkmark over which you cannot step, and then more and more like a witch's spell, the white tape around the church, around the dead bodies in the square, around the casks of wine in the farmer's barn, and then in the open fields the sign with its skull and crossbones marking the dead animals, the cows, the heavy plow horses, all blown upside down by the land mines, their bellies torn open for the sun. And how one morning, the new strange town was so quiet, so still, and how for some reason he had been afraid, though the fighting was still some miles away. And then suddenly, far off, the church bells tolled, and they could see the square filled with people, and he knew it was Sunday. On that same day, the fear gone, in some place where the skull and crossbones were not seen, where some child had forgotten to make his white mark in chalk, where by some human error the magic white tape was not where it should be, he had suffered the first violation of his flesh and bone and come to know the meaning, the terror of annihilation.

He said nothing. He could feel Hella turning over on her stomach and bury her face in the pillow. He shoved her roughly and said, "Go sleep on the couch." He moved over against the wall, feeling its coolness against his body draw the heat of fever. He pressed against it.

In his dream the trucks moved through many lands. The countless women sprang from the earth, stood on tiptoe in the streets, searched with hungry faces. The emaciated men danced like scarecrows in their joy, and then, as the women before them began to weep, bowed their heads and bodies to be kissed. The white tape circled them, the trucks, the men, the women and the world. The sick terror born of guilt was everywhere. The white flowers withered and died.

Mosca woke. The room was shot through with shadows, the last ghosts of night, and he could make out a vague outline of the wardrobe. The air was cold, but the fever and chill had left his body. He felt a gentle tiredness that was pleasant. He was very hungry, and he thought for a moment how good breakfast would taste later in the morning. He reached out and felt Hella's sleeping body. Knowing that she had never left him, he put his cheek against her warm back and fell asleep.

# 9

GORDON MIDDLETON watched the children march down the street past his house in a neat column of two's. They swung their paper lanterns in time to the slow chant that came faintly to Gordon's ears through the closed window. Then the two files marched inward on its front and became a group, the lit yellow-red lanterns like a cluster of fireflies in the cold and pale October dusk. Gordon felt a pang of homesickness for the dying New Hampshire village he had left so long ago, the cold, bare beauty of its countryside, the night air lit only with fireflies, and where it seemed, there as here, that everything was dying as winter came.

Without turning his head, Gordon asked the Professor, "What are they singing, the children with the lanterns?"

The Professor sat by the chess table, surveying with satisfaction the ruin he had brought to his opponent. In the leather brief case beside him were the two sandwiches he would take home with him and the two packs of cigarettes that were his weekly tuition fee for giving lessons in German to Gordon Middleton. The cigarettes he would save for his son, when he could visit him in Nuremberg. He must again ask permission to visit. After all, if the great men could have visitors, why not his son?

"They are singing a song for the October *Fest*," the Professor said absently. "To show that the nights are getting longer."

"And the lanterns?" Gordon Middleton asked.

"Really, I don't know, an ancient custom. To light the way." The Professor suppressed his irritation. He wanted to summon the American back to the game, complete the slaughter. But though the American never presumed on his position as conqueror, the Professor never forgot his place as one of the conquered or, far back in his mind, his own secret shame about his son.

Gordon Middleton opened the window, and floating up the street from the lanterns, filling the room with a crystal-clear tone, like the October air, came the children's sing-song voices. He listened intently, testing his newly acquired German, and the simplicity of the words and the clarity with which they sang made understanding easy. They sang:

*Brenne auf mein Licht*

*Brenne auf mein Licht*

*Aber nur meine liebe Laterne nicht*

"You'd think their parents would have more important things to worry about instead of making lanterns." Gordon waited, listening to the song again.

*Da oben leuchten die Sterne*

*Hier unten leuchten wir*

and then on a long note without sadness but sounding so in the falling light.

*Mein Licht ist aus, wir geh' nach Haus*

*Und kommen Morgen wieder*

Gordon Middleton saw Mosca crossing the Kurfürsten Allee, walking through the cluster of lanterns and still-singing children, scattering the light.

"My friend is coming," Gordon said to the Professor. Gordon walked over to the chess table and with his forefinger toppled over his king.

The Professor smiled at him and said out of politeness,

"It was yet possible to win." The Professor was afraid of all young men—the hard, sullen German youths with their years of warfare and defeat—but even more of all these young, drunken Americans who would beat or kill without provocation, purely out of drunken malice and the knowledge that they were safe from retaliation. But any friend of Middleton would surely not be dangerous. Herr Middleton had assured him of this, and Herr Middleton was himself reassuring. He was almost a caricature of the Puritan Yankee with his tall, awkward, loosely knit frame, prominent Adam's apple, long bony nose and square mouth. And in his little New England town a schoolteacher. The Professor smiled thinking how in the past these little grade-school teachers had fawned on the Herr Professor, and now in this relationship his learning and title meant nothing. He was the courter.

The bell rang and Gordon went to the door. The Professor stood up and nervously straightened his coat, the frayed tie. He pulled his short body with its swollen potato stomach to an erect position and faced the door.

The Professor saw a tall, dark boy, not more than twenty-four, certainly not older than his own son. But this boy had serious brown eyes and a grave, almost sullen face that just missed being ugly. He was dressed very neatly in officer green and had the white-and-blue patch denoting his civilian status sewed on his lapels and left sleeve. He moved with an athletic carelessness that would have been contemptuous if it had not been so impersonal.

When Gordon made the introduction, the Professor said, "I am very happy to meet you," and thrust out his hand. He tried to keep his dignity but realized that he had said the words obsequiously and betrayed his nervousness with his smile. He saw the boy's eyes go hard and noticed the quick withdrawal after their hands touched. The knowledge that he had offended this youth made the Professor tremble, and he sat down to arrange the chess pieces on the board.

"Do you care to play?" he asked Mosca and tried to suppress the apologetic smile.

Gordon waved Mosca toward the table and said, "See what you can do, Walter, he's too good for me."

Mosca sat in the chair opposite the Professor. "Don't expect too much, Gordon taught me this game just a month ago."

The Professor nodded his head and murmured, "Please take the white pieces." Mosca made the opening move.

The Professor became absorbed in the game and lost his nervousness. They all used the simple opening, these Americans, but where the little schoolteacher had played a cautious game, sound but uninspired, this one played with all the impetuosity of youth. Not without talent, the Professor thought, as with a few expert moves he broke the force of the headlong attack. Then swiftly and ruthlessly he swooped on the unprotected rooks and bishop and slaughtered the pawns standing forward without support.

"You're too good for me, Professor," the boy said, and the Professor noted with relief that there was no rancor in the voice.

Then without any transition Mosca said abruptly in German, "I'd like you to give English lessons to my fiancée twice a week. What does it cost?"

The Professor flushed. It was humiliating, this common bargaining, as if he were a shopkeeper. "Whatever you wish," he said stiffly, "but you speak quite a good German, why not teach her yourself?"

"I have," Mosca said, "but she wants to learn the structure, grammar and all that. A pack of cigarettes for every two lessons O.K.?"

The Professor nodded.

Mosca borrowed a pencil from Gordon and wrote on a slip of paper. He gave it to the Professor and said, "Here's a note in case anyone in the billet questions you. The address is there too."

"Thank you," the Professor almost bowed. "Will tomorrow evening be suitable?"

"Sure," Mosca said.

Outside the house a jeep horn began a steady honking. "That must be Leo," Mosca said. "We're going over to the officers' club. Feel like coming, Gordon?"

"No," Gordon said. "Is that the boy that was in Buchenwald?" And when Mosca nodded, "Have him come in for just a second, I'd like to meet him."

Mosca went to the window and pushed it open and the horn stopped. "Come on in," Mosca shouted. It was very dark now, the children and their lanterns out of sight.

When Leo came in he shook hands with Gordon and said to the Professor stiffly, "*Angenehm.*" The Professor bowed, picked up his brief case and said to Gordon, "I must go." Gordon took him to the outer door, and they shook hands in farewell. Then Gordon went to the kitchen in the rear of the house.

His wife was sitting at the table with Yergen, haggling over the price of some black-market goods. Yergen was polite, dignified and firm; they both knew she was getting a good bargain. Yergen believed in quality. On a chair beside the table was a foot-high stack of rich-looking, rusty-colored woolen material.

"Isn't this lovely stuff, Gordon?" Ann Middleton asked in a pleased voice. She was a plump woman, her features good-natured and kind despite the determined chin and shrewd eyes.

Gordon in his slow, deliberate way made a sound of assent and then said, "If you're through here I'd like you to come and meet some friends." Yergen hurriedly gulped the cup of coffee before him and began to fill his leather brief case with the round tins of fats and meats that rested on the table. "I must go," he said.

"You won't forget the material for my husband's coat next week?" Ann Middleton asked warningly.

Yergen made a gesture of protest. "Dear lady, no. Next week at the latest."

When she had locked the back entrance after Yergen, Ann Middleton unlocked a cupboard and took out a bottle of whiskey and some bottles of Coca-Cola. "It is a pleasure to do business with Yergen, he never wastes your time with anything shoddy," she said. They went into the living room together.

After the introductions Gordon rested in one of the armchairs, not listening to the usual small talk his wife made. He felt almost painfully the alien atmosphere of the requisitioned home, living with belongings which had no memories, no associations, not knowing who had picked out the pictures on the wall, the furniture scattered through the rooms, who had played the piano which rested against the far wall. But these feelings were traitorous to his intellect and not new. He had felt it most keenly on his visit home to his parents before he entered the Army. In that home, surrounded by furniture from ancestors long dead, as he kissed the dry cheeks of his mother and father, cheeks dried out and tough by the vigorous northern climate, he had known that he would never go back, as others would not, the young people who had gone to war and to the factories; and that this land, glacial in its stark and wintry beauty, would be inhabited only by old people, their hair white as the snow which covered the bony hills. And in his bedroom the large picture of Marx that his mother had thought was just a painting. How proud he had been of his cleverness and a little contemptuous of her ignorance. It was probably still hanging there.

His wife had prepared drinks, weak ones, since whiskey was rationed and since she sometimes used it to trade on the black market. Gordon asked Leo, "Wasn't it in your camp that some prisoners were killed by an Allied air raid?"

"Yes," Leo answered, "I remember. We did not resent it, believe me."

"I read that Thälman, the Communist leader, was killed in that raid. Did you know him?" For once Gordon's voice had lost its calmness. There was a vibrant note in it.

"That was a curious thing," Leo said. "Thälman was brought to the camp two days after the raid in which he was supposed to have been killed. Then he was taken away in a short time. We heard about the announcement of his death; of course it was a joke among us."

Gordon took a deep breath. "Did you meet him?"

"No," Leo said. "I remember because many of the *kapos*, the trusties, were Communists. They were the first ones sent to the camps and naturally they had the good jobs. Anyway, I heard that they had managed to secure some delicacies and even liquor and planned to welcome Thälman with a secret banquet. But it never came off. He was always under special guard."

Gordon was nodding his head with a solemn, sad pride. He said to his wife with quiet anger, "You see who were the real enemies of fascism?"

Leo said with irritation, "The Communists were not

bargains. One, a *kapo*, had great pleasure beating old men to death. He did many other things I cannot say before your wife."

Gordon became so angry that it showed on his usually well-controlled face, and his wife said to Mosca, "Why don't you come over for dinner some night with your girl. And Leo too." They settled details, giving Gordon time to recover. Suddenly Gordon said to Leo, "I don't believe the man was a Communist. He may have been at one time. But he was either a renegade or an impostor." At this Ann and Leo burst out laughing but Mosca turned his sharp, dark face toward Gordon and said, "The guy was in camp for a long time. Don't you know what that means, for Christ's sake?" And Leo said almost comfortingly, "Yes, he was one of the oldest inmates."

In a room above them a baby began to cry, and Gordon went upstairs and brought down a great big healthy boy who looked much larger than his six months. Gordon changed the diaper, proudly showing off his skill.

"He's better than I am," Ann Middleton said, "and he enjoys doing it which I'm sure I don't."

"Why don't you fellows spend the evening here instead of going on to the club?" Gordon asked.

"Yes," Ann said, "please do."

"We can stay a little while," Mosca said, "but we have to meet Eddie Cassin at the club about ten o'clock. He went to the opera."

Ann Middleton sniffed, "I'll bet he's at the opera."

"And besides," Mosca said, "it's stag night at the club and the show should be terrific. Leo here never saw a stag show. He can't miss it."

When Gordon went to the door with them he said to Mosca, "We never use up all our allowance on our commissary card. Any time you need some groceries and want to use it, just let me know."

Gordon locked the door and went back to the living room. Ann said to him, "Really that was quite shameful, you were downright rude to Leo." Gordon, knowing that this from her was a stern rebuke, said without defiance but resolutely, "I still think the man was an impostor."

This time his wife did not smile.

The soft, rose-colored lights went out. Eddie Cassin leaned forward in his seat, applauded with the rest as the old, white-haired conductor entered the pit and tapped the music stand sharply with his baton. The curtain went up.

As the music started slowly, yet with passion, Eddie Cassin forgot the school auditorium he was in, the Germans all around him, the two monstrous Russian officers almost blocking his view. The familiar figures on the stage were now all his life, and he gripped his jaw and mouth with his hands to control the emotional workings of his face.

On the stage the man and woman who at the beginning had sung of their love for each other, now sang of their hate. The man in his peasant costume cried with anger in hard beautiful tones, rising and ascending, the orchestra playing beneath the voice, rising and falling with it, as a wave might, yet falling completely away when need be. The woman's voice, shrill, cut through his, mingled, the orchestra circling what they said. The man threw the woman away from him with so much force that as she spun away she fell to the floor, really slamming against the wood of the stage. She was up on her feet instantly, screaming reproaches, yet musically, and as the man threatened her and she denied his accusations, suddenly the man's voice, the voices of the chorus, the orchestra, all fell away and the woman's voice found itself alone, admitted her guilt, hurled back defiance, and falling to a lower and sweeter tone sang of death and sorrow and a bodily love that led all men and women. Before Eddie Cassin's eyes the man took the woman by the hair and thrust into her body with a dagger. On a loud clear note she called for help, and her lover died with her; the horns and violins rose to a high, crescending wave, and the man's voice made its final utterance, a long clean note of revenge, passion and inconsolable grief. The curtain came down.

The Russian officers in their green-and-gold uniforms clapped enthusiastically, seeming to lead the applause. Eddie Cassin pushed his way out of the auditorium and into the fresh night air. He leaned against his jeep, feeling exhausted and yet content. He waited until everyone had left, waited until the woman who had died on the stage came out. He saw that she was plain, with heavy German features, dressed all in black, loosely; lumpy as a fifty-year-old housewife. He waited until she was out of sight and then got into the jeep and drove across the bridge into the Altstadt, Bremen proper, and as always the ruins rising up to meet him awakened a feeling of kinship. Mingled with this was the remembrance of the opera and how closely this physical world resembled—with the same element of the ridiculous—that interior make-believe world he had seen on the stage. Now that he was free of the music's spell, he was ashamed of the easy tears he had shed, tears for a tragedy so simple, so direct, a child's story of guiltless and unfortunate animals come to disaster, and his own tears a child's tears he would never understand.

The officers' club had been one of the finest private homes in Bremen. What had been its lawn was now a parking lot for jeeps and command cars. The garden in the rear supplied flowers for the homes of the higher ranking officers.

When Eddie entered the club the dance floor was empty, but ringed around it, seated on the floor and leaning against the wall, the officers were three rows deep. Others watched from the barroom, standing on chairs so that they could look over the crowd before them.

Someone brushed past Eddie and went on to the dance floor. It was a girl, stark nakedness exposed on tiny, silvery platforms of ballet slippers. Her pubic hair had been shaved to an inverted triangle, dark red on her body like a shield. In some way she had fluffed out the hair so that it was a formidably thick and matty bush. She danced without skill, coming close to the officers seated on the floor, almost thrusting the triangle of hair into their faces so that some of the young officers started involuntarily and turned their crew-cut heads away. She laughed when they did this and laughed and danced away when some of the older officers made a half-joking grab. It was an exhibition curiously unsexual, with no element of lust. Someone threw a comb out on the floor, the girl continued to dance like a draft horse trying to gallop. The officers began to shout jokes she did not understand, and humiliation made her face and dance more strained, ludicrous, until everyone was laughing, throwing combs, handkerchiefs, butter knives, olives from their drinks, pretzels. One officer shouted "Hide this," and it became a refrain. The club officer came out on the floor holding an enormous pair of scissors, clicking the shears suggestively. The girl ran off the dance floor, past Eddie back to the dressing room. Eddie went to the bar. At one corner he saw Mosca and Wolf and went over to them.

"Don't tell me Leo missed the show," Eddie said. "Walter, you guaranteed he wouldn't."

"Hell," Mosca said, "he already latched onto one of the dancers. He's in."

Eddie grinned and turned to Wolf. "Find the gold mine?" He knew Wolf and Mosca went out nights and traded in the black market.

"Business is tough," Wolf said, his dead-white face shaking dolefully from side to side.

"Don't kid me," Eddie Cassin said. "I hear your *Fräulein* wears diamonds on her pajamas."

Wolf was indignant. "Now where the hell would she get pajamas?"

They all laughed.

The waiter came and Eddie ordered a double whiskey. Wolf nodded toward the dance floor and said, "We expected you in the front row tonight."

"Nah," Eddie Cassin said. "I'm cultured, I went to the opera. Anyway the broads there are better looking."

From the other room officers flooded into the bar, the show was over. The room became crowded. Mosca stood up and said, "Let's go up to the dice table and play a little."

The dice table was almost completely surrounded. It was a crudely constructed affair with four unpainted wooden joists for legs and a green cloth stretched over the wooden top. Boards half a foot high formed a rectangle to confine the dice.

The Colonel himself, a small, plump man with a blond mustache, extremely neat, was rolling the dice awkwardly, the square cubes slipping clumsily from his clenched hand. All the other players were officers, mostly flyers. On the Colonel's right stood the Adjutant, watchful, not taking any part in the game while the Colonel played.

The Adjutant, a young Captain, was an ingenuous-looking man with a bland face and a smile that was attractive when not meant to menace. He gloried in his position as Adjutant, the petty power that enabled him to select the officers who would perform the more irksome duties on the base, especially on week ends. The Colonel relied on him, and the Adjutant did not forget an affront easily. But he was fair, and only vindictive when the affront was one to his position, not to himself personally. The rigidity of Army life and Army procedure was his religion, and any breach of it sacrilegious and blasphemous. Anyone who tried to get something done without going through channels—those straight and narrow paths clearly defined in Army regulations—would suddenly find himself a very busy man, and no matter how hard he worked, busy for a few months at least. He brought to his religion the fanaticism of the young; he was no older than Mosca.

A white-jacketed waiter stood behind a small bar in the corner of the room. When the players called out for a drink he set it up, and whoever had called would step over for the glass and take his drink back to the game, resting it on the wooden ledge made by enclosing boards.

Wolf, who did not gamble, sat in one of the easy chairs, and Eddie Cassin and Mosca squeezed into places around the table. When Eddie's turn to shoot came, Mosca bet with him. Eddie, a cautious gambler, slipped the one-dollar bills from his metal clip almost regretfully. He had a good roll and made five passes before he sevened out. Mosca had made even more money than Eddie.

Since they were standing beside each other, it was Mosca's turn to shoot, the dice going around the circle clockwise. Already ahead and feeling confident, he put twenty dollars worth of scrip on the green felt. Four different officers took five dollars each. Mosca threw the great square cubes backhanded. They came up seven. "Shoot it," he said. He was sure now, and exhilarated. The forty dollars was faded by the same four officers. Eddie Cassin said, "And ten goes with him."

The Colonel said, "I'll take that." They laid the money on the table.

Mosca threw the dice as hard as he could against the side of the table. The cubes bounced off the wooden board, tumbled over the green felt and spun like two red tops; then the edges caught in the felt and they stopped dead. It was another seven. "Shoot the eighty bucks," Mosca said.

"And the twenty goes with him." Eddie Cassin left the money on the table. The Colonel covered it.

This time Mosca released the dice gently, as if turning loose a pet animal, so that they bounced off the wall and rolled a few inches coming up square red and enormous in the middle of the green felt. It was another seven and one of the officers said, "Rattle those dice." He said it without malice, a superstitious prayer against Mosca's luck. Mosca grinned at the officer and said, "The hundred and sixty goes."

The Adjutant still stood with a drink in his hand, watching Mosca and the dice. Eddie Cassin said cautiously, "Ten goes with him." And picked up the other thirty dollars he had won.

The Colonel said, "I'll bet you twenty." Eddie reluctantly laid down another ten-dollar bill, and catching Mosca's look, shrugged his shoulders.

Mosca picked up the dice, blew on them, and slammed them backhanded against the opposite wooden board. The red dice with their white dots came up a four.

One of the officers said, "I'll lay ten to five he doesn't."

Mosca took the bet and several others. He let the dice lay on the table and, unconsciously arrogant, sure of his luck, held his sheaf of bills ready to cover any bets. He was happy, he enjoyed the excitement of the game, and it was rare that he gambled with luck. "I'll take a hundred to fifty," he said, and when no one answered he picked up the dice.

Just before he threw, the Colonel said, "I'll bet twenty you don't make it." Mosca threw down a ten-dollar bill and said, "I'll take that."

"You only put down ten dollars," the Colonel said.

Mosca stopped rattling the dice and leaned against the table. He couldn't believe that the Colonel, an old Army man, didn't know the proper odds in dice. "You have to lay two to one against a four point, Colonel," he said and tried to keep the anger out of his voice.

The Colonel turned to one of the officers beside him and asked, "Is that right, Lieutenant?"

"That's right, sir," the officer said, embarrassed.

The Colonel threw down twenty dollars. "All right, shoot."

The red cubes slammed against all four sides of the table, raced swiftly across the green felt and stopped with a surprising suddenness, each red square framing two little white dots. Mosca looked at them for a moment before picking up the money and spoke his mind aloud, "I never saw a prettier sight."

There was no sense pushing his luck too far, he thought. He threw a couple of bills on the table and after a few rolls he sevened out. He continued to play with mediocre luck. When the Colonel picked up the dice to shoot, Mosca faded him. The Colonel threw a point and then sevened out on the second roll. Mosca picked up the money. The

Colonel said without rancor, "You're too lucky for me," and smiled, then walked out of the room and they could hear him going down the stairs. Mosca realized that he had been wrong, that the Colonel really hadn't known the correct odds, hadn't been trying to pull rank.

The atmosphere around the table became more relaxed, the conversation of the officers more natural. The waiter was busy with the many shouted orders for drinks. The Adjutant went over to the bar, sat on one of the stools until his glass was filled, tasted it, and then called, "Mosca, come here for a minute." Mosca looked over his shoulder. Eddie Cassin already had the dice and it was his turn next. "After my shot," he said.

Eddie had a good roll, but Mosca sevened out quickly and then went over to the patiently waiting Adjutant.

The Adjutant looked him in the eye with a calm, level glance and said, "Where do you come off telling the Colonel what the odds are?"

Mosca was surprised and a little confused. "Hell," he said, "the guy wanted a bet. Nobody'd bet him even money on a four."

The Adjutant, in a quiet voice, as if he were addressing a stupid child, said, "There were at least ten officers at the table. They didn't tell him the odds, and if they had they would have done so in a more courteous manner. Why do you think they didn't tell him?"

Mosca could feel himself flushing. For the first time he realized that there was no sound of dice, the men around the table were listening. He felt a familiar uneasiness that reminded him of his first months in the army. He shrugged. "I figured he didn't know so I told him."

The Adjutant stood up. "You may think because you're a civilian you can get away with that sort of thing. You showed pretty plainly that the Colonel was trying to use his rank to cheat you out of ten dollars. Now just remember one thing; we can ship you back to the States pretty damn quick if we really want to, and I understand you have reasons for not wanting that to happen. So watch yourself. If the Colonel doesn't know something, his fellow officers can tell him. You insulted the Commanding Officer and every officer in this room. Don't let anything like that happen again."

Unconsciously Mosca hung his head, the shame and anger washing over him. He could see Eddie Cassin watching him, and Eddie had a little smile of pleasure on his face. Mosca through the fog of anger heard the Adjutant say in a contemptuous voice, "If I had my way I wouldn't let you civilians into an officers' club. You don't know what Army means."

Without thinking Mosca lifted his head. He saw the Adjutant's face very distinctly, the gray candid eyes, the bland earnest face, stern now.

"How many battle stars you got, Captain?" Mosca asked. "How many landings you make?" The Adjutant had sat down on his stool again, sipping his drink. Mosca almost raised his arm when the Adjutant spoke.

"I don't mean that. Some of those officers there are bigger war heroes than I imagine you ever were and they didn't do what you did or take your attitude." The Adjutant's voice was dead calm, cold with reasonableness that was not conciliatory.

Mosca relinquished his anger and adopted the other's cold calm, as if imitating him as they imitated each other in age and height and bearing. "O.K.," he said, "I was wrong telling the Colonel, I apologize. But don't *you* give me that civilian shit."

The Adjutant smiled, no personal insult reaching him, the priest suffering for his religion. "As long as you understand about the other thing," he said.

Mosca said, "O.K., I understand." And despite all he could do the words were a submission, and when he went back to the dice table he felt his face burning with shame. He saw Eddie Cassin suppressing another smile, winking at him to cheer him up. The officer rolling the dice, a big easy-going southerner, said in his soft drawling voice, loud enough for the Adjutant to hear, "It's a good thing you didn't win another ten bucks, we'd have to take yuh out and shoot yuh." The officers around the table laughed, but Mosca did not. Behind him he could hear the Adjutant talking easily and occasionally laughing, drinking with his friends as if nothing had happened.

# 10

MOSCA AND GORDON MIDDLETON stopped working to eavesdrop; through the slightly ajar door of Eddie's office they could hear a young girl's voice. "Eddie, I wanted to see you for just a minute, it is very important." Her voice was a little shaky.

Eddie's voice, cold and formally polite said, "Sure, go ahead."

The girl said hesitatingly, "I know you told me I was not to come to your office, but you never visit me any more."

Gordon and Mosca grinned at each other. Gordon shook his head. They listened.

The girl said, "I need a carton of cigarettes."

There was a silence. Then Eddie asked with cold sarcasm, "What brand?" But the girl did not catch the inflection, the implied rejection.

"Oh, you know that doesn't matter," she said. "I need them for the doctor. That is his price."

Eddie's voice was polite, impersonal, "Are you ill?"

The girl laughed coyly. "Oh, Eddie, you know very well. I am going to have a baby. For a carton of cigarettes my doctor will help me lose it." Then reassuringly, as if anxiety for her welfare might make him refuse, "There is no danger."

Mosca and Gordon nodded at each other, laughing noiselessly, not at the girl but at Eddie, at what they imagined to be his embarrassment and the fact that this liaison would cost him a carton of cigarettes. Eddie's next words wiped their smiles away.

The voice was still cold, polite, but there was a horrible note of joyous hatred in it. "Tell your German boy friend to help. You won't get any cigarettes from me. And if you come to this office again you will not be working on this Air Base. Now get back to your job."

The girl was crying. Finally she protested in a weak voice, "I have no boy friend. It is your child. It is three months, Eddie."

"That's all," Eddie Cassin said.

The girl had regained her courage and drawn some anger from his contempt. "You didn't come to me for a whole month. I didn't know if you would come again. That man just took me to some dances. I swear it. You know you were the one. What is a carton of cigarettes to you?"

Gordon and Mosca could hear Eddie pick up the phone and ask the operator for the base Provost Marshal. Then the girl's voice with a note of terror in it said, "Help me, Mr. Cassin, please help me." They then could hear the hall door open and slam shut and Eddie saying, "Never mind," to the operator.

Eddie Cassin pushed through the door to their room and his delicate pale-gray face wore a pleased smile. "Did you enjoy our little scene?" he asked.

Mosca leaned back in his chair and said contemptuously, "You're a real prick, Eddie."

Gordon Middleton said, "I'll give you the cigarettes for her, Eddie." He said it with none of the contempt Mosca had shown, simply as a statement of fact, as if the only reason Eddie had refused was because of the value he would lose.

Eddie looked them both over with a derisive smile. "Gee, what nice guys. Willing to help a poor kid like that. Listen. That little tramp had a guy on the side all the time. He smoked the cigarettes I gave her, ate the chocolate bars and food I meant for her." He laughed with real good humor. "Besides, I've been through this before. And I know that the black-market fee for abortions is only half a carton."

The door of the office opened and Wolf came in. He said, "Hi ya fellas." He put his brief case on the desk and sat down with a weary sigh. "What a bunch of cheerful bums," He grinned at them, his pasty-white face lit with genuine happiness. "Caught two krauts stealing coffee. You know that soup the mess officer lets them take home in their little pots? Well they put the ground coffee on the bottom, sand over that, then the soup over. Don't ask me how they get the sand out later."

For some reason this soured Eddie. He said gloomily, "Wolf Tracy always gets his man. Tell us how you do it, Wolf."

Wolf grinned. "Hell, who would ever figure it out? Same as usual. Stool pigeon."

Middleton rose. "Guess I'll go home early. O.K., Eddie?"

"Sure," Eddie said.

Wolf raised his hand. "Wait a minute, Gordon." Gordon stopped by the open door. "Don't say I told you, and you other guys keep it quiet. But you'll be getting your shipping orders back to the States in about a week. O.K.?"

Gordon lowered his head to stare at the floor. Wolf said kindly, "Hell, you expected it, didn't you, Gordon?"

Gordon raised his head and smiled slowly. "I guess so," he said. "Thanks, Wolf." He went out the door.

Eddie said quietly to Wolf, "That security check came back from the States?"

"Yeah," Wolf said.

Eddie Cassin began to clear off his desk. Twilight darkened the windows of the personnel office. He opened his brief case and filled it with two bottles of gin, a large tin of grapefruit juice and some chocolate bars he took from a desk drawer.

Wolf said, "Why don't you give me your cigarettes and booze, Eddie. You'll wind up with money in the bank instead of a dose."

Eddie put the brief case under his arm and went to the door. "I'm living," he said. "Wish you scavengers luck. I'm off to tame a gorilla."

During supper Wolf said to Mosca, "You know, I must have been the first to spot Gordon. I gave him a lift to town one day and on the road he told me to stop. He got out of the jeep and walked back. Then he picks up a jagged hunk of metal that my wheel had just missed. He throws it off into the bushes and says with that nice, quiet smile, a little embarrassed, 'Save a guy a flat tire.' Now, you say that's a nice thing to do, and sure Gordon is a nice guy. But that's going to a little too much trouble. He puts himself out too much. So when my boss told me he had to keep an eye out for Gordon because he was a Party member I wasn't surprised. They eat up guys like that. Poor stupid bastard."

Mosca lit up a cigar and took a sip of coffee. "He's got balls," he said.

Wolf swallowed the food in his mouth. "Wrong attitude. Use your head now. How many times a day do we get Germans that want to join our Army? They want to fight the Russians. How many times there been rumors Russian troops invaded the British and American sectors? I see the secret reports. It won't be long now, I give it two years before everything blows up. So guys like Gordon have to get the ax. Right here." He made a chopping motion at his throat. "And me I'm going back to the States. I won't wear that PW in Siberia."

Mosca said slowly, "I hope I can get out of here before then."

Wolf wiped his mouth and leaned back to let a waiter pour coffee. "Don't worry," he said. "I got some inside dope they have to lift the marriage ban so we can make honest dames out of the *Fräuleins*. Lots of pressure from the churches back home. Don't want anybody screwing dames without a fighting chance of getting hooked."

They left the mess hall and went out to Wolf's jeep. Outside the wire fence of the air base they took the turn in the road that led away from town and to a far end of the Neustadt. It was only a short ride, and Wolf pulled up in front of an isolated house that was extraordinarily narrow, as if it consisted of one strict line of rooms from front to back. There were three other jeeps parked nearby, a few German Opel cars with wood-burning motors and tin smokestacks. Some bicycles were chained to an iron bar cemented into the stone steps.

Wolf rang the bell, and when the door opened Mosca was startled. The tallest and largest German he had ever seen stood before them. "We have an appointment with Frau Vlavern," Wolf said. The giant stood aside to let them enter.

The room was almost full. Two G.I.'s sat close together with a stuffed green duffel bag between them. There were three officers, each of them with a bulging brief case of shiny pigskin. There were five Germans with empty flaccid brief cases of black leather. They all waited patiently; everyone went in turn, Germans and Americans alike. There were no conquerors here.

The giant took them one by one into the next room and also took care of the door as more officers and G.I.'s and Germans arrived. Some Mosca recognized as base personnel, crew chiefs, a Mess Sergeant, the PX officer. All acted as if they did not know each other after the first nod of greeting.

The windows were heavily shuttered but the sound of jeep motors starting and dying to a halt could be heard in that room. When someone disappeared with the giant, they never returned. At the other end of the house was a door that served as exit.

Their turn came, and the giant took them into the next room. He indicated they were to wait. The room was empty save for two wooden chairs and a small table on which was an ash tray. When they were alone Mosca said, "That's a big guy."

"Her protection," Wolf said, "but if she has the scrip that won't mean nothing. That giant is nearly a moron. She keeps him here to scare people, like drunken G.I.'s and krauts. But for the real McCoy he can't do much." He smiled at Mosca.

After a short wait the giant came in again. He said, in German, in a huskily soft voice that did not fit his body, "Would you care to see something I personally wish to sell?" He took out a band of gold in which was fastened a large diamond. He gave it to Mosca. "Only ten cartons."

Mosca handed it over to Wolf and said, "That looks like a good buy. A carat at least."

Wolf turned it over and smiled. "It's not worth anything," he said. "See, it's flat backed. I told you this guy was a moron." He threw the ring to the giant who snatched at it clumsily but missed and had to stoop down from his great height to pick it up from the floor. Then determinedly he gave the ring to Mosca again. "Ten cartons, a bargain, but do not tell the old Frau." He put a huge finger, childlike, on his lips.

Mosca tried to give the ring back to him but the giant refused to take it. "Ten cartons, keep it for ten cartons," he said over and over again. Mosca put the ring on the table. Slowly, sadly, the giant picked it up.

Then he motioned them to follow and opened the door to the next room. He stood by the door to let them pass, first Mosca, then Wolf. But as Wolf went by he gave a malicious push that sent the American hurtling to the center of the room. Then the giant closed the door and stood by it.

A small, stout, gray-haired woman sat in a wide wicker chair, beside her a desk on which stood an open ledger. There were stacks of PX goods against one wall, hundreds of cartons of cigarettes, yellow boxes of chocolate bars, bars of toilet soap and other toilet goods with bright wrappers. A small German man was arranging the goods neatly into piles. The pockets of his black, ill-fitting jacket bulged with German currency, and when he turned to watch them a bundle of it fell to the floor.

The woman spoke first and she spoke in English. "I am very sorry," she said. "Once in a great while Johann takes a dislike to someone and does such a thing. There is nothing to be done."

Wolf had been taken by surprise and stood in momentary bewilderment. But now his heavy dead-white face turned crimson. The woman's insolent tone angered him even more. He saw Mosca smiling at him and that Mosca had stepped to a wall where he could command everyone in the room if he showed a weapon. Wolf shook his head, then turned to the old woman and saw the glint of amusement in her shrewd eyes.

"It is a small thing," Wolf said calmly. "You know what I have come for. Can you help us?"

The woman looked him up and down and still speaking English said, "My dear man, your story has a stink to it. I don't know of this million dollars in scrip. If I did I would be very careful in my dealings with you and your friend. Really, you insult my intelligence."

Wolf kept his smile. Business before pleasure, he thought. He said, "If you make a contact and deliver that contact to me it may well mean a small fortune for you. For such a little thing."

There was contempt in the woman's voice and disdain in her puffy, fat cheeks. "I am a woman of business and will have no part in such affairs. And make certain I will warn my friends against you." She gave a snort of laughter. "*You* have five thousand cartons."

Wolf was still smiling. He asked, "Can either of these two men understand English? It is important."

The woman, surprised by the unexpected question, said, "No, they do not."

The smile faded from Wolf's face and into it, as if it were a mask he had always ready, came the look of power, a confident quiet sternness.

He put his brief case on the table and leaned over it to look directly into the old woman's circled eyes.

"You are too clever and too proud," he said with measured harshness. "You think you have some power, that you are safe, that your age and your men protect you. I don't like insolent Germans. You don't understand Americans, you and your giant." The woman was alert now, her eyes a beady, flashing black. The little German with his bulging coat had a frightened look. The giant at the door moved toward Wolf. Mosca drew the Hungarian pistol from his brief case and clicked off the safety catch. They all turned to him.

He didn't point the gun, held it down to the floor. In German he said to the giant, "Turn around." The giant moved toward him. Mosca took a step forward and the old woman seeing his face called out a sharp command to the giant. He gave her a bewildered look, then retreated to the far wall and turned his back.

Wolf leaned toward the woman again. "Do you like my friend?" he asked her.

She didn't answer. She kept her eyes on Mosca. The little German, without a command, joined the giant against the wall. Wolf went on. "My friend is a very prideful and irritable man. If your giant had pushed him instead of me there would be no speeches, you would be very sad people here. There would be no words, words I speak so calmly. Now listen. I am reasonable. I hold no grudge for this incident. But if on my rounds I learn you have given information about me, then you can see the other side of my face."

He stopped and looked into the old woman's eyes. There was no fear in them. She was regarding him quite calmly, without compliance. But this was in his province, this was his life work, this challenged the genius he knew he had. He understood that look as no one else could. That words meant nothing, threats no hindrance or persuasion to the human will. He smiled because he knew the answer. He went over to the giant and pushed and turned him around.

"You lump, take off your belt and stand before your mistress," he said. The giant did so. Wolf stepped away.

He drew his gun from his brief case, for effect really, and said to the woman. "Tell him to give you three hard strokes on your back." He made his voice malignant. "If you cry out I'll kill the three of you. Now. Tell him three strokes."

The old woman was still calm. "You do not understand," she said. "If I order him he will take me quite seriously and injure me terribly. He will strike with all his power."

Wolf said good humoredly, "I understand that perfectly."

Her fat cheeks creased with a faint doubtful smile. "You have made your point, it is not necessary to go any further. I will say nothing, I promise. Now, please, I have many people waiting."

Wolf paused for a long moment, and then with a deliberately cruel smile he said, "One stroke. To seal our bargain."

For the first time the woman seemed frightened. Her face sagged, there was a quaver in her voice. "I shall scream for help," she said.

Wolf didn't answer her. He spoke to Mosca, slowly, so that the woman would be sure to understand. "When the woman goes down, kill the big man." He swung the gun up to the woman's face. She turned her head away. She said to the giant in German, "Johann give me one hard stroke across the back." She sat on the chair with her head bowed on the table, her rounded fat shoulders hunched for the blow. The giant swung his belt down and when it hit, they could hear a terrible crackling split of skin and meat beneath cloth. The woman raised her head. Her face was bloodless with pain and fright and shock. Wolf looked at her with cold, emotionless eyes. "Now you understand," he said. Then, mimicking her insolent voice and manner,

"There is nothing to be done." He walked to the door and said, "Come on, Walter," and they went through the rooms they had come by and out the front door.

In the jeep going back to town, Wolf laughed and said to Mosca, "Would you have shot that big guy if I gave the word?"

Mosca lit a cigarette. He was still tense. "Hell, I knew it was an act. I got to hand it to you, Wolf, you put on a hell of a show."

Wolf said in a satisfied voice, "Experience, boy. Some of our officers were too chicken to use real pressure on prisoners. So we had to use the scare technique. And you looked real mean there on the wall."

"I was surprised," Mosca said. "When that big guy pushed you and the old dame was so snotty, I figured a trap. Then I was mad. Christ, don't they know some of these G.I.'s would butcher the whole crew for a stunt like that?"

Wolf said slowly, "I'll tell you how people are, Walter. This old dame, she thinks she's clever. And she has this big giant and all these officers and G.I.'s treat her with respect because she can make their fortune. Now get this: She forgets. She forgets what it is to be afraid. That one stroke she got was the key. Remember that. Without that one stroke she couldn't be afraid. People are like that."

They went across the bridge and into the Bremen town. In a few minutes they were before the billet.

They smoked a cigarette together in the parked jeep.

Wolf said, "In a week or so we make the most important contacts. We'll have to stay out most of the night. So be ready for a call any time. O.K.?" He slapped Mosca on the back.

Mosca stepped out of the jeep, took a last puff on his cigarette. "You think she'll squawk to her friends?"

Wolf shook his head. "This is the one thing I know about. She'll never open her mouth to anybody." He grinned at Mosca. "She'll never forget that stripe she wears on her back."

# 11

WALTER MOSCA, dressed in civvies, stared out of the window of the Civilian Personnel Office. He watched the people of the base going by, the airplane mechanics in their green fatigues and fur-lined leather jackets, natty flying officers in dark greens and violet overcoats, the German laborers in their old clothing, all hunched against the sharp November wind. Behind him Eddie Cassin said, "Walter." Mosca turned around.

Eddie Cassin leaned back in his chair. "I got a job for you. I had an idea and the Lieutenant thinks it's pretty good. We're having a food conservation drive all over the European Theatre, you know, try to tell the chowhounds that they shouldn't eat themselves sick. Not to starve but not to load up their trays, then leave a lot of stuff that has to be thrown out. Now here's the idea. We want a picture of a G.I. with a big heaping tray of food and caption it 'Stop This.' Next to it we want a photo of two little German kids sniping butts in the street and the caption, 'And You Stop This.' How does it sound?"

"It sounds like real shit to me," Mosca said.

Eddie grinned at him. "All right. But it looks clever as hell. Real public-relations stuff. Headquarters will eat it up. Maybe *Stars and Stripes* will print it. Who knows? It could turn out big.

"For Christ's sake," Mosca said.

"O.K.," Eddie Cassin said, a little annoyed. "Just get a picture of kids sniping butts. The jeep is outside and you can pick up that photographer, the Corporal, at the lab."

"O.K.," Mosca said. He went out and watched the afternoon flight from Wiesbaden come down out of the sky, as if appearing by magic from nothing but air. Then he got into the jeep.

It was late afternoon before he drove the jeep over the bridge into Bremen proper. The Corporal had been goofing around the hangars, and it had taken Mosca an hour to track him down.

The streets of the city were full of hurrying Germans and the Strassenbahns clanged their way through dense traffic, passengers hanging on to the step poles. Mosca parked the jeep in front of the Glocke.

In the gray workaday afternoon all was still. The front of the Red Cross Club was empty of beggars, streetwalkers and children; activity would begin after the supper hour. Two German policewomen strolled slowly up and down the sidewalk, slowly as if bemused by the melodious clanging of streetcar bells.

Mosca and the Corporal waited in their jeep for some begging children to appear, smoking cigarettes but not talking. Finally the Corporal said, "What goddamn luck. This is the first time I didn't see some kraut kids hangin' around."

Mosca got out of the jeep. "I'll take a look," he said. It was very cold and he turned up the collar of his jacket. He walked around the corner and seeing no children, continued to walk until he was in the rear of the Glocke Building.

Serenely perched on a great hill of rubble, looking down

on half the great city that lay in ruins before them, were two small boys. They were wrapped in coats reaching to their shoes and on their heads were caps that came down almost over their ears. Through their bare hands they strained the loose dirt out of the rubble they scooped up, and then threw stones and fragments of brick out across the prairie and valley of ruins below them; throwing at nothing in particular and not hard enough to lose balance on top of the hill.

"Here," Mosca called in German, "do you two want to earn some chocolate?"

The children looked down at him gravely, judging him, recognizing him as one of the enemy, despite his civilian clothes, then slid down the hill, not afraid. They followed him, leaving their vast, silent, empty playground, clasping each other's hand when they came into the busy square before the Glocke.

The Corporal was out of the jeep, waiting for them. He slipped a plate into his camera and adjusted the range finder. When he was set he said to Mosca, "O.K., tell them what to do." The Corporal could speak no German.

"Pick up those cigarette butts," Mosca told the boys. "Now look up so that man can take your picture." They bent obediently but their long, peaked caps shadowed their faces.

"Push their caps back," the Corporal said. Mosca did so, exposing two grinning gnomelike faces to the camera.

"Those butts are too small," the Corporal said. "They won't show up." Mosca took out some whole cigarettes and threw them into the gutter.

The Corporal had made a few shots but was not satisfied. He was preparing for another when Mosca felt someone's hand on his arm and he was spun around.

Before him were the two policewomen, the one who had spun him around nearly as tall as he, her hand still on his arm. He gave her a push that was nearly a blow, feeling the soft breast beneath the rough, blue wool of her uniform. She staggered back, her hand falling away from his arm, then said defensively, "That is not allowed here." She turned to the boys and said in a warning voice, "You two leave here instantly."

Mosca grabbed the children by their coats. "Stay here," he said. He turned on the two women, his lean, dark face ugly and vicious with anger. "Do you see that uniform?" pointing to the Corporal. He held out his hand. "Give me your identification." The two women began to stutter explanations, that it was their job to keep the children away, keep them from begging. A German man going by stopped, the boys edged away from the quarrel, and the man said something to them in an angry, scolding voice which frightened them, and they began to run. Mosca caught them again as the Corporal let out a warning shout. The man began to walk away quickly to get to the throng of fellow Germans waiting on the corner for a streetcar. Mosca ran down the street after him and when the German heard the pounding feet he turned around, his eyes blinking with fright.

"Did you tell those children to leave?" Mosca shouted at him.

The German said quietly, apologetically, "I did not understand. I thought they were begging."

"Give me your identity pass," Mosca said. He held out his hand. The German, trembling with nervousness and shock, reached into his jacket pocket and pulled out the usual enormous wallet stuffed with papers. He fumbled unseeingly, trying to watch Mosca at the same time until Mosca took the papers out of his hand and found the blue card himself.

Mosca handed the wallet back. "Come to the police station in the morning for your pass," he said, and turned to walk back to the jeep.

Across the street, on the other side of the square, he saw in the failing November light a dark, silent mass of Germans watching him; tall, giantlike, black as the outline of a forest. For one moment he knew fear and terror as if they could see into his heart and mind, and then his anger flared up again. He walked slowly, calmly, to the jeep. The two boys were still there but the policewomen had disappeared.

"Let's go," he said to the Corporal. He drove down to the Metzer Strasse and got out. He said to the Corporal, "Take the jeep back to the base for me."

The Corporal nodded and said quietly, "I think those shots will be enough." And Mosca realized that he had forgotten to renew the taking of pictures and had left the children standing in front of the Glocke, not given them the chocolate he had promised.

When Mosca entered the room, Hella was warming soup on the electric plate, a red-labeled empty can open on the table. A pan full of bacon waited its turn. Leo sat on the couch reading.

The room was warm with the smell of food, comfortable in its well-filled largeness. The bed and its night table in one corner, on the table a lamp and small radio; the great white wardrobe in the corner near the door, and in the middle a great round table surrounded by wicker chairs. Along one wall the enormous, empty china closet helped give the room a coziness that was not crowded, that yet gave plenty of space to move around in. A hell of a big room, Mosca always thought.

Hella looked up from her cooking. "Oh, you're home early," she said and rose to kiss him. Her face always changed when she saw him, he could see the happiness there, giving him always a sense of guilt and fear because she built so much of her life on him. As if she did not know the many dangers he felt in the world around them.

"I had something to do in town and didn't go back to the base," Mosca said. Leo raised his head and nodded to him, then continued to read. Mosca reached into his pocket for a cigarette, and his fingers touched the German's identity card.

"How about giving me a lift to the police station after we eat?" Mosca asked Leo. He threw the card on the table.

Leo nodded and said, "What have you there?" Mosca told them what had happened. He noticed that Leo was watching him with a curious, amused smile. Hella poured the hot soup into cups and said nothing. Then she put the bacon on the electric plate.

They drank the soup carefully, dipping crackers into it. Hella lifted the blue identity card from the table. Holding the cup in one hand she flipped the card open with the other. "He's married," she said. "He has blue eyes and brown hair and works as a printer. That is a good job." She studied the picture. "He doesn't look like a bad man, I wonder if he has children."

"Doesn't it say on the pass?" Mosca asked.

"No," Hella said. "He has a scar on his finger." She let the card drop back onto the table.

Leo tilted his head back and drank the last of his soup,

then leaned over the table, the tic in his face working a little. "Tell me," he said, "why didn't you go to the police station with the man right away? It was close by."

Mosca smiled at him. "I just wanted to scare the guy, I'm not going to do anything. I guess I just wanted to scare the son of a bitch."

"He'll have a very bad night," Hella said.

"He deserves it," Mosca said angrily, defensively. "Where does that bastard come off putting his two cents in a deal like that."

Hella lifted her pale, gray eyes to him. "He was ashamed," she said, "and I think he felt it his fault that these children beg and pick up cigarettes in the streets."

"Ah hell, let him sweat," Mosca said. "How about some bacon before you burn the hell out of it?"

Hella put the bacon and a loaf of gray German bread on the table. When they had finished eating the grease-soaked sandwiches Leo and Mosca rose, Leo searching for his jeep keys on the trunk. Hella picked up the identity card and looked at the address. "See," she said eagerly, "he lives on Rubsam Strasse. That is closer than the police station."

Mosca said curtly, "Don't wait up for me. We're going to the club after." Then he smiled at her as she leaned her head to be kissed, her thin, closely drawn light-brown hair like a helmet. The sentimental action always endeared her to him though he smiled at it and never made the first move himself. "Do you want me to bring some ice cream?" She nodded. As he went out the door she called after him, "It's on the way to the club."

In the jeep Leo said to him, "Where do we go?"

"O.K., for Christ's sake, take me to the guy's house." Mosca shook his head. "You and her give me a big pain in the ass."

"I don't give a damn," Leo said, "but it is on the way to the club. And besides I know what it is to 'sweat,' as you say. That is a very accurate word." He turned his big-boned face to Mosca and smiled with a touch of sadness.

Mosca shrugged. "I don't even want to see the bastard. How about you going in the house, Leo?"

"Not me," Leo said with a grin. "You took it away from him? You give it back."

They had no trouble finding the house, a private, two-family home cut up into a tenement to provide much-needed housing. On the vestibule door was a list of all the tenants, including every member of the family, and what apartments they occupied. Mosca looked at the identity pass and compared names. Then he went up to the second floor. He knocked sharply and the door was opened immediately. He realized that he had been seen from the window and his knock waited for. The man at the door had the same bullet head and stern features but his face was set in a constrained mask and softened by the now naked baldness of his skull. The German stood aside and Mosca went in.

He had interrupted the evening meal. The table in the large room held four dishes filled with black gravy in which floated dark, shredded vegetables and large pasty white potatoes. In one corner was a bed, further along the wall a sink hung awkwardly, above it a great framed painting in dark greens and browns. A woman, light hair drawn against her skull, was trying to bring two small boys through the door to the other room of the apartment. But as she turned to see Mosca she let the children escape her. They all looked at Mosca and waited.

He handed the German the blue identity card. The man took it and said falteringly, "Yes?"

Mosca said, "You don't have to go to the police station. Forget about everything."

The blunt, stern face turned ghastly white. The relief from fear, the shock of the day, the jeep screaming to a stop in front of his house, all combined now—a poison disintegrated his blood. He trembled visibly and his wife hurried to his support, helped him to one of the four empty wooden chairs surrounding the table. Mosca, alarmed, said to the woman, "What's the trouble, what's the matter with him?"

"Nothing," the woman said, her voice dead, completely empty of emotion or any life. "We thought you came to take him away." Her voice wavered slightly.

One of the children began to cry with quiet fright, as if the strength and walls of his world had been destroyed. Mosca, thinking to quiet him, took a few steps forward and brought out a bar of chocolate. The child was terrified and began to scream great hysterical screams, so high pitched they were barely audible. Mosca stopped and looked at the woman helplessly. She was bringing her husband a small glass of schnapps. As the man drank, the woman ran over to the child, slapped him full in the mouth and then picked him up in her arms. The child was still. The father, still terribly agitated said, "Wait, please wait," and almost ran to the cupboard for a bottle of schnapps and a small water glass.

He poured Mosca a drink and forced it into his hands. "It was all a mistake, you see, all a mistake, I thought the children were annoying you. I did not mean to interfere." And Mosca remembered the man's angry tone when he had scolded the two boys in front of the Glocke, the angry shame and guilt, as if its owners were himself the cause of the children's degradation.

"It's all right," Mosca said. He tried to leave the drink on the table but the German kept hold of his arm and forced the drink on him again.

Forgetting his wife and children watching him, as if he were pleading for his life, the father went on feverishly, "I was never a Nazi. I joined the Party to keep my job, all printers must join. But I paid my dues. No more. I was never a Nazi. Drink. It's good stuff. Drink it. I save this for when I feel ill." Mosca drank and broke away for the door but the German caught him, shook his hand, "I am very grateful for your kindness. That is from the heart. I will never forget this. I have always said the Americans were good. They are kindhearted, we Germans are fortunate." He wrung Mosca's hand for the last time, his head shaking up and down with nervousness and passionate relief.

At that moment Mosca felt an almost uncontrollable urge to strike him down, to make the blood flow from that bald skull and twitching face, and turned his head away to hide his contempt and disgust.

Framed against the brown door, in the room beyond, Mosca saw the wife's face. The flesh was drawn tight around the separate and distinctly seen bones. The skin was dead white and her head was slightly lowered, the shoulders hunched by the weight of the child in her arms. Her gray eyes, almost black now, were dark pools of unforgetting hatred. Her hair, too, seemed dark beside the child's golden one and her gaze did not flinch as it met Mosca's. Not one muscle of her face moved.

As the door closed behind him, Mosca heard her voice, quiet but sharp, speaking to her husband. Out in the street, by the light of the lamp-lit room, he could see her looking down at him, the child still in her arms.

# 12

WOLF ATE his cold supper German-peasant fashion, picking up the long, blood-red wurst and slicing off a thick, glutinous chunk with his pocketknife. Then he cut a block of dark bread from the enormous loaf resting before him. The German girl he lived with, Ursula, and her father, took the bread and wurst in their turn. Each had a can of American beer beside their plates with which they filled small wine glasses when necessary.

"When do you have to go?" Ursula asked. She was a small, dark girl with an ungovernable temper. Wolf had taken pleasure in taming her. He had already put in his marriage papers, and it was with this understanding that he had been allowed to move into the father's house to live with her. There were other considerations.

"I have to meet Mosca at the Rathskellar in about an hour," Wolf said, looking at the watch he had taken from the Polish refugee after the war. The dead Polack, Wolf thought.

"I don't care for that man," Ursula said. "He has no manners. I don't know what that girl sees in him."

Wolf cut another slice of wurst and said jokingly, "The same thing you see in me."

As he knew she would, Ursula flared up. "You damn Americans think we'll do anything for your goods. Try treating me as your Ami friends treat their girls. See if I keep you. Out the house you go."

The father, munching on the hard bread, said placatingly, "Ursula, Ursula," but he said it out of habit, thinking of something else.

When Wolf had finished supper he went into the bedroom and stuffed his large, brown leather brief case with cigarettes, chocolate and a few cigars. He took these from a locked wardrobe to which he had the only key. As he was about to leave Ursula's father came in.

"Wolfgang, before you leave. A word if I may." The father was always polite and respectful, always remembering the lover of his daughter was an American. Wolf liked this in him.

The father led Wolf to their cold storeroom in the back of the basement apartment. The father threw open the door and in a dramatically concerned voice said, "Look."

From the wooden beams hung bare bones of hams with tiny shreds of dark meat clinging to them, small ends of salamis, and a white cheese like a thin quarter moon.

"We have to do something, Wolfgang," the father said, "our supplies are very low. Very, very low."

Wolf sighed. He wondered what the old bastard had done with all that stuff. They both knew damn well it hadn't been eaten. A regiment couldn't have done such damage. As always when the old man had outgeneraled him he thought grimly, wait until Ursula and me get back to the States. I'll teach them both a lesson. The old man would expect packages. Balls he'd get. Wolf nodded his head as if he had been thinking over the problem.

"All right," he said. They went back to the bedroom and he gave the father five cartons of cigarettes. "These are the last I can give for a few months," Wolf said warningly. "I have a very big deal ready."

"Don't worry," the father said, "this will last a long time. My daughter and I get along as sparingly as we can, you know that, Wolfgang." Wolf nodded his head reassuringly, and also in admiration of the man's nerve, thinking, the old robber will make his fortune out of me yet.

Before he left the room, Wolf took the heavy Walther pistol from his bureau drawer and slipped it into the jacket of his coat. This always captured the father's attention, made him more respectful, and this also pleased Wolf.

As they left the room together the older man threw his arm in a confidential, fatherly way around Wolf's shoulders. "Next week I am getting a great supply of brown and gray gabardine. I'll have some beautiful suits made for you, as a present. And if any of your friends wish to buy I will give them a special price. As a favor to you."

Wolf nodded gravely. As he went out the door Ursula called out, "Be careful." He left the basement and walked up a few steps to the street. Then he strode briskly in the direction of the Rathskeller. It was only fifteen minutes away, he would be in plenty of time. As he walked he marveled over the father. A load of gabardine. *His* gabardine really. And then he was supposed to sell it without commission. He'd fix that. He'd make himself a little something. He'd give Mosca, Cassin and Gordon a good break, maybe even the Jew, but still earn a little something. But he should be able to sell a lot of it. At a nice cut for himself. Well, that was chicken feed, but every bit helped.

In the Rathskeller, the great underground restaurant that before the war had been one of Germany's finest, he found Eddie Cassin and Mosca at a table by the giant wine casks.

These huge barrels reaching to the ceiling formed a shadow over the two men, cutting them off from the rest of the olive-drab officers and the few women who spotted the vast, cavernous room. A string orchestra played quietly, the lights were dim, and small white-clothed tables stretched out as far as the eye could see; then clustered in white eddies like foam; in alcoves and small private dining rooms.

"Wolf, the living cigarette tree," Eddie Cassin shouted. His voice rose above the music and rose to the almost invisible ceiling high above them and became lost there. No one paid any attention. He leaned over the table and whispered, "What you two hustlers got planned tonight?"

Wolf sat down. "Just making a little trip around town. See if we can pick up any bargains. Stop using your butts for gash, and I'll make you a few pennies." Though he joked, Wolf was worried. He could see Mosca was nearly as drunk as Eddie and he was surprised. He had never seen Mosca drunk before. He wondered if he should cancel the whole deal for this night. But it was all set up, this was the first night they would hit the big black-market wheels, they might even get a lead on who had the dough. Wolf ordered a drink, watching Mosca to see if he would be O.K.

Mosca noticed this and smiled. "I'll be all right, a coupla minutes fresh air. I'll be O.K." He tried to enunciate carefully but the words slurred together. Wolf shook his head with an impatient disgust he could not hide.

Eddie shook his head in drunken mimicry. "The trouble with you, Wolf, is you think you're clever. You wanna be a millionaire. Wolf, you'll never make it. Never in a million years. One, you got no brains, just a little cunning. Two, you havn't got real guts. You can slap kraut prisoners around but that's all. That's all, that's all."

"How can you stand this gash hound?" Wolf asked Mosca, his voice deliberately quiet, insulting. "He's had so many dames sitting on his head, his brain's gone soft."

Eddie jumped up angrily and shouted, "You lousy butt hustler—" Mosca pulled him down to the chair. Some of the people at the other tables turned around. "Take it easy, Eddie, he's only kidding. You too, Wolf. He's drunk. When he's drunk he hates everybody. And besides, his wife wrote him she's leaving England with the kid and coming here, and he can't stand giving up all his dames."

Eddie turned on Mosca with drunken reproachfulness and said, "That's not so, Walter, I really gave her some raw deals." He shook his head dolefully.

Mosca, to cheer him up, said, "Tell Wolf about your gorilla."

Wolf drank his whiskey down, and some of his good humor returned. He grinned at Eddie Cassin.

Eddie said solemnly, almost reverently, "I'm screwing a gorilla." He waited for Wolf's reaction.

"I'm not surprised," Wolf said and laughed with Mosca. "What's the deal?"

"I'm screwing a real honest-to-God gorilla," Eddie insisted.

Wolf looked questioningly at Mosca. "It's a dame," Mosca said, "he claims she looks just like a gorilla, she's that homely."

Eddie looked down at the table and then turned earnestly to Mosca. "I got a confession to make, Walter, she's really a gorilla, I was ashamed to admit it. But she's a real gorilla. I lied to you. She lives right near the air base and she works for Military Government. She's an interpreter." He smiled at them and Wolf, his spirits completely restored, laughed so heartily that the people at the nearby tables turned around again.

"How about bringing her around and giving us a break?" Wolf asked jokingly.

Eddie shuddered. "Christ, I never go out in the street with her even. I sneak into the house when it's dark."

"It's time for us to leave, Walter," Wolf said briskly, "this is the big night and it's going to be a long one." Mosca leaned over Eddie and asked, "You all right? Can you get home O.K.?" Eddie mumbled that he was and as they walked to the door they could hear him shouting to the waiter for another drink.

Wolf waited for Mosca to get ahead of him, noticing the unsteady walk. Going up the steps he could not help saying, "You picked a hell of a night to get stewed."

The cold winter air sliced through Mosca's cheek bones, freezing the red pulp of his gums and palate, flesh already raw from too much alcohol and cigarettes. He lit a cigarette to warm his mouth and throat and thought, "Screw you, Wolf," and thought if this son of a bitch makes another crack I'll rap him or walk away. He could feel the cold working through his coat and below it, freezing his knees and thighs, feeling his whole torso itch with the beginning chill as if it were glazed with frost, and he felt nausea as the frozen air hit the souring whiskey in his belly, sending it spinning up to his brain. He wanted to vomit but knotted his stomach muscles, held it down, not wanting Wolf to see him so. Knowing that Wolf was right, it was a hell of a night to get stewed. But for the first time he'd had a real quarrel with Hella, not the kind of an argument that made you mad or resentful but one in which neither could understand the other. Just depressing and sad.

The street Wolf and Mosca followed led down a hill

from the Rathskellar, past the area of light shed by the Red Cross Club, the music from it trailing after them like a ghost through the ruins. Past the Police Building with its searchlight that imprisoned the jeeps in a white blinding pool of light cut from the surrounding darkness, and then descending the hill, steep as a well, they left the heart of the city and became part of the black night, and though they must have walked for some time it seemed almost a moment to Mosca before Wolf had knocked on a door, and they were inside some place, out of the cold.

In the room there was a large table, four chairs around it. These were the only pieces of furniture. Against the walls were stacks of merchandise over which brown Army blankets had been hastily thrown. There were no windows, and the room was hazy with smoke.

Mosca could hear Wolf saying something, introducing him to the little almost dwarflike German before him, and though the closeness of the room brought the nausea back he made an effort to listen, bring everything into focus.

"You know what he is interested in," Wolf was saying. "Money, only money. American scrip."

The German shook his head. "I have asked, I have asked all around. No one has the amount you say. That I know. I can buy a few hundred dollars, but that is the most possible.

Mosca broke in, enunciating slowly what he had been taught to say. "I am interested in selling a great quantity at one time. Five thousand cartons minimum."

The little German looked at him with respect and awe and his voice was filled with envious greed. "Five thousand cartons, OH OH OH." He thought of it dreamily and then said with a brisk, businesslike air, "However, I will keep an eye out, have no fear. A drink before you go?

Friedl," he called. A woman opened an inner door and peered out. "Schnapps," the German shouted as if he were calling a dog's name, bringing it to heel. The woman disappeared and reappeared a few minutes later with a thin, white bottle and three small water glasses. Behind her came a small boy and girl, golden-haired but with dirty, red-splotched faces.

Wolf crouched on his haunches, "Ah, what beautiful children," he exclaimed. From his brief case he took four bars of chocolate and extended a pair to each.

The father stepped between them and reaching out took the chocolate into his own hands. "No," he said, "it is too late for them to eat candy." He went to one of the footlockers resting against the wall and when he turned to face them his hands were empty. "Tomorrow, my children," he said. The boy and girl turned away sullenly. As Wolf and Mosca lifted their drinks the woman said something sharply in a dialect they could not understand. The man gave her a warning and threatening look, "Tomorrow, I have said. Tomorrow."

Mosca and Wolf left, and in the dark street, lit only by a single yellow window pane they could hear the shrill voices of man and wife, voices raised in menacing anger, fear and hate.

The white, homemade potato schnapps, almost as strong and raw as alcohol, warmed Mosca but added to the blackness of the winter night. He was unsteady and stumbled often. Finally Wolf stopped and held his arm and asked in a concerned voice, "You wanta call it off for tonight, Walter, and go home?" Mosca shook his head at Wolf's pasty-white face, luminous and cold as death in the darkness before him. They started to walk again, Wolf slightly ahead, Mosca following, straining against the cold wind and the physical nausea in his body. He thought of how Hella had said the same words to him that afternoon.

She had been wearing one of the dresses he had given her for the Christmas just past. Ann Middleton had let him use her clothing card at the Army store. Hella had watched him take the little Hungarian pistol from the wardrobe and slip it into the pocket of his short coat. Then she asked him quietly, "Don't you want to go home?"

He knew what she meant. The marriage ban against Germans had been lifted a few days before Christmas and now more than a month later he had done nothing about putting in his papers for permission to marry. And she knew that this was because once they were married they would have to leave Germany and go back to the States. And he answered, "No, I can't right now, I have six months to go on my job contract."

She had been hesitant, almost fearful, and when she came to kiss him good-bye, as she always did when he left her, even for a few hours, she said, "Why don't you read the letters from your family? Why don't you answer them with more than a little note?"

Against his own body he could feel the slight swelling of her rounded stomach and filling breasts. "We have to leave here sometime," she said. And he knew that this was true. But he couldn't tell her why he couldn't go home now. That he had no real feeling for his mother or Alf, and reading their letters would be like hearing their voices crying out. That the sight of the ruined city pleased him, the gaping wounds left in streets by destroyed buildings, the ragged and torn skyline as if a great, jagged ax had chopped off the top of the city's skull. That when he was home the solid, unending, wall-like streets, unmarred, secure, had made him angry, uneasy.

"We have time," he said. "After the baby comes in June, we'll get the papers and marry."

Hella stood away from him. "I'm not worried about that. But you shouldn't treat your family so, you should at least read their letters." He had flared up at her and said, "Look, don't keep trying to make me do things I don't want to do." And she had kissed him and said, "Be careful tonight," and he knew she would wait up for him though he had told her not to.

He could hear Wolf's voice say, "Here we are," and see the white face before him. There was a high stoop and they were standing in a pool of light formed by a naked bulb fastened into the face of the house. Its yellow light weakly stained the fabric of night. Mosca climbed the steps warily, holding fast to the iron rail.

"This guy is a long shot," Wolf said as he rang the bell. "But I want you to know him. He's a jeweler, and if you want something for your girl, he'll be a right guy."

A window above their heads, above the nakedly lit bulb, was thrown open. Wolf tilted his head back and said, "Ah, Herr Furstenberg, good evening."

"Please, just one moment, Herr Wolfgang." The voice was mellow with sadness and age, and a despair that came natural to it.

When the door opened a small bald-headed man, dark and with enormous black eyes waited to greet them, and when Wolf introduced Mosca the German clicked his heels and bowed. "Please come up," he said, and they climbed the stairs and went through a door to a large living room with many pieces of furniture which included two large sofas, three or four stuffed chairs and a grand piano. There was a large table in the center of the room and several smaller ones against the walls. On one of the sofas two young girls not more than sixteen were sitting, not close to each other but with a space between them. Herr Furstenberg sat in this space.

"Please," he said, motioning to the empty chairs nearest him. Wolf and Mosca sat down.

"I wanted you to meet the man I have spoken about," Wolf said. "He is a very good friend of mine and I know you will treat him well if he should ever need your help."

Herr Furstenberg, his arms around both girls' waists, bowed his bald head courteously and said with equal formality and graveness, "There can be no question of that." Then turning his great, black hollow eyes directly to Mosca he said, "Please come to me any time if I can help you."

Mosca nodded and sank back into the comfortable chair, feeling his legs quiver with fatigue. Idly, hazily through the fog of his tired mind, he noticed that the two young girls were fresh looking, without make-up, and wore heavy woolen stockings that rose to their kneecaps. They sat soberly beside Herr Furstenberg in daughterly fashion, and one had pigtails braided down each side of her shoulder, long golden ropes which piled into her rough, woolen-skirted lap and coiled into Herr Furstenberg's waiting hand.

"In that other matter," the German said, turning to Wolf again, "I am truly sorry, but I cannot help you. None of my friends have heard of such a thing, this theft of a million dollars of scrip. It is a fantastic story." He smiled kindly at them both.

"No," Wolf said firmly, "the story is true." He rose, extended his hand. "I'm sorry I disturbed you at so late an hour. If some information should come, please let me know."

"Of course," Herr Furstenberg said. He rose, bowed to

Mosca and shook his hand, saying to him, "Please come to me any time." The two girls rose from the sofa and Herr Furstenberg put his arms around their waists as a fond father might, and the three of them walked Mosca and Wolf to the staircase. One of the girls, not the one with long hair, ran down the steps and showed them out. They could hear the door being bolted behind them. Then the naked bulb above the stoop went out and they were in total darkness.

Mosca, dead tired, disgusted at leaving the comfortable room, asked Wolf curtly, "Do you think we'll ever find these bastards?"

"I'm just looking for a lead tonight," Wolf said, "and letting these people look you over. That's the big thing."

Now in the darkened streets they passed other hurrying forms, saw jeeps parked in front of deserted-looking houses. "Everybody is on the hunt tonight," Wolf said. He waited for a moment and then asked, "How did you like Furstenberg?"

The wind had died away and they could talk easily. "He seems like a nice guy," Mosca said.

"He's damn nice for a Jew especially," Wolf said. "No offense against your buddy." He waited for Mosca to say something and then went on. "Furstenberg did his time in a concentration camp. His wife and kids are in the States. He thought he was going to join them, but he has TB so bad they won't let him in. And he got it in the camp. Funny, huh?" Mosca didn't answer. They crossed a well-lighted avenue, coming back to the heart of the city.

"He's gone a little crazy," Wolf almost shouted. The wind had started up again and they were walking into it, tripping over rubble. They turned a corner and the wind was gone again. "You see those two girls? He gets them fresh from the country, new ones every month or so. His agent told me the story, we do business together. Furstenberg goes along for weeks living with the girls, they have their own room. And then, bang, after treating them like daughters all this time, one night he goes into their room and humps their ass off. Next day he ships them away with some real valuable presents and a week later he gets a fresh set. These are new ones, I haven't seen them before. That must be a nice little scene when he slips them the business. Real wild. Like a guy chasing chickens to cut off their heads."

Another guy, Mosca thought. Everybody going off their nuts. And he wasn't much better. So they wouldn't let the poor bastard in because he had TB. That was a law for the books. Sensible, all laws were sensible. But they always screwed somebody. But screw that son of a bitch Furstenberg, that heel-clicking prick. He had his own troubles. And that's what he had wanted to tell Hella this afternoon. That every day he lived he broke a law. Having her with him in the billet, buying clothes for her with Middleton's Army card, sleeping with her, and he could be sent to jail for loving her. And he wasn't complaining, that was the world, he wasn't indignant. But when they pulled all the other shit with this and tried to make you feel ashamed and tried to say it was right, justice, then it was shit. When they wanted him to act as if everything the world told him was so, then he just said fuck you in his mind. He couldn't stand listening to his mother, and Alf and Gloria. He couldn't stand reading the newspapers, they made him puke. They said this is good today and tomorrow they said you're evil, a murderer, a wild animal, and they made you believe it so much you helped hunt yourself down. He could get away with murdering Fritz but go to jail for taking care of a woman he wanted. And a week ago he had watched them shoot the Polacks against the wall, the hand-ball court behind the air base, the three brave Polacks who had massacred a small German village, men, women and children, but those poor bastard Polacks had made a mistake, they murdered a few days after the occupation had begun instead of a few days before, and instead of receiving their medals from the General as brave guerrillas, the top half of their bodies had been shrouded in brown cord sacks, and they were tied to wooden stakes driven into cracks in the cement, and the firing squad stood almost on top of them, shooting down into the slumped bodies a few feet away. And you could say it any way you wanted, you could prove a million times how necessary it was, the murdering, backwards and forwards, and he didn't give a shit about the whole business anyway. Didn't he eat a good breakfast after watching the Polacks?

But he couldn't tell Hella why he practically hated his mother, his girl, his brother now and why he loved her. Maybe because she had been afraid as he had been afraid, that she was as frightened of death as he was, and maybe really it was because she had lost everything as he had except that he had lost everything inside himself and she hadn't. That he hated all the mothers and fathers and sisters and brothers, sweethearts and wives that he saw in the newspapers, the newsreels, in brightly colored magazines, receiving medals for their dead sons, their dead heroes, the proud smiles, the proud weeping, the brave dress for the occasion showing real grief, painful but sweet in its very release of pain, and all the stern faces of the bestowing dignitaries in their blazing-white shirts and black ties, and he could imagine them all over the world the loved ones of the enemies too receiving the same medals for their dead sons and heroes weeping and smiling bravely, accepting in exchange the beribboned metal disc in its satin-lined box—and suddenly wriggling into his throbbing brain came an image of all the monstrously sated worms raising their pulpy white heads to bow in thanks to the dignitaries, the mothers, the fathers, the brothers, the sweethearts.

But you couldn't blame them because our cause was just; that's true, he thought, but how about Fritz? That was an accident, really an accident. And everybody would forgive him, his own dignitaries, his mother, Alf and Gloria. They would all say you couldn't help what you did. The worms would forgive him. Hella had wept but she accepted because there was nothing else she had left. And he couldn't blame any of them but don't try to tell me what's wrong, don't say I should read their letters, don't say the world shouldn't come to an end because men are holy and have immortal souls, don't say I should smile and be polite to every son of a bitch who does me a favor and says hello. All of Hella's hints about being nicer to Frau Meyer and Yergen and my own friends and answer and read my family's letters. It's all mixed up and it's nobody's fault and why blame them for being alive?

He had to stop walking, he felt really ill, his head was spinning, and he could not feel his own legs move. Wolf was holding his arm, and he rested against Wolf's shoulder until his head cleared so he could walk again.

White streaks and shadows ran through the night and Mosca, following them, raised his head and saw for the first time the cold and distant winter moon, and saw that they were in the Contrescarpe park, skirting around the little lake. Icy moonbeams glinted over water and webbed the black trees with frosted light, and as he watched, great dark-blue shadows raced across the sky and drowned the moon, its light, and now he couldn't see anything at all. Then Wolf spoke to him saying, "You looked real bad, Walter, keep going a few minutes, and we'll make a stop where I can fix you up."

They came suddenly into the city and to a square on a little rise of ground. On one corner stood a church, the great wooden doors barred shut. Wolf led the way to a side entrance and they climbed a narrow staircase to the steeple, and flush with the top step was a door which seemed to be cut out of the very wall. Wolf knocked, and through his nausea, Mosca still felt a shock to see that it was Yergen and thought, Wolf knows Yergen won't believe I have the cigarettes. But he was too sick to care.

The closeness of the room made him lean against a wall and then Yergen was giving him a green pill and hot coffee, shoving the pill into his mouth and holding a burning cup to his lips.

The room, Yergen and Wolf sprang into focus. The nausea left Mosca's body, and he could feel the cold sweat over his whole body running down between his thighs. Wolf and Yergen were watching him with little knowing smiles on their faces and Yergen patted him on the shoulder and said kindly, "You're all right now, eh?"

The room was cold. It was large, square, with a very low ceiling and one corner had been made into a cubicle by a wooden partition painted pink and covered with illustrations cut from a book of fairy tales. "My daughter is sleeping behind there," Yergen said, and as he spoke they could hear the little girl moaning, then wake and begin to cry softly, as if she were alone and the sound of her own fear would frighten her. Yergen went behind the partition and came back out carrying his little daughter in his arms. She was wrapped in an American Army blanket, and she looked at them gravely with her wet eyes. She had jet-black hair, a sad, mature face.

Yergen sat on the couch against one wall and Wolf sat beside him. Mosca drew up the only other chair in the room.

"Can you go out with us tonight?" Wolf asked. "We're going over to Honny's place. He is the man I am counting on."

Yergen shook his head. "I can't tonight." He rubbed his cheek against his daughter's wet one. "My little girl had a fright earlier this evening. Someone came up and kept knocking on the door, and she knew it wasn't me because we have a special signal. I have to leave her so much alone and the woman who takes care of her goes home at seven. When I came she was so frightened and in such shock I had to give her one of the pills."

Wolf shook his head. "She is too young. That should not be done often. But I hope you don't think we came. You know I respect your wishes and come only by appointment."

Yergen held his daughter closely. "I know, Wolfgang, I know you are dependable. And I know I should not give her drugs. But she was in such a state that I was frightened." Mosca was surprised to see the look of love on Yergen's proud face, and the sadness and despair.

"Do you think Honny has some news yet?" Wolf asked. Yergen shook his head. "I don't think so, but, forgive me for saying this. I know you and Honny are very good friends. But if he does have news I am not so sure that he will tell it immediately."

Wolf smiled. "I know that. So I'm bringing Mosca to see him tonight, to convince him I have a man with five thousand cartons."

Yergen looked into Mosca's eyes and for the first time Mosca realized that Yergen was their accomplice, a partner. And he saw that in Yergen's eyes was a look of fascinated fear as if he were looking at someone he knew would perform an act of murder. For the first time he realized concretely the exact role his two partners had given him. He stared back at Yergen until Yergen bowed his head.

They left. Out in the street the blackness of the night had become thinner as if the moon had spread itself against the sky and diluted the shadows without giving light. Mosca felt refreshed, alert, and the cold wind cleared his head. He walked briskly beside Wolf. He lit a cigarette and the smoke was mellow and warm on his tongue. They were silent. Once Wolf said, "This is a long walk, but one more stop will end the night and we'll get treated good. Combine business with pleasure."

They took short cuts through ruined buildings until Mosca lost all sense of direction, and then suddenly they were in a street that seemed cut off from the rest of the city, a little village surrounded by a desert of rubble. Wolf stopped at the last house at the end of the street and gave a quick series of raps on the door.

It opened, and facing them stood a short, blond man, the front of his head completely bald, the golden hair covering the back and top of his head like a skullcap. He was very neatly dressed.

The German grasped Wolf's hand and said, "Wolfgang, just in time for a midnight snack." He let them in and bolted the door. He put his arm around Wolf's shoulder and hugged him. "Ah, it is good to see you. Come in." They went into a living room that was luxurious, with a china closet stuffed full of cut glass and tableware, the floor covered by rich, dark-red rugs. There was a wall of books and glowing yellow lamps and soft armchairs, and in one of the armchairs, her feet over a yellow hassock, sat a thick-bodied, thick-lipped woman with bright-red hair. She was reading a brightly covered American fashion magazine. The blond man said to her, "Here is our Wolfgang and the friend he told us about." She extended a limp hand to both of them. She let the magazine fall to the floor.

Wolf peeled off his coat and put his brief case on the chair beside him.

"So," he said to the blond man. "Any luck, Honny?"

"Ah," the woman said, "I think you are making a little joke with us. We have been able to find out nothing." She spoke to Wolf, but she looked at Mosca. Her voice was peculiarly sweet, softening the meaning of everything she said. Mosca lit a cigarette, feeling his face tighten with the desire she aroused in him with her look, the complete frankness of her eyes and the memory of her hand which had been burning hot when it touched his. And yet now, raising his eyes, watching her through the cigarette smoke, he saw that she was ugly; despite her careful disguise with make-up she could not hide her voracious mouth, the cruel tiny blue eyes.

"It is a true story," Wolf was saying. "I know. I need only to make contact with the right people. Whoever helps me with that contact will earn a pretty reward."

"And this really is your rich friend?" the blond man asked with a smile. Mosca noticed that his face was covered with large freckles, giving him a boyish look.

Wolf laughed and said, "There sits a man with five thousand cartons," burlesquing it but making his voice sound really envious. Mosca, enjoying himself, gave the two Germans a smile as if he already had a truck loaded with cigarettes outside the house. They smiled back at him. He thought, you kraut bastards, smile later.

The sliding door to the next room opened and there was another German, slight, in a dark business suit. Behind him Mosca could see a dining table set with snowy white tablecloth and napkins, gleaming silver, and tall, beautifully cut drinking glasses.

The blond man said, "Please join us in our late supper. On your business, Wolfgang, I cannot help. But surely, a man with such a fortune in cigarettes as your friend can give me a little business for other items besides scrip."

Mosca said gravely, "That is very possible." He smiled, and the others laughed as if he had made a very clever joke. They went into the dining room.

The servant brought in a platter on which was a large, dark-red ham such as was sold in American Army commissaries. On a silver dish there were evenly cut slices of fresh white American Army bread. It was still warm. Wolf buttered a piece, raised his eyebrows in complimentary astonishment and said, "I see yours is delivered even before it gets to the American commissary." The blond man made a gesture of delight, laughing meanwhile. The servant brought several bottles of wine and Mosca, very thirsty from the long walking and feeling much better, drank his glass down in one gulp. The blond man was amused and pretended to be pleased.

"Ah," he said, "a man to my taste. Not like you, Wolfgang, a cautious sipper and plodder. Now you see why he has five thousand cartons and you do not."

Wolf smiled back at him and said banteringly, "Superficial psychology, my friend, very superficial. You forget how I eat." And he started to help himself from the ham platter and then the long dish on which lay a dozen sticks of different kinds of wurst. From the cheese and salad dish he treated himself liberally and then looked at the blond man, saying, "Well, Honny, now what do you think? What can you say now?" Honny, his blue eyes sparkling with pleasure in his freckled face, almost shouted with great good humor, "I can only say one thing. Good appetite."

The red-haired woman laughed as did the rest of them and bent down to feed the huge dog lying beneath the table. She fed him an enormous slice of ham, and then from the servant took a large wooden bowl into which she poured a whole liter bottle full of milk. As she was bending, she let her hand slide carelessly along Mosca's leg and then pressed his thigh to lift herself again to a sitting position. She did it casually with no attempt at concealment.

"You're too fond of that dog," Honny said. "You really need children. They would be an interest."

"My dear Honny," she said, looking him straight in the face, "then you must change your tastes in love-making." But the sweetness of her voice flooded the words.

Honny murmured, "And that is too high a price to pay." He winked at Wolf. "Every man to his tastes, eh, Wolfgang?" Wolf nodded, continuing to chew on the enormous sandwich he had made for himself.

They ate and drank. Mosca, watchful, ate more and drank less. He felt fine. There was a long silence, then the woman snapped out of her moody trance and said with sudden verve, excitement, "Honny, shall we show them our treasure? Please?"

Wolf's face appeared alertly, comically, from behind his

sandwich. Honny laughed and said, "No, no, Wolfgang, there is no profit in this. And besides it is very late and perhaps you are too tired."

Trying not to sound eager, Wolf said cautiously, "Tell me what it is."

The blond man smiled at him. "There is no gain involved. This is a curiosity. In our back yard I am building a little garden. The house from the other side of the street is destroyed and part of it flowed over my property. I started to clear it away and I was enjoying the exercise. But then I found something very strange. I found a hole in the rubble and underneath it the basement is intact and the rest of the house has fallen into it. Now. This is interesting. By some freak some beams have fallen in such a way as to hold up the building and form a great room underneath." He smiled and the red freckles stood out like blood on his face. "I assure you it is unique. Would you care to go?"

"Sure," Mosca said and Wolf nodded his head with indifferent consent.

"You won't need your coats. It is just across the garden and once underneath it is very warm." But Wolf and Mosca took their belongings from the other room, not wanting to go out defenseless and not wanting Honny to know they carried weapons. Honny shrugged. "Wait till I get my flashlight and some candles. Will you come, Erda?" he asked the woman.

"Of course," the woman said.

The four of them went through what was to be the garden, the blond man using his flashlight to show the way. The garden was a square piece of hard ground bordered by a brick wall so low they could step over it with ease. They climbed a little hill of rubble and could see over the top of the house behind them, but a cloud hung veil-like before the moon, the city below was invisible. They descended into the valley formed by two mounds of shale and fragmented brick and came to the wall which supported and hedged in another heap of ruins.

The blond man crouched down. "Through here," he said, and showed a hole in the wall that looked as dark and opaque as a deep shadow. They entered in single file, the blond man first, then the woman, Wolf and Mosca.

Unexpectedly, when they had taken a few steps inside, they were going down steps. Honny called out a warning behind him.

At the end of the steps Honny waited. The woman lit two candles and gave one to Mosca.

By yellow candlelight they could see before them, below them, breaking away from the concrete on which they stood as the sea breaks away from cliffs, a great subterranean room, their candles lighting it as a lighthouse the ocean, leaving great depths of shadows. There was a shifting floor and sloping walls of rubble. Another staircase in the middle of the room led upward and disappeared, blotted out by the ruins which had fallen into it, as if someone had built stairs running blindly into a ceiling.

"This was an SS billet when they made a hit, your bombers. Just before the war ended," Honny said. "They have been buried now over a year. How glorious."

"There may be something valuable," Wolf said, "have you searched?"

"No," Honny said.

They dropped off the ledge, their feet sinking into the floor. The woman remained by the wall, resting against the end of a huge wooden beam, one end of which had fallen and jammed into the floor, the other end wedged against the ceiling. She held the candle high, and the three men spread out into the enormous room.

They moved cautiously, their feet dragging through a treacherous shale of glass, dirt and pulverized brick, like men wading through a swiftly moving stream. Sometimes when they hit a soft spot and sank alarmingly into the rubble their frantic scrambling was like treading water.

Before him Mosca saw a shiny, black boot. He picked it up, it was unexpectedly heavy. He realized there was a leg inside it, the top sealed off by a cover of pressed brick and stone glued together with blood and marrow of crushed bone. He let the boot drop and went to the farthest corner, sometimes sinking down through the rubble halfway to the knee. Near the wall he stumbled over a long body trunk with no head or neck or legs or arms. He pressed against it with his fingers, the black cloth unrecognizable, and inside it he felt flesh out of which all the fat and blood had been squeezed by the enormous pressure of the falling building. The flesh felt very firm against the bone, but he could feel the bonelike rock underneath. The two extremities of the trunk were sealed off in the same way as the boot.

There was nothing horrible in these remnants of human beings. No sight of blood or flesh. They had been so crushed that the clothing they wore had been pressed into the place of skin. The blood had been absorbed by the tons of brick turned to blotting dirt. Mosca kicked the rubble around a bit and, when his other foot began to sink, moved away hastily. Wolf was busy alone in a far corner, without illumination, almost invisible.

Suddenly Mosca felt oppressively warm. A hot dust rose in the air and a curious smell, like charred flesh, came from that dust, as if under the shifting floor, underground fires were raging all through the city, hidden by similar ruins.

"Give me a light," Wolf said from his corner. His voice was like a great hollow whisper. Mosca threw his lit candle across the room. It made a great arc of yellow flame and landed beside Wolf. He let it rest there.

They could see Wolf's shadow fumbling with a torso. The quiet voice of Honny said conversationally, "It is very curious that these bodies have no heads. There are six or seven I have found, some have a leg or arm, but none have heads. And why have they not decomposed?"

"Here," Wolf said, his voice reverberating now from the far corner, "I have something." He lifted up a leather holster in which hung a pistol. He drew the gun out of its holster and parts of it crumbled away and fell into the shale of the floor. Wolf flung the holster away from him and resumed his poking around, meanwhile speaking to the blond man.

"Like the mummies, those old mummies," he said. "All the stuff pressed into them. And maybe they were sealed off and the building just shifted so we could get in. And their heads were crushed right into the floor, into little bits, shreds, part of the floor we walk on here. I've seen that before." He had worked himself away from the candle and was now deep in the far corner and he said again, "Give me some light." The woman at the wall lifted her candle high and Wolf held something aloft so that the weak yellow ray would fall on it. At the same moment the blond man swung his flashlight toward him.

Wolf's scream was short, more one of surprise, the woman's hysterical, trilling off to a sob. Caught in the light of the flashlight and candle, was a gray hand, tremendously elongated fingers patinaed with paintlike dirt. The light of the candle fell away from it almost in the instant Wolf flung the hand away. They were silent, all now feeling the heat of the room, the oppressiveness of the air from the dust they had stirred from the shifting floor. Then Mosca said to Wolf teasingly, "Aren't you ashamed?"

The blond man laughed softly, but it echoed through the room. Wolf said apologetically, "I thought the goddamn thing was a rat."

The woman by the ledge said, "Let's go quickly, I need air," and as Mosca started to move toward her and the light, part of the wall shifted.

A wave of rubble swept him off his feet. His head fell against one of the torsos. His lips touched it and that touch told him there was no cloth over the body, but skin burned and charred hard as leather. Underneath that skin the body was hot as if already burning in hell. He pushed away with his hands and when he tried to rise a great black wave of vomit gushed out of his mouth. He heard the others moving to help and almost screamed, "Stay away from me. Stay away." He knelt, clutching great handfuls of the sharp fragments of glass and brick and bone and vomited out everything, the putrified food, the alcohol turned to bile. He could feel his hand stinging as the rubble cut into his flesh.

He was empty of everything. He rose. The woman helped him up to the ledge out of the room. By the light of the candle she held, he could see on her face a strangely distraught look of excitement and pleasure. She held on to the back of Mosca's short coat as they went up the stairs.

They came out into the cold night air and breathed deeply. "It is good to be alive," the blond man said. "That, below, that is the after death."

They climbed the little hill of rubble from the defile

they were standing in. The moon was out across the city and made it like a gray deserted fairyland, with wisps of fog and dust interlacing, spinning cobwebs to form a room above the earth, as if everyone were sleeping in a living death. Up the slope of the hill on which stood the *Polizeihaus* they could see the yellow light of a streetcar climbing slowly, and they could hear lightly on the winter air the soft, muted tone of its bell, cold and crystal clear. Mosca realized they must be quite close to his billet in the Metzer Strasse for he had seen this streetcar often at night, climbing the same hill, hearing the same bell.

The woman clung to the blond man as they stood there on the rubble heap and asked, "Will you come in for a drink?"

"No," Mosca said and to Wolf said, "Let's go home." He felt lonely and afraid, afraid of the people he was with including Wolf, afraid that something had happened to Hella alone in the billet. Now, completely sober, it seemed a very long time ago that he had left Eddie Cassin drunk and alone in the Rathskellar and started the long walking through the streets with Wolf.

He wondered if Eddie had made it home all right, and how late it was, surely long after midnight. And Hella would be waiting up for him, alone, reading on the couch. He thought for the first time with emotion of his mother and Alf and Gloria, of their letters that he hadn't read. For the first time he knew that the safety he imagined they felt, they did not feel; they dreamed in their own terror. Suddenly he felt they were all in danger, everyone that he knew, and that there was nothing he could do about it. He remembered his mother going to church and knew what he wanted to say to her that would explain everything and make him accept everything, because it was true. "We are not made in God's image," and that was all of it, and now he could go on living, trying hard to make himself happy and Hella too.

Tiredness washed everything out of his mind. He started down the hill of rubblé his chin buried in the collar of his coat, feeling the cold, the ache in his bones, and as he and Wolf walked through the streets, the pale flooding light of the moon showed the wounds of the city as cruelly as the sun, but without color or pity, bloodlessly; as if it were a light shed by some lifeless and metal instrument, mirroring its own image in the earth, its own arid craters and lifeless scars.

# 13

THE BRILLIANT MORNING SUN of early spring washed the ruined city in colors of bright yellow and gold, glinting off smashed red brick; a light-blue sky curtained maimed and disfigured buildings on the horizon.

Yergen's daughter pushed the cream-colored baby carriage, her sad little face proud and happy, yet concerned; her pretty blue dress matched the sky. Yergen walked beside her, watching her, enjoying her happiness, sensing the coming alive of the great city after a long, terrible winter.

Coupled *Strassenbahnen* made a great clanging as they went through the streets, filling the golden morning air with a sound of bells. Turning into the Metzer Strasse, Yergen saw far down the street Mosca and his friends working on a jeep. Then he saw Hella standing under a tree. Coming closer he saw that Mosca, Leo and Eddie were loading the jeep with Mosca's possessions. There were suitcases and Val-packs full of clothing, a wooden box full of tinned food and a small coal stove which he, Yergen, had procured for them.

Yergen touched his daughter's shoulder. "Giselle, push the wagon right under their noses, surprise them." The little girl smiled happily and pushed faster. Hella saw them first and Yergen could hear her squeal of delight before she took a few awkward running steps to meet them.

"How do you like it?" Yergen asked with pride. "Isn't it every bit as good as I promised?"

"Oh, it is wonderful, Yergen, it's beautiful," Hella exclaimed. The thin, serene face had such a look of joy that Yergen was really and truly touched. He looked at the carriage again and saw that it was beautiful, low slung with lines like a racer, its lovely, creamy paint, framed by the green earth on which it rested and the light-blue sky above them.

"My daughter Giselle," Yergen said, "she wanted to bring it herself." The shy little girl bowed her head. Hella knelt clumsily, the loose overcoat she wore folding around her onto the earth. "Thank you very much," she said and kissed the little girl on the cheek. "Will you help me bring it to my new home?" The child nodded.

Mosca came over from the jeep. He was dressed in old, wrinkled sun tans. "I'll pay you later, Yergen," he said, barely glancing at the carriage. "We're moving over to Kurfürsten Allee. Why don't you walk over there with Hella and the carriage. We'll be there soon as we get loaded."

"Of course, of course," Yergen said. In high spirits he lifted his hat to Hella and said in German, "Dear lady, may I accompany you?" She smiled at him and took the arm he offered. They let the child go before them.

They walked into a spring breeze that smelled of flowers and grass, and Hella buttoned her coat. Yergen could see it stretch tight across the front of her stomach and felt an unaccountable content mixed with sadness. His own wife dead, his daughter without a mother, and now walking beside the mistress of the enemy, he thought of how it would be if Hella belonged to him, her tenderness and love given to him and his child and carrying a new life within her that would belong to both of them. How sweet it would be on this sweet morning, how the sadness and fear would wash away inside himself and how Giselle too would be safe. And as he thought this, Giselle turned her head to give them both a smile.

"She looks much better now," Hella said.

Yergen shook his head. "I am bringing her away to the country this very day. For a month. On the doctor's advice." Yergen slowed his walk so that Giselle would not hear what he said next. "I think she is very ill. It was a bad winter for her."

Giselle was far ahead of them now, pushing the carriage through a great patch of sunlight. Hella slipped her arm into Yergen's again. He said, "I must get her away from the ruins, anything that makes her think of her mother's death, away from Germany." He hesitated and then matter of factly, casually, as if repeating something he did not even remotely believe, "The doctor says she may become insane."

Giselle was waiting for them where the shade of the street began again, as if afraid of walking alone among the shadows of a tree. Hella walked ahead of Yergen so that she would come first to the little girl and said to her gaily, "Do you want to ride in the carriage?" Giselle nodded and Yergen helped her into it, letting her long legs dangle over the side. Hella pushed, saying laughingly, "Oh, what a big baby I have," tickling the child under the chin. Then she tried to run to make an impression of speed, but she was too awkward. Giselle didn't laugh, but she was smiling and making little sounds that were the shadows of laughter.

They came to a long row of white stone houses beaded along the Kurfürsten Allee. Hella stopped by the first house, by a little gate that barred a cemented path leading to the door. Hella called out, "Frau Saunders," and a woman appeared at the open window. She had a sad, stern face with the hair severely done, and they could see from the upper part of her body visible to them that she was wearing a plain black dress.

"Forgive me for calling out," Hella said smilingly. "I walk so badly now. Could you throw me the key, they will be here in a few minutes." The woman disappeared and then reappeared to drop the keys into Yergen's waiting hand. Then she disappeared again into the house.

"Oh. Oh," Yergen said, "you may have some trouble in that quarter. She looks very respectable." And then realizing what he had said, embarrassed, he paused, but Hella laughed and said, "She's very nice, she'll understand. She recently lost her husband with cancer. That's how she has two empty rooms. They had special privileges because of his illness."

"And how were you fortunate enough to find them?" Yergen asked.

"I went to the housing officer of the district and inquired," Hella said. "But first I offered a little present of five packs of cigarettes." They smiled at each other.

Yergen saw the loaded jeep coming down the Allee. Leo parked as he always did, bumping against a tree on the sidewalk. Mosca jumped down and Eddie and Leo got out of the front seats. They began to carry stuff into the house, Hella showing them the way. When Hella came out again, she had a large brown parcel which she handed to Yergen. "Ten cartons," she said, "is that right?" Yergen nodded. Hella went to Giselle who was now leaning against the carriage. She took from her coat pocket a handful of chocolate bars and gave them to the child, saying, "Thank you for bringing me such a beautiful carriage. Will you come to see me when the baby comes?" Giselle nodded her head and handed the chocolate to Yergen. He took one and broke it into small pieces so that she could hide them in her hand as she ate. Then as Hella watched them walk down the Kurfürsten Allee she saw Yergen stop to pick up his daughter, she holding the brown parcel balanced on his shoulder. Hella went back into the house and climbed the flight of stairs to the second floor.

The floor consisted of a four-room apartment; a bedroom, a living room, then another bedroom and a small room that was to be made into a kitchen. Mosca and Hella, it was understood, were to have the small bedroom and the kitchen and were to be allowed to use the living room on special occasions. Frau Saunders had her bedroom and a stove in the living room to do her cooking.

Hella found Mosca, Leo and Eddie waiting for her. There were two bottles of Coke and two glasses of whiskey on the small table. The bedroom was cluttered with suitcases and everything else they had brought. Hella noticed that Frau Saunders had hung pretty blue-flowered curtains on both windows.

Mosca lifted his glass, Hella and Leo lifted their bottles of Coke. Eddie was already sipping his whiskey, but then waited for them.

"To our new home," Hella said. They all drank together. Eddie Cassin watched Hella take one sip from her Coke and then open the suitcases to put her clothes away in a great mahogany dresser.

He had never made his play for Hella, though he had been in Mosca's room alone with her many times. He wondered why and he realized that partly she had never given him the opportunity. She had never moved close to him, or given him any sort of opening, verbally or physically. She had no coquetry. And all in a very natural manner that was not provoking. He realized that it was partly his fear of Mosca, and trying to analyze that fear, he thought it was grounded in his knowledge of Mosca's carelessness of other people and the stories he had heard about Mosca from some other men in the outfit, a fight he had had with a Sergeant for which he had been transferred to Military Government and for which he had just escaped court-martial. The Sergeant was so badly hurt that he was sent back to a hospital in the States. But it was a queer story, hushed up, and just rumors. Basically it was the carelessness, a lack of interest so complete that it was frightening. His friends, Eddie thought, myself, Leo, Wolf, Gordon, we think we're his buddies. If we were all killed tomorrow he wouldn't give a good goddamn.

"The carriage," Hella exclaimed suddenly, "where did you put the carriage?"

They all laughed. Leo clapped his hands to his head and said in German, "My God, I left the wagon in the street." But Mosca said quickly, "It's in the small room, Hella, the kitchen." And Eddie Cassin thought, he can't even stand to see her anxious as a joke.

Hella went into the other room. Leo finished up his Coke. "The next week I leave for Nuremberg," he said. "They want me to testify about those people who were guards and officials at Buchenwald. At first I said no, but then they told me a certain doctor was among the defendants. He is the one who used to tell us, 'I am not here to cure your aches and pains. I am not even here to keep you alive. My job is to see that you are able every day to work.' That bastard I will testify against."

Mosca filled the glasses again and gave Leo a fresh bottle of Coke. "If I were in your shoes I'd want to kill those bastards."

Leo shrugged. "I don't know. I have only contempt but no hatred any more. I don't know why. I just want to get out of here." He took a long slug from his Coke.

"We'll miss you at the billet, Walter," Eddie said. "How do you think you'll like living kraut style?"

Mosca shrugged. "It's all the same." He filled Eddie's glass, then said. "Scram, Eddie, after that one. I don't want you scaring the hell out of my new landlady. No more drinks."

"I've reformed," Eddie Cassin said. "My wife is coming from England with the kid." He looked at them with mock pride. "My family is coming to join me."

Mosca shook his head. "Poor dame, I thought she gave up when you were in the Army. What the hell are all your chippies going to do?"

"They'll get along," Eddie said. "Don't worry about them, they always get along." Suddenly, unreasonably, he was angry. "I'd like to give 'em all a boot in the ass." He took his jacket and left.

Eddie Cassin went down the Kurfürsten Allee, walking slowly. The curved, tree-shaded avenue was pleasant in the warmth of the early spring afternoon. He decided to take a shower in the billet and then go on for supper at the Rathskellar. He glanced across the Allee before he turned into the Metzer Strasse, a flash of color attracting his eye, and there he saw a young girl standing underneath a wide, green tree, four little children dancing around her. Across the broad avenue he could see the delicate lines of her face, the purity of youth in them. As he watched, she lifted her head to the yellow light of the afternoon sun and turning away from the children looked directly at Eddie Cassin.

He saw on her face that smile which, in its innocence and instinctive knowledge of sexual power, always excited him. It was a smile of youth, Eddie thought, a smile they wear when being flattered, and yet innocent, curious, wondering what the power really was that they possessed, and a little excited. To Eddie Cassin it denoted virginity, a virginity of mind, of body too, but primarily a mental innocence which he had seen and corrupted before, the struggle and courtship sweeter to him than the actual taking.

Now staring across the street, he was moved to a sadness that was sweet, and also a wonder that this young girl in her white blouse could move him so. He hesitated to go to her; he was unshaven, dirty, and he could smell his own sweat. Hell, I can't screw 'em all, he thought, knowing that across the broad avenue, even in the bright sunlight, she could only see the delicate cut of his features and not the fine lines of age. What would seem to her old age, decay.

She had turned to the children, and that graceful, youthful motion of her head and body, the picture they made as they all sat on the green carpet of grass, burned into his brain. Under that dark-green tree, the young girl in her white shirt, the white sleeves rolled up nearly to her shoulder, the two bulges of white cloth that were her breasts, her golden head bending over the seated children, these were not to be borne. He strode quickly away down the Metzer Strasse and into the billet.

Eddie showered and shaved and found himself hurrying, but he paused long enough to put a great deal of sweet-smelling talcum powder over his body and face. He combed his hair carefully, regretting its grayness on the sides, and in his room put on his olive-green officer's uniform with the civilian patch, knowing that he would not appear as old in her eyes in these as he would in civilian clothing.

There was a knock on the door and Frau Meyer came in. She was in a bathrobe. It was an old trick of hers. When she knew Eddie was bathing she would bathe also, and smelling sweetly of perfume come to the room as he was dressing. Usually it would work.

"Have you a cigarette for me, Eddie?" she asked and sat on the bed and crossed her legs. Eddie, tying his shoelaces, motioned toward the table. She took a cigarette, lit it, and sat again on the bed.

"You look very handsome, are you seeing someone?"

Eddie stopped for a moment, surveyed the almost-perfect body, the pleasant, buck-toothed face. It was known. He lifted her off the bed, carried her out of the room and set her down in the hall. "Not today, baby," he said and ran down the stairs and out of the building. There was a tremendous excitement and exultation in him, a quivering of the heart. He trotted up the Metzer Strasse, slowing to a quick walk as he came to the corner and, puffing a little, turned into the Kurfürsten Allee.

As far as he could see, the trees along the Allee stood all alone, no children underneath them. The strip of grass was a continuous green line with no foreign body to mar its harmony with the trees above it. His eye singled out the exact spot in the row opposite him and it was as if it were a picture hanging on his wall, familiar, known every day, out of which the human figures he had always seen had magically faded. Eddie Cassin crossed the Allee and went to the nearest house. He knocked on the door and inquired in bad German about the girl taking care of four children, but no one knew anything about her, in that house or the others. The last house was an apartment billet for American civilians and the man who answered the door Eddie recognized as someone he had seen often at the Rathskellar. "No," the man said, "she doesn't come from this street. The guys in here are laying all the dames in the block, and I know them all. I felt like going out my-self. You're out of luck, fella." And he grinned sympa-thetically at Eddie Cassin.

He stood in the center of the Allee, not knowing which way to go. The spring evening fell upon him, fresh breezes blowing away the afternoon heat. On the other side of the Allee and beyond it, he could see the gardens with their newly sprouting green, the even patches and the mottled brown wooden and paper huts in which the gardeners kept their tools and in which some of them lived. He could see some men working in that small, farmlike area, and he could smell the river behind the hill which rose above the gardens. Patched through the rubble and from the sides of ruined houses he could see wild little streaks of dark green. He knew he would never see the girl again and would not recognize her if he did, but suddenly the ex-hilaration returned and he started the long walk down the whole length of the Kurfürsten Allee until it ended where the city ended and he could see the country un-marked, the slightly rolling, restful hills, the moist green of spring over them like fresh-grown skin; and where no blemish of gray and blackened ruins could mar the beauty of the day.

That evening Hella tacked the woodcut illustrations of fairy tales on the walls. She had bought them for the com-ing child, she said, but Mosca felt that it was some sort of superstition, a magic that would make everything go well. When she finished she said, "I think we should go in to see Frau Saunders."

"Christ, I'm too tired tonight," Mosca said. "We did a hell of a lot of work."

Hella sat still on the bed, her hands folded, inspecting the almost square room. The cream-colored carriage rested against one light blue flowered curtain, looking like a picture on a wall. There was a blue cloth on a small round table, and the two chairs were upholstered in light gray. On the floor was a maroon rug, faded with age. Bed and dresser were both mahogany, and on each wall there was a small painting of a country scene in light greens, violets, blues and the white silvers of running streams. A great surge of joy went through her body. Then she noticed Mosca's face set, strained, and she knew he felt uneasy. She took his hand and held it in her lap. "Now it seems really true, that we'll always be together."

"Let's go in and pay our respects to the landlady," Mosca said.

All the rooms had doors that opened on the hall, and the hall itself had a door that locked the floor off from the stairs. To go from one room to the other they had to go out in the hall and knock on the door of the living room. They heard a voice telling them to come in.

Frau Saunders was sitting on the sofa reading a newspaper. She stood up when Hella introduced them and shook Mosca's hand. Mosca saw that she was not as old as he had thought from the glimpse he had had of her. The hair was severely done and her face was lined, but there was a curious youthfulness in the movements of her lanky body, in its straight flowing black.

"I hope you will feel free to use the living room whenever you wish," Frau Saunders said. She had a low, sweet voice but she said the words out of politeness.

"Thank you," Hella said. "I wanted to thank you for the curtains and the extras you put in the rooms. If there is anything we can help you in, please tell us."

Frau Saunders hesitated. "I hope only that there will be no trouble with the authorities." She gave Mosca a doubtful glance as if she wished to say something else.

Hella guessed what it was. "We're very quiet people, he's not one of these wild Americans always giving parties." She smiled at Mosca but he did not smile in return. "We just came in for a few minutes," Hella went on, "we had a hard day, so—" She rose and they said good night awkwardly, Mosca giving a polite smile, Frau Saunders giving the same smile in return, and in that moment Mosca realized that this woman was shy despite her age, and that she was a little frightened by the thought of the enemy living in her home.

As they undressed in their room Mosca told Hella a bit of news he had almost forgotten. "Orders finally came in to ship the Middletons back to the States. They leave next week."

Hella was surprised. "Oh, that is too bad," she said.

"Don't worry," Mosca said, "I can get some other people's commissary cards, and we can trade out in the country like real Germans."

In bed Hella said, "So that is why you looked so worried today." Mosca didn't say anything. After she had fallen asleep he lay awake for a long time.

He felt strange that now, finally, as if this had been the purpose behind everything, he lived as one of the enemy. The house was full of Germans and the houses in the streets around him; in his bed, carrying his child. He missed the sound of parties that went on in the billet, the throbbing of jeep motors, radios tuned to the Armed Forces Network giving out American music. Here all was still. The bathroom in the hall gave a small sudden roar of water. Frau Saunders, he thought, and then had to get up and go himself, waiting a little to give the woman plenty of time to get back to her own room. Then he stood by the curtained window, smoking a cigarette, trying to see in the darkness outside. He tried to think back to when he had been given his first weapon, his first steel helmet, his first combat orientation lecture to protect himself against the enemy. But that now too seemed unreal and unimportant. What finally was real was this room, the carriage, the woman in the bed.

# 14

THE EVENING before the Middletons were to leave Germany, Hella and Mosca went for a walk through the city before visiting them. Leaving the house on the Kurfürsten Allee, Hella stopped to say good evening to the women in their doorways. Mosca stood by her patiently, a polite smile on his face.

They began the walk to the center of town. "Let's get Frau Saunders some ice cream from the Red Cross Club," Hella said. Mosca looked at her.

"You two sure became awful good buddies in a week," he said. "What goes on anyway? I know you give her part of your meals and some of the sugar and coffee we have. When the Middletons leave you'll have to get stingy, baby. That stuff will be hard to get."

She gave him an amused smile. "If I thought you really cared I wouldn't do it. I know it's just that you want me to have everything. But I can't do it, Walter. When I cook some meat the smell fills the whole hall, and I think of her in the living room with just dry potatoes. Besides I'm too fat. Look at me."

"That's not from eating," Mosca said. She laughed and gave him a push. He grinned at her and said. "But you're pretty big. At least now you can't wear my shirts any more." She had on a blue maternity dress Ann Middleton had given her.

They walked along, Mosca holding her arm when they had to climb over rubble that overflowed onto the walk. The trees were all heavy with leaves and the rays of the setting sun only occasionally glanced over them. Hella said thoughtfully, "Frau Saunders is really fine. You wouldn't think it to look at her, but she is a lot of fun to talk to and she does nearly all my work for me. And not because I give her things, she really wants to help. Will you get her some ice cream?"

Mosca laughed and said, "Sure."

She had to wait outside while he went in to the Red Cross Club. On the way back they went by the *Polizeihaus* and on the outskirts of the Contrescarpe park below they were blocked off by a small crowd listening to a man standing on a park bench. He was lecturing, waving his arms, shouting. They paused. Mosca shifted the cold box of ice cream to his right hand and Hella leaned on his shoulder.

"The guilt is on every one of us," the man was shouting. "This godless age, this godless land. Who thinks of Christ, of Jesus? We accept his blood as our salvation and do not believe. But I tell you, I tell you, his blood has washed away so many sins, that blood is weary, the Lord God is weary of our ways. How much longer will he be patient? How much longer will the blood of Jesus save us?" He paused and his voice became soft, pleading. "The love of Jesus is no longer enough, the blood of Jesus is no longer enough. Please believe me. Save yourselves and me and our children and our wives, our mothers, our fathers, sisters, brothers and our country." His voice became calm, factual, reasonable, and his body relaxed. He spoke conversationally.

"You see this land in ruins, the continent, and Christ sees further than we, he sees a destruction of soul universal, evil triumphant, Satan looking over the world in glee, seeing with his laughing eyes the death of man and everything man has done since the beginning of time."

A plane passed overhead on its way to the air base. The roar of the motor made him stop. He was a small man with a pouter-pigeon chest accentuated by the way he threw back his head to glare with his rolling, brilliant, birdy eyes. He went on.

"Picture to yourself a world innocent of life. In the polar regions the snow and ice everywhere untracked, unmoved upon. In Africa, in the jungles, where the sun gives, from God, innumerable and diverse forms of creation, there everything is still." The voice now was madly rhetorical, pompous, the brilliant eyes bulging from his small head. "The carcasses of dead beasts lie putrifying in the rotting vegetation. On China's plains, by the fertile rivers, not even the crocodile lifts his grinning head to return the leer of Satan. And in our cities, in the many hearts of what is known as civilization, there is nothing but ruins. Hills of stone out of which no life will ever grow, a soil of broken glass. For eternity."

He stopped and waited for a sign of approval but instead a surprising shout rose from different parts of the crowd. "Where is your permit? Where is your permission from Military Government?" Three or four male voices could be heard shouting this. The preacher was stunned.

Hella and Mosca found themselves standing now almost in the middle of the crowd, a pile of people bunched up behind them. On their left was a young man dressed in a blue, washed-out shirt and heavy working trousers. He carried in his arms a pretty girl of six or seven whose eyes were curiously blank and whose sleeve on the side facing them was pinned to her flowered frock. On their right was an old worker puffing a stubby pipe. The young man was shouting with the others, "Where is your permit, where is your permission from Military Government?" Then he turned to Mosca and the old worker and said, "We're bawled out by everybody now that we've lost, even by swine like this." Mosca, in civilian clothes, smiled at Hella, amused that he had passed as German.

Now the preacher pointed his arm slowly toward the sky and said in a great solemn voice, "I have permission from our Creator." The sun, red with its last, dying fire bathed the upraised arm with crimson light. The sun began to sink below the earth, and gray in the soft summer twilight, springing up on the horizon like a great ragged circle of spears, the ruins of the city rose like magic before their eyes. The preacher bowed his head in thanksgiving.

He raised his head to the sky. He embraced them all with a sweep of his arms. "Come back to Jesus Christ," he shouted, "Come Back to Jesus. LEAVE YOUR SINS BEHIND. LEAVE THE DRINKING. LEAVE THE FORNICATION. RENOUNCE THE GAMBLING, THE PRIDE FOR WORLDLY SUCCESS. BELIEVE IN JESUS AND BE SAVED. BELIEVE IN JESUS AND BE SAVED. YOU HAVE BEEN PUNISHED FOR YOUR SINS. THE PUNISHMENT IS BEFORE YOUR EYES. REPENT BEFORE IT IS TOO LATE. SIN NO MORE."

The deafening voice stopped for breath. The crowd was stunned, rolled back by the great volume of sound from that little man. He returned to a normal shout.

"Each one of you, think of the lives you led before the war, are you not to believe that the suffering, the ruin you see is God's punishment for the sins you committed then?

"And now the young girls fornicate with enemy soldiers,

the young men beg for cigarettes. Puff Puff." He blew out imaginary smoke with maniacal hatred. "On our Sabbath people go to the country to steal or bargain for food. The house of the Lord is empty. We invite destruction. Repent, I say again. Repent. Repent." The words began to run together, hysterically. "Believe in the Lord Jesus Christ Believe in the Lord the one and only God Believe in the One Lord Believe in Christ."

He paused and then in a threatening and scolding voice shouted at them. Harshly. Accusingly. "You are all sinners, you are all condemned to everlasting hell. I see some of you smile. You pity yourselves. Why should God make us suffer so? You ask that?"

Someone in the crowd shouted mockingly, "It wasn't God, it was the Ami bombers." The crowd laughed. The man on the bench waited for them to be still and then peering through the failing light, savagely, vindictively, he pointed to a woman wearing black. "You, woman, do you laugh at God? Where is your husband, your children?" He pointed to the young man beside Mosca. "Look," he said to the crowd and they all turned and followed that pointing finger. "There is another scoffer, one of the young men, the hope of Germany. For HIS sins his child is mutilated and he laughs at the wrath of God. Wait, scoffer, in your child's face I see another punishment. Wait. Look at your child and wait." With spite and malice he pointed out other members of the crowd.

The young man with the child set her down and said to Hella, "Please look after her." Then they could see him push through to where the preacher stood on his bench, break through to the open space. With one violent blow he struck the little preacher to the ground. He knelt on the preacher's chest, grabbed a handful of hair and slammed the bird-shaped head against the cement walk. Then he rose.

The crowd dispersed. The young man picked up his child and walked into the Contrescarpe park. As if by magic most of the people had disappeared. The preacher lay still and alone in the falling twilight.

Some men helped him up. There was blood running out of his thick curly hair, many tiny rivers flowed down his forehead to form a red mask over his face. Hella had turned away and Mosca took her arm and walked her down the street. He saw that she looked ill, the sight of blood, he thought. "You'd better stay home with Frau Saunders tonight." And then, as if he owed her an excuse for not interfering, he said, "It's not our business."

Mosca, Leo and Eddie Cassin sat around the Middleton living room. The household furniture belonged to the requisitioned house so there were still chairs to sit on. Everything else was packed in wooden crates lined against the wall.

"So you're really going to the Nuremberg trials tomorrow?" Gordon asked Leo. "What time are you leaving?"

"Oh, in the evening," Leo said. "I would rather drive at night."

"Give it to the bastards when you get there," Ann Middleton said. "Lie if you have to but make sure they all get what's coming to them."

"I won't have to lie," Leo said. "My memory is very good."

"I want to apologize about the way I acted the last time you were here," Gordon Middleton said. "I'm afriad I was very rude."

Leo waved his hand. "No, I understand. My father was

a political prisoner, a Communist. My mother was Jewish, that is why I was sent away. But my father was a political. Of course, after the Stalin-Hitler pact he lost his faith. He realized one was no better than the other."

The Professor, who was sitting in a corner by the chess table and had a polite smile of interest on his face, became frightened by this tactless remark. He saw, with panic and embarrassment, the anger rising in Gordon Middleton and did not wish to witness a scene of verbal violence. All violence distressed him. "I must go," he said. "I have an appointment to give a lesson." He shook hands with Gordon and Ann. "Allow me to wish you a good trip to America and good fortune. I have been very happy to know you."

Gordon escorted him to the door and said earnestly, "I hope you won't forget to write me, Professor. I'm depending on you to tell me what happens to Germany." The Professor nodded his head. "Certainly, certainly." He had already decided not to communicate in any way with Gordon Middleton. Any tie with a Communist, however innocent, could in the unpredictable future do him great harm.

"Wait a minute, wait a minute," Gordon led the Professor back into the room. "Leo, I just remembered the Professor is going to Nuremberg the end of the week. Can you give him a lift or would that be against your outfit's regulation?"

"No, no," the Professor said in great agitation. "That is not necessary, please."

"It's no trouble," Leo said.

"No," the Professor said, and now he was almost hysterically frightened. "I have my train tickets, everything is arranged. Please, I know it would be too much trouble for you."

"O.K., Professor, O.K.," Gordon said soothingly, and took him to the door.

When Gordon came back into the room, Mosca asked, "What the hell did he get so excited about?"

Gordon glanced at Leo. "He's a very correct man. His son is under arrest as a minor war criminal, I don't know exactly what, except that he's being tried by a German court, not the occupation so it can't be too bad. I guess he was horrified that Leo might find out and think it was something to do with the concentration camps, which of course it couldn't be. You don't mind do you, Leo?"

"No," Leo said.

"I'll tell you what," Gordon said. "I'll go to his place tomorrow, I'll have time. I'll say you'll pick him up tomorrow night. Once he knows you know, he'll be willing. Is that O.K.?"

"Sure," Leo said, "it is very nice you should worry so about that old man."

Ann Middleton looked at him sharply, but there was no irony on Leo's hawklike face. He was sincere. She smiled. "Gordon always takes care of his converts," she said.

"I haven't converted him, Ann," Gordon drawled in his slow, even voice, "but I think I've put a few ideas in his head. He listens." Gordon paused and in a calm tone in which there was a gentle reproof he said. "I don't think 'convert' is the right word to use." They were all silent.

"When do you think you'll be back," Mosca asked Leo.

Leo grinned at him. "Don't worry, I won't miss it."

"Miss what?" Ann Middleton asked.

"I'm going to be a godfather," Leo said. "I already have the present."

"It's a shame I won't be here to see the child when it

comes," Ann said. "Too bad Hella couldn't be here tonight. I hope she isn't too ill."

"No," Mosca said. "She just took too long a walk this evening. She wanted to come but I told her she'd better not."

"After all, we're not that important, Walter," Ann said jokingly but with a touch of malice. Eddie Cassin in his corner armchair opened his eyes. He had dozed off. Visiting married couples was something he hated. He nearly always detested wives when they were with their husbands and in their own homes. And he disliked Ann Middleton. She was plain, she was strong willed, and she treated him with contempt.

Mosca was grinning at her. "You know damn well I'm right."

"It just irritates her that you aren't concerned about other people," Gordon said. "I wish I could be like that sometimes."

Mosca said, "Gordon, maybe I'm being out of line but I'll take a chance. Everybody around the base knows that you're being sent home because you held a Communist party card. I don't know anything about politics. I was a kid when I went into the Army. I guess in some ways I still am. What I'm trying to say is this. I have a lot of respect for you because you have guts. You know things are screwed up. I think you're wrong because I wouldn't trust anybody who can make me do what he wants, no matter what the reason is. That includes the United States Army, the Communist party, Russia, that fat bastard of a Colonel, right on down the line." He turned to Eddie Cassin. "What the hell am I trying to say?"

Eddie said dryly, "That you like him even if you didn't let Hella come." They all laughed.

Gordon didn't. His long Yankee face expressionless, he said to Mosca. "Since you've spoken maybe I can say something I've always wanted to say to you before, Walter." He paused a moment, rubbed his great, bony hands together. "I know how you feel or think I do, and maybe you can't help yourself. You say I'm wrong, but I have a belief I can hold no matter what happens. I believe in the human race, that life on earth can be extraordinarily beautiful. I believe that this can be accomplished through the efforts of the Communist party. You build everything on a few people you care about. Believe me that is a fallacious way of life."

"Yeah? Why?" Mosca bowed his head and when he raised it to look at Gordon there were dark-red spots of anger on his face.

"Because those people and you yourself are controlled by forces that you refuse to concern yourself with. You exercise no free will when you fight on your level, in your narrow circle, your little, personal, arena. When you do that you put those people you care about in terrible danger."

Mosca said, "This talk about controlling forces that affect my life. Christ, don't you think I know about it? I don't believe anything can help. But nobody is going to move me around, make me think one thing one day, and then, all of a sudden, bang on the other side we go. I don't care if it's right or wrong. Every day some kraut at the air base or in the billet or working in the Rathskellar tells me how happy he'll be when we march together against the Russians and expects me to give him a cigarette. And on the other side I guess it's the same. You know what I'm glad about?" He leaned over the table at Gordon, his face flushed with excitement and liquor. "That this time there's a good chance of everything going up in smoke. Everybody gets it up the ass."

"Hey, hey," Ann Middleton applauded, clapping her hands. Eddie Cassin was laughing and said, "Jesus Christ, what a speech." Leo seemed shocked. Mosca burst out laughing and said to Gordon. "Look what you made me do."

Gordon had been smiling too, thinking how he always forgot how young Mosca was, and was always surprised when that youthful, immature sincerity flashed through Mosca's reserve. And trying to help he said, "How about Hella, then, and your kid?"

Mosca didn't answer. Ann got up to fill their glasses. Leo said, "He doesn't mean what he says." And then Mosca, as if he had not heard, said to Gordon, "I make myself responsible." And only Eddie Cassin felt that he had said these words as dogma, something he would have to live by. Mosca smiled at them and said it jokingly this time. "I make myself responsible." He shook his head. "Who can do better than that?"

"And how is it you don't feel that way?" Ann Middleton asked Leo.

"I don't know," Leo said. "I went to Buchenwald when I was quite young, and I met my father there and we were for a long time together. And people are different. Besides Walter is changing. I caught him bowing, actually bowing good evening to his German neighbors."

The others laughed, but Mosca said impatiently, "How a guy can spend eight years in a concentration camp and come out the way you did I'll never understand. If I were you and a kraut looked at me crosswise I'd send him to the hospital. And every time he gave me an answer I didn't like I'd kick him in the balls."

"Please, please," Ann said in mock horror.

"Too bad about you," Mosca said, but he grinned at her. She had used worse language cursing black-market operators who had cheated her.

Leo said slowly. "You forget I am part German. And the things the Germans did, they did not because they were Germans but because they were human beings. My father told me that. And then I am having a good time, I live a new life, it would poison that life if I were cruel to other people."

"You're right, Leo," Gordon said. "We need a more intellectual approach, not emotional reactions. We have to reason, to change the world by logical action. The Communist party believes in that."

There was no doubting his sincerity, the purity of his belief.

Leo gave him a long look. "I know one thing only about communism. My father was a Communist. The camps could never crush his spirit. When the word came into the camp that Hitler and Stalin had signed a pact, my father died easily afterward."

"And if that pact was necessary to save the Soviet Union?" Gordon asked. "If that pact was necessary to save the world from the Nazis?"

Leo bowed his head and put his hand up to his face to hold the muscles tight and stop the tic. "No," he said, "if my father had to die that way the world isn't worth saving. That is emotional, I know, not your intellectual approach the party favors."

In the silence that followed they could hear the baby crying upstairs. "I'll go change him," Gordon said. His wife gave him a grateful smile.

When he had left Ann said, "Don't mind him," to Leo,

keeping the tone of her voice absolutely without inflection so that she could not be thought disloyal. She went out into the kitchen to make coffee.

When the evening ended everyone shook hands all around. Ann said, "I'll drop around tomorrow to say good-bye to Hella." And Gordon said to Leo, "Don't forget the Professor, Leo, will you?" Leo nodded. Gordon added slowly and sincerely. "I wish you luck."

Gordon locked the door behind them and went back into the living room. He found Ann sitting thoughtfully in her chair. "I want to talk to you, Gordon," she said.

Gordon smiled at her. "Well, here I am, talk." He felt a sharp pang of fear. But he could talk to Ann without becoming angry when they discussed politics, even though she never agreed with him.

Ann got up and walked nervously up and down the room. Gordon watched her face. He loved the broad, honest planes, the blunt nose and the pale-blue eyes. She was a pure Saxon type, he thought, and yet she looked almost Slavic. He wondered if there were any connection. He would have to read up on it.

Her words smashed against his mind. She said, "You'll have to give it up, you will just have to give it up."

"Give up what?" Gordon asked innocently.

"You know what," she said. And the shock of understanding, the pain that she should say such a thing, was so great that there was no anger in him, only a sinking in his stomach, a despairing hopelessness. When she saw his face she came and knelt beside his chair, and it was only when they were alone that she relinquished her strength, that she was tender, supplicating. She said, "I'm not angry you lost this job because you were a Communist. But what are we going to do? We have to think of our child. You have to be able to work and earn money, Gordon. And the way you lose all your friends when you get so angry about politics. We can't live like this, darling, we just can't."

Gordon rose from his chair and moved away from her. He was profoundly shocked, not so much that she was capable of saying such a thing but that she knew him so little, the human being closest to him. That she could think he would leave the party as one would give up tobacco or a special food. But he had to answer her.

"I'm thinking of our child," Gordon said. "That's why I'm a Communist. How would you like to have him grow up and suffer what Leo went through or become someone like Mosca who cares nothing for his fellow human beings? I didn't like the way he talked in front of you, but he doesn't care about that though he professes to be fond of me. I want our son to grow up in a healthy society that won't send him to wars or concentration camps. I want him to grow up in a moral society. That's what I'm fighting for. And you know that our society is corrupt, Ann, you know it."

Ann rose to face him. She was no longer tender or supplicating. She spoke to him factually. "You don't believe anything bad that has been written about Russia. I believe some of it, enough of it. They won't make my son safe. I have faith in my own country, as people have faith in their brothers and sisters. You always say that is nationalistic. I don't know. You're prepared to make sacrifices for what you believe in, but I'm not prepared to have our child suffer for your beliefs. And Gordon if I thought you fitted in with them I wouldn't try to make you stop. But what happened to Leo's father is exactly what will happen to you. I felt that when he told us, and I felt he told us for that reason, to warn you. Or even worse, you'll become corrupt.

You have to quit, you just have to quit." Her broad-planed face was stubborn and he knew that stubbornness to be invincible.

"Let me see if we understand each other," Gordon said slowly. "You want me to get a good job, live like a good middle-class citizen and not place my future in jeopardy by remaining in the party. Is that correct?"

She didn't answer and he went on. "I know your motives are irreproachable. Basically we both agree. We want to do the best thing for our son. We disagree on method. The security you want for him is only a temporary one, a security at the mercy of the capitalists who run the country. My way, we fight for a permanent security, a security that can't be shattered by a few members of the ruling class. Don't you see?"

"You'll have to give it up," Ann said stubbornly. "You'll just have to give it up."

"And if I can't?"

"If you don't promise to give it up—" Ann paused and composed herself to say the words, "I'll go back to England with the baby instead of to America."

They were both frightened by what she had finally said, then Ann went on in a low voice close to tears. "I know you'll keep your promise once you've made it. You see, I trust you." And for the first time since they had been together Gordon was truly angry with her, because he knew her faith was justified; he had never lied to her, never broken a promise. His New England conscience had always functioned in personal relationships. And now she was using his honesty to trap him.

"Let me get this straight," Gordon said deliberately. "If I don't promise to leave the party, you'll take our son and go to England. You'll leave me." He kept the pain and anger out of his voice. "If I do promise, you will come to the States with me." Ann nodded her head.

"You know that's not a fair thing to do," Gordon said, and he couldn't hide the pain. He walked over to the chair and sat down again. Calmly and patiently he sorted out everything in his mind. He knew Ann meant what she said. He knew he never could give up the party, that he would only grow to hate her if he did, and he knew he could not give her and the child up, possibly her but not the baby.

"I promise," he said, and he knew he lied. And when she came to him, her face flooding with tears of relief, and knelt and put her head in his lap, he felt for her pity and compassion and felt also a sense of dread for what he had done. For he had full knowledge of his deed, that once in America it would take her some time to discover his deception, and once she had discovered it she would not have the money or the will to go back to England. Their roots in each other would be too strong. He knew that for both of them their lives would now be mixed with hate and distrust and contempt and that for the rest of their years there would be a struggle between them. But there was nothing he could do. He stroked her coarse and heavy hair, which always excited him, as did her sturdy peasant body. He turned her heavy-planed almost Slavic face upward so that he could kiss it through the tears.

He thought, there was nothing I could do, and the kiss he gave her was painful to him.

# 15

IN TWILIGHT, the ruins of Nuremberg had a quiet grandeur, as if all this destruction was a thing of long ago, and by forces of nature—fire, earthquakes, centuries of rain and sun—and parts of it were tarry black as if the earth had been bled, and caked lava had formed enormous mounds.

Leo drove through it and for the first time found pleasure in the sight of this desolation. In the suburbs he stopped in front of a little, square white-painted house absolutely identical with the houses beside it. He hoped the Professor was ready; he was anxious to leave Nuremberg, glad to leave the trial behind him. He had given his testimony honestly, factually, against the guards and the *kapos* he had known. He had met some of his old friends, old inmates, and shared their grim satisfaction in this long-awaited vengeance. But curiously enough he had disliked being with his former comrades, as if they had not been victims but had all participated in some shameful act in which they all now felt an equal guilt. He tried to reason this out and knew that he did not wish to be with people who remembered and shared the degradation, the terror, the hopeless misery of his life in that time. And just a face associated with that life made it real again. He pressed the horn of his jeep and shattered the evening stillness.

Almost immediately he saw the Professor's small, slight

figure leave the house and come down the walk toward the jeep. He had a little surprise for the Professor, Leo thought grimly, but he made an effort to be polite. "Did you have a good visit with your son?" he asked.

"Yes, yes," the Professor said, "a very nice visit." He said the words politely, listlessly. He looked ill, dark circles pouched beneath his eyes, an almost bloodless mouth and gray skin.

Leo drove slowly so that they could talk, the slight breeze pleasant against his face. Later he would go at the fullest speed and then because of the rushing night wind they would not be able to speak. He took a pack of cigarettes from his shirt pocket with his right hand, controlling the wheel with his left. He gave one to the Professor, and the Professor lit a match, cupped it in his hand and leaned over to light Leo's cigarette, then lit his own. After a few puffs Leo said, "I know about your son, one of my friends testified against him last month." He saw the Professor's hand shake as it brought the cigarette up to the mouth but the old man said nothing.

"If I had known about him I would never have taken you here," Leo said, and wondered why then he was taking the man back to Bremen.

The Professor said nervously, excitedly, holding tightly to the open side of the jeep, "I did not want you to help me. I knew it was not proper. But Herr Middleton said he explained everything to you, that you understood."

"When will they execute your son?" Leo asked cruelly and then felt ashamed.

"In a few weeks," the Professor said. He had lost the cigarette and his hands were tugging at each other in nervous spasms. "This was my last visit." He sat and waited for pity, hoping that Leo would not question him.

Leo was silent. They were in the open country, the smell of fresh grass and growing trees untainted by dust. The jeep was moving very slowly. Leo turned his head toward the old man. He spoke slowly. "He was convicted by a German court, your son, for killing a fellow German, not for his crimes as a camp guard. That is ironic. You will never be able to think in your heart that the damn Jews killed him. That hatred can never be your consolation. What a pity."

The Professor bowed his head and watched his hands. "I never thought such things," he said. "Truly, I am an educated man."

"Your son deserves to die," Leo said. "He is a monster. If ever a man deserved to have his life taken away, that monster does. Do you know the things he did? An evil creature, the world will be better without him. I say that with a clear conscience. Do you know the things he did?" The hate in his voice and in his heart made him stop the jeep on the side of the road and turn for an answer.

But the Professor did not answer. He had buried his head in his arms as if to hide as much of himself as he could. His whole body was shaking. There was no sound coming from the old man, but his small body was weaving backward and forward, continuously, aimlessly, as if severed from the motor of his brain.

Leo waited for it to end, and as pity and compassion began to wash away the hate, he thought *no no* and called to his mind the image of his own father, the tall emaciated figure, head shaven, walking down the gravel path and Leo in his own uniform walking to meet him, not knowing him, and his father suddenly stopping and saying, "What are you doing here?" and Leo at that time remembering, and remembering now, how in an even earlier time he had been caught by his father in the Tiergarten when he was supposed to have been in school and his father saying in the salfsame tone, *"Was machst Du hier?"* Only now here along the gravel path with its white-painted stones, the barbed wire ringing the horizon all around them, now the father saying these words was weeping, stooping down to his son, the red stripe of the political prisoner across his breast, the boy with the green diagonal denoting his race. And Leo in the jeep, remembering this, only now knowing what his father must have suffered at that time ten years ago, felt only contempt for this old man before him paying for his father's grief with his own. This man, well educated, knowing right from wrong, who out of fear, cowardice, impotence, did not come to the help of his father. Slept warm in his bed, ate well, and earned it all with a helpless shrug, an easy resignation. Leo looked away from the Professor and across the road and down into a green valley growing black with the falling night. He knew he could never remain in Germany, that he could never live with these people, could not even hate them, they who had kept his youth behind barbed wire, burned a number into his arm that he would carry to his grave, killed his father, made his mother flee into the night thousands of miles away, robbing her mind of the co-ordination necessary to live so that finally a time had come when she had died because she could not sleep, literally could not sleep.

And now in this land, and with this people, he lived in peace and did not rage with fire and sword. Slept with their daughters, gave chocolate bars to their children, gave them cigarettes, drove them around the countryside. With his contempt for himself Leo drove out the last pity he felt for the old man. He put the jeep in motion, making it go at top speed, wanting to get back to Bremen. The Professor had wiped his face with a handkerchief and sat passively, bracing his feet against the floor, his body rigid, fighting the swaying of the jeep.

In the early morning hours, the countryside becoming shadowy with the first beginning light, Leo stopped at one of the coffee-and-snack bars the Americans had set up on the *Autobahn*. He took the Professor in with him, and they sat at a long wooden table. Along it some G.I. truck drivers were sleeping, their heads pillowed on their arms.

They drank their first cup of coffee in silence but when Leo returned with the cups filled a second time and a handful of doughnuts the Professor began to talk, slowly at first, then more quickly, his hands trembling as he hurriedly sipped coffee.

"You don't know yet how a father feels, Leo, a father is helpless. I know all about my son, and he confessed to me something else. When his mother was dying he was on the Russian front, and I managed to get him leave—he was a hero, he had courage, many decorations, but he never came. He wrote that his leave was canceled. Now he told me everything, that he went on through to Paris. That he wanted a good time. He explained to me that he could feel no pity, no love for his mother. And after that was when everything went bad, and he began to do all those terrible things. But," the Professor paused as if bewildered and then more intensely, "but how is that, a son not weep for his mother's death? He was never unnatural, he was like all the other boys, perhaps more handsome, more intelligent. I taught him to be generous, to share his things with his little playmates, to believe in God. We both loved him, his mother and I, we never spoiled him. He was a good son. Now, even now, I can't believe the things he's done, but he confesses, he confessed to me." The pouched eyes filled with tears. "He told me these things, and last night he cried in my arms and said 'Poppa, I'm glad to die, I'm glad to die.' We talked all week about our lives together, and then last night he cried as he used to when a child." The Professor stopped suddenly and Leo realized that his face must be showing the mixture of repulsion and pity that he felt.

The Professor began again but now his voice was calm, reasonable, and slightly apologetic as if showing his grief had been the extreme of bad manners. He spoke very slowly. "I go over our life together and try to find out where did it start? I can't find it. I can see nothing. It all happened by itself that he became a monster. It's terrifying to think that. That makes you stop. You called him that, Leo, and it is true. Your son could be such a monster." The Professor smiled to show that this was impersonal, mere theorizing, and this smile was so ghastly in that grief-masked face, the bloodless lips twisted so unnaturally, that Leo had to bow his head over his coffee not to see.

And this smile taking all of his strength the old man became more intense. "I say these things to you because you are the victim. My son and I, I too, we were the ones who did these things to you. What can I say? That it was an accident, as if I drove a car and was careless and ran you down. Without malice. My son caught a terrible fever, as if he lived in a swamp, do you understand that? He must die of this illness, I know that. But I believe he is good in spite of everything, I believe he is good." The Professor began to weep and said loudly, hysterically, "God have pity on him, God have pity on him."

One of the G.I.'s lifted his head from the table and said, "Pipe down for Chrissake." The Professor became silent.

Leo said, "Sleep a little and then we'll go on, first smoke

a cigarette." When they had finished they both pillowed their heads on their arms and the Professor fell asleep immediately, but not Leo.

He raised his head again and stared at the brown-skinned doughnuts scattered on the dirty wooden table. A black pool of coffee in its tin mess kit caught a few golden glints from the weak yellow bulbs in the room. He felt no pity for the old man; he could not. His own suffering rose in his blood as antidote. But he knew now his mother and father's grief on his account, a cruel suffering. Sleepily his mind made a circle around a half-formed dream of countless evil men put to death with perfect justice and that death spreading like a disease to countless more innocent. There was no other way, but before his head dropped onto the wooden table he thought hazily of a wonderful solution, at every execution a drug be given to the loved ones, a drug of forgetfulness, and in a full dream he dipped a great steel needle into the black pool of coffee, drew the golden glints up into the glass tube with the black liquid and finally in the back of the Professor's head with its little fleshy neck he stabbed until the steel hit bone and watched the needle empty itself. The Professor turned his face up to him, humbly, gratefully.

It was almost dawn when they woke, and they made the long ride to Bremen without further conversation than was necessary. The afternoon sun had just begun its voyage west when they rode through the outskirts of Bremen, and Leo stopped the jeep at the house where the Professor had his room.

Leo raced the motor to drown out the old man's polite gratitude. He drove away quickly. He felt cold, fatigued, but not ready for sleep. He drove through the town, past the *Polizeihaus* and down the Schwachhauser, then made the turn into the Kurfürsten Allee. He drove slowly down the long, curved tree-lined avenue, the sunlight and warm afternoon breeze giving him new strength. As he approached Mosca's house he took his foot off the gas pedal and bumped over the curb so that the jeep was tilted, one side on the street and one on the walk. He steered into the tree to stop the slowly rolling jeep but he had been going faster than he thought and the shock of contact snapped his head back. He cursed, leaned against the cushion and lit a cigarette, then honked the jeep horn three times.

The window went up quickly, but instead of Hella it was Frau Saunders who put her head out. She called down to him, "Frau Mosca is not here. She was taken this morning to the hospital. The child came early."

Leo in his excitement stood up in the jeep. "Ah, no, is she all right?"

"She's fine," Frau Saunders said. "The child is a boy. Everything went well. Herr Mosca is there now."

Leo didn't wait to answer her. He roared the jeep into action and made the turn that would take him to the city hospital. On the way he stopped by the officers' club and gave a German servant a pack of cigarettes for a great bouquet of flowers.

# 16

MOSCA HEARD Inge calling him to the phone in the outer office. He went in, picked up the receiver and said hello. A woman's voice answered in German. "Herr Mosca, here is Frau Saunders. They took your wife to the hospital an hour ago. I think it is the baby."

Mosca paused, looking at Inge and Eddie, as if they could hear the voice over the phone. They were both busy, bent over their desks.

"But it's two weeks early," Mosca said and saw Eddie look up and Inge turn around to watch him.

"I think it is the baby," Frau Saunders was saying. "She had pains this morning after you left. I called the hospital and they sent an ambulance."

"O.K.," Mosca said, "I'll go right away."

"Will you telephone me when you find out?" Frau Saunders asked.

"All right," Mosca said and then before he hung up he heard Frau Saunders say, "She told me to tell you not to be worried."

Eddie Cassin raised his eyebrows when Mosca told him the news. Eddie picked up the phone and ordered a vehicle from the motor pool.

When the jeep came Eddie said, "I'll meet you at the Rathskellar for supper if you can make it. Give me a ring if anything happens."

"It may not even be the baby," Mosca said, "she's not too rugged."

"She'll be O.K.," Eddie said reassuringly. "It's the baby all right. They come early and they come late. I've gone through all that." He put out his hand to shake Mosca's and said, "Here's luck."

On the drive to town, Mosca became anxious, really worried. Without warning a great wave of fear flooded over him, so powerful that he was sure that she was ill and said to the driver, "Go faster."

The driver said, "I have my orders, the regulations." Mosca threw his half-full pack of cigarettes into the German's lap. The jeep leaped forward.

The city hospital was a group of red brick buildings scattered over a great area of tree-lined walks and green lawns, and all encircled by an iron fence crawling with ivy to hide the defending spikes. Along the perimeter of the fence were little iron doors. The main entrance for visitors, however, was an enormous gateway through which entered vehicles and pedestrians. The jeep went through this gate, moving slowly through eddies of German men and women.

"Find out where the maternity ward is," Mosca said. The jeep stopped. The driver leaned out and spoke to a passing nurse, then put the jeep in motion. Mosca leaned back and tried to relax as they rolled slowly through the hospital grounds.

Now he was in a German world. Here there were no uniforms, no military vehicles except the one he rode in. The people around him were all the enemy; their clothes, their speech, the way they walked, the very atmosphere. As they rode, he could see from time to time the iron spears enclosing this world. Near the fence was the maternity building.

Mosca went in and found a small office in which sat an elderly nurse. Against the wall stood two men wearing American Army fatigues but on their heads the peaked caps of the Wehrmacht. These were ambulance drivers.

"I'm looking for Hella Broda, she entered here this morning," Mosca said. The nurse consulted a record book on her desk. For a moment Mosca was afraid she would say no and his fears would be realized. She looked up at him and smiled. "Yes," she said. "Wait, I'll call up about her." As she spoke over the phone one of the ambulance drivers said to Mosca, "We brought her here," and both men smiled at him. He smiled back politely and then saw they were hoping for cigarettes as a reward. He reached in his pocket; he had given his driver the last pack. He shrugged and waited for the nurse to finish.

She hung up the phone. "You have a baby boy," she said to him.

Mosca said impatiently, "Is my wife all right?" Then he was self-conscious about the word wife.

"Yes, of course," the nurse said. "If you wish you can wait and see her in about an hour. She's sleeping now."

"I'll wait," Mosca said. He went out and sat on the wooden bench that ran along the ivy-covered building.

He could smell flowers from a nearby garden, a burning sweetness mixed with the reddish light of the burning midday sun. White-clad nurses and doctors passed to and fro, crossed over green lawns and entered blood-red brick buildings fastened squarely and without visible scars in the fresh, living earth. Filling the air was a muted trilling of insects and new-born birds. He felt a sense of absolute peace, a quiet restfulness, as if the iron fence were a barrier to the noise and ruin and dust of the city on the other side.

The two ambulance drivers came out and sat near him. The bastards never give up, Mosca thought. He was dying for a smoke himself. He turned to one of the men and asked, "Have you a cigarette?" They were stunned, the one nearest him actually gaped, his mouth open. Mosca grinned. "I have none with me. I'll leave a few packs for you both when I come again."

The nearest man took out a dark-colored pack of German cigarettes and extended it to Mosca, saying, "If you really wish to smoke one of these—?"

Mosca lit one up and choked on his first breath. The two ambulance drivers burst out laughing and one said, "These take getting used to." But after that first puff, it tasted good to Mosca. He lay back on the bench, letting the afternoon sun strike his face, resting. He felt tired.

"How was she when you brought her?" He spoke with his eyes closed.

"Fine, like all of them," the driver who had given him the cigarette said. He had a face that was perpetually set in an expression of good humor, a half-smile that was formed by the very structure of facial bone. "We've had hundreds like her, no trouble."

Mosca opened his eyes to look at him. "Not nice work, carrying women around every day, listening to them cry and scream." He realized as he spoke that he felt resentment toward these two men because they had seen Hella defenseless, that for a period of time she had been helpless in their hands.

The same driver said, "It's nice carrying around people who can make noise. In the war I was with a burial squad. We used to take a truck out and pick up the dead. In the winter they were stiff, we had to pack them in carefully, like cordwood, in neat stacks, sometimes you could bend their arms a little and there was a nice little trick of hooking arms in one pile to arms in another so you could stack them higher."

The other driver left the bench and went back into the building. "He's heard these stories before," the German continued. "And he was with the Luftwaffe; they empty a can of garbage, they have nightmares for weeks. Anyway, as I was telling you. In the summer, terrible. Terrible. I used to pack fruit before the war, maybe that is why the Army gave me the burial squad. I used to pack oranges, sometimes they were rotten, we have to import them you know, so I'd repack them. The bad ones I'd squeeze into small boxes to take home. In summers that was the way with dead men. They would be all squashy, we'd press them in against one another. It would be like a big pile of garbage in the truck. So this job is fine. The other one, winter or summer, we had no conversation, nothing interesting, you understand." He gave Mosca a huge grin.

Mosca thought, how about this bastard. He felt a genuine liking for the man, recognized the intended kindliness.

"I like conversation," the man went on, "so I didn't care for my Army work. Now here, it is a pleasure. I sit with the woman, and when she screams I say go ahead and scream, nobody will hear. When they cry, like your wife, I say, Cry, it will do you good. Anybody who has children must get used to tears. My little joke. I don't always say things the same. I think of something new usually and it is almost always true. I don't talk much, just enough so they won't feel alone, as if I were their husband."

Mosca closed his eyes. "Why did my wife cry?"

"Man, it is a painful business." The German tried to give him a reproachful look but only succeeded in making a kindly grimace, the bones of his face working against him. "The pain made her cry but that means nothing because you could see she was very happy. I thought then, her husband is a lucky man. I didn't say anything to her, I couldn't think of anything to say. I wiped her face with a wet towel because the pain made her sweat, and she cried a great deal. But when she got out of the ambulance she smiled at me. No, she was fine, there was nothing for me to say."

A tap on the window behind them made the driver turn; the nurse was motioning for him to come in. The German left and a few moments later both drivers came out. The German shook Mosca's hand. "All the best, don't forget our cigarettes when you come again." They got into their ambulance and drove slowly toward the main gate.

Mosca closed his eyes, leaned back, and the heat of the June sun made him doze off. It seemed as if he slept for a long time, even dreamed, and then he was awake. There was a tapping on the windowpane behind him. He turned his head and saw the nurse motioning him to enter.

She gave him the floor and room number and he ran up the two flights of stairs. When he came to the room he saw outside a long table on rollers and on the table nearly twenty small white-clothed bundles from which came an overwhelming din. One of them might be his and he stopped to look for a moment. A nurse came out of the room and started to wheel the table away. "You can go in," she told him. He pushed open the door and stepped into a large, square, green-walled room in which were six high hospital beds filled with women, none of them Hella. Then in one corner he saw a bed so low it was nearly level with the floor.

She was lying flat, her eyes open, watching him, and

she was more beautiful than he had ever seen her. Her mouth was the dark redness of blood and her face very white except for two crimson spots on her cheeks. Her eyes were shining and alive and except for her body, which was curiously lifeless and immobile, she did not look as if she had had a child only a few hours before. Conscious of the other women in the room, he went to her and bent down to kiss her cheek, but she twisted her head so that her mouth met his. "Are you happy?" she whispered. Her voice was peculiarly hoarse, as if she had a heavy cold. Mosca smiled down at her and nodded.

"It's a beautiful baby, so much hair," she whispered. "Like yours." He didn't know what to say and stood there wondering how all this could make her so happy and leave him so untouched.

A nurse came in and said, "That's all, please, you can come back tomorrow, in the regular visiting hours." Mosca leaned down to Hella and said, "I'll see you tomorrow, O.K.?" She nodded and tilted her head for him to kiss her again.

Outside the nurse asked if he would like to see the baby and he followed her down a long corridor to where it ended in a glass wall. There were some men looking through this wall at babies held up in turn by a small, pert-looking nurse who obviously enjoyed her work and the antics of the visiting, newly made fathers. She opened a small pane in the glass wall and the nurse with Mosca said, "The Broda child." The nurse disappeared into a room behind the glass wall and came out with a small bundle. She took the cloth away from its face, holding up the baby proudly.

Mosca was shocked by the baby's ugliness. It was the first time he had ever seen a new-born infant. The face was wrinkled, puckered up sourly, the small black eyes almost closed but still emitting malignant gleams toward the new and hostile world, and over its head like an untidy shawl, a great shock of black hair gave it an animal-like appearance.

Beside Mosca a small, bald-headed German man was going into ecstasies over another baby held by another nurse behind the glass wall. Mosca saw with relief that this baby looked almost exactly like his own. The German was exclaiming and cooing, "Oh, what a sweet child, what a lovely child," making sucking noises with his mouth and twisting his face into extraordinary grimaces to get a reaction from the infant. Mosca watched curiously and then stared at his own child, trying to feel some emotion, then signaled to the nurse to take it away. The nurse gave him a long, angry look; she had been waiting impatiently for his performance. Mosca thought, Screw you, sister.

He ran down the steps and walked through the hospital grounds toward the gate. He saw Leo driving slowly against the waves of Germans going out. He stopped in front of the jeep and climbed up over the hood, stepped over the windshield and into the jeep. He saw the great bouquet of flowers in Leo's lap, and as their sweet, cool fragrance hit his face, he was suddenly free of tension and felt extraordinarily happy.

When, finally, they met Eddie at the Rathskeller, Eddie was already drunk. He said, "You son of a bitch, why didn't you call? I had Inge phone the hospital and they gave me the dope. Then your landlady called and I told her the news."

"Christ, I forgot," Mosca said with a foolish smile.

Eddie threw an arm around his shoulders. "Congratulations. Now, tonight we celebrate."

They ate and then went to one of the tables in the bar.

"Do we buy the drinks or does Walter?" Leo asked as if this were a very serious point.

Eddie gave them both an amused, paternal look. "Tonight I'll buy everything. If I know Walter he won't even give out cigars. Look at that sad face."

"Jesus," Mosca said, "how the hell can I act like a big-wheel father. We're not even married. They kept calling the kid by Hella's last name. That made me feel funny. I was thinking I'll put in the marriage papers."

"Let's see," Eddie said. "You can figure three months. But then thirty days after you're married, back to the States. You going to leave all this gravy?"

Mosca thought it over. "I figure I can get the papers and hold off the marriage for a while. But I'd like to have everything set, just in case."

"You could do that," Eddie said, "but you have to go back sometime. Especially now the Middletons are gone, you can't get the right food for a wife and kid." He gave Mosca a strange, peering look. "You sure you want those papers, Walter, you ready to go back?"

Mosca said to Leo. "How about you, you made up your mind yet, U. S. A. or Palestine?"

"I'm doing well here," Leo said. He thought of the Professor. "But soon I must decide."

"You ought to come back with me," Mosca said. "You could stay with me and Hella until you get set. That is, if I can get a place myself."

Eddie asked curiously, "What will you do when you get back to the States?"

"I don't know," Mosca said. "I figure I'll go to school maybe. I'm an ignorant guy, I went right from high school into the Army." He grinned at them. "You wouldn't think it but I used to be a good student. But I enlisted, you know that, Eddie, you used to break my balls about it when we were G.I.'s. Now I want to learn what goes on." He stopped, trying to think of how he could put it into words. "Sometimes I wanta fight like hell against everything around me, but I don't know what to fight. It seems like I can't get out of a straight line to a trap. Like now. I want to do something but I'm not allowed. My own personal business. I can't marry a kraut and I can see why the Army makes it tough. I don't give a crap about the Germans but that stops me. All right, screw it." He took another drink.

"You know, when I was a kid I thought everybody was wonderful. I had definite ideas and now I can't even remember them. In a street fight when I was a kid I always used to fight like I was a hero in the movies, always fight fair, never hit the other guy when he slipped or was off balance. A real jerk. But that wasn't for real. Now it seems like that life before I got into the Army was never really real. Like you could never believe the war would end. You knew you would go on to Japan, and then they would find somebody new to fight, the Russians maybe. Then after that maybe the men on Mars. But always somebody new so that you could never go home. Now for the first time I believe that it is over, that I'll have to go back to that dream life or whatever it was. I can start by going back to school."

Leo and Eddie were embarrassed. It was the first time Mosca had ever spoken to them about his feelings, and they were surprised by the boyishness of the emotions behind the lean, dark, almost cruel-looking face. Leo said, "Don't worry, Walter, when you lead a normal life with a wife and children everything will be O.K."

"What the hell do you know?" Eddie demanded in drunken anger. "Eight years in a concentration camp without dames. What the hell do you know?"

Leo said with a quiet contempt, "I know one thing. You'll never leave here." This stunned Eddie.

"You're right," he said. "Goddamn if you're not right. I wrote my wife again that she gotta come and bring the kid or I'll never leave this goddamn continent. That's my only hope. But she's screwing for her boss, she thinks I don't know about it. But I've got her figured all the way."

Leo said to Mosca, "Maybe I will come with you, who knows what will happen by that time? I can't stay here forever. Maybe we go into a business together with our black-market profits and you could go to school too, how would that be?"

"That's right," Eddie said. "Go into business with Leo and you can't lose, Walter." He smiled at them and saw that neither of them had understood or perhaps had not heard because the liquor was twisting the words as they came out of his loose mouth and also perhaps because about that, they had always trusted him. He felt ashamed. "You guys are dreaming," he said and realized that he was angry because they were making plans together and leaving him out, with no malice, assuming that he would never leave here. He felt, suddenly, concern for both of them. Leo for his innocence of the real world, Mosca for what he sensed was an endless struggle that raged behind that seemingly indifferent, dark proud face; a struggle to hold to the world with the help of one thin thread. And he felt an overwhelming drunken sorrow for himself. To the amazement of Leo and Mosca, he put his head down on the table and began to cry. Then he fell asleep.

# 17

WOLF EASED his pudgy body down the basement steps and sighed wearily, glad to be out of the hot summer sun. He was tired, as there had been a lot of work to catch up after a month's vacation. He had taken his wife to visit a sister in Bavaria, a last visit before they went to the States. Now he went directly to the kitchen where Ursula was preparing supper. "They have a baby boy," he said.

Ursula turned around and exclaimed happily, "Isn't that wonderful, just what she wanted. Is she back from the hospital yet? I must go to see her."

"It happened the day after we left," Wolf said. "The baby came early. So she's been home three weeks now." And he thought, they barely know each other and yet Ursula is happy. Something about children being born always touched him too. He wanted kids of his own, when he was all set. That was one thing you were sure of and he could teach them how to take care of themselves. They'd be the sharpest kids in the neighborhood, they'd know what the score was.

"Have you heard anything about our marriage papers?" Ursula asked.

"They haven't come back from Frankfort," Wolf said. This was a lie. The papers were now in his desk at the air base. But if Ursula knew she would insist on getting married immediately and he would have to leave Germany within thirty days after the ceremony. He wanted to re-main a few months longer and complete a few deals.

Ursula's father spoke behind him. "Ah, Wolfgang, home at last." Wolf swung around. "You had a telephone message. You must get in touch with a man named Honny, at once." The father had just come in from the storeroom and carried a great ham which he now put on the kitchen table. He took a large carving knife and lovingly cut off medium-thick slices to be fried with their potatoes.

One thing, Wolf thought wryly, the old man always made himself useful around the house. He asked, "Did the man say anything else?"

"No," Ursula's father said, but he kept repeating that it was very important.

Wolf went into his bedroom and dialed the number. When someone picked up the phone and said hello, he recognized Honny's voice and said, "Here is Wolfgang."

Honny's voice, very excited and effeminate in its higher register said, "Wolfgang, it is good you called so quickly. That contact you were looking for during the winter. I have it."

"Are you sure?" Wolf asked.

Honny's voice became lower, more guarded. "I saw enough of the evidence to think so." He stressed the word "evidence."

"Ah so," Wolf said, "very well. I will be there in about an hour. Can you have him there then?"

"In two hours," Honny said.

"All right," Wolf said and hung up. He called out to Ursula that he would not be eating supper and hurried out of the house. He heard her exclamation of surprise and disappointment before he closed the door. He walked quickly down the street and arrived just in time to catch a *Strassenbahn*, making it on the run.

Wolf was excited. He had given up hope on the whole deal, hadn't even thought about it for several months except when Mosca had kidded him. And now everything was breaking just right. The marriage papers were all set, he could get plane tickets, the hell with free government transportation. And it would be a perfect out on the old-man deal. Ursula and her father had been breaking his balls about taking the old man with them to the States, and he had almost laughed in their faces. But you had to lie to women all the time, he had promised Ursula he would try his best. And he wouldn't mind if the old man was on the ball. But the father had taken a nice shellacking when he had tried to put over a swindle on some black-market operators. He spent a week in the hospital recovering. Since then the father had stayed in the basement apartment like a mole, eating a whole twenty-pound ham in less than a week, three or four ducks at a sitting, almost an entire goose during the course of a Sunday. He must have gained forty pounds in the last two months. The wrinkles of his skin had been filled out with layer on layer of lard and he had let out his prewar suits to contain a great, new paunch.

He must be the only fat kraut in Bremen, Wolf thought, the only one who could pose for those posters and travel folders showing the tremendous, jolly German who illustrated the good living of his country. In his basement he had the fattest kraut in Germany. A goddamn cannibal. A twenty-pound ham in three days. Jesus Christ.

Wolf jumped off the *Strassenbahn* as it passed the mouth of the Kurfürsten Allee and walked briskly past the Metzer Strasse to further on where Mosca lived in the white stone house. Though the sun was going down the air was still hot and Wolf kept under the shade of the trees that lined the Allee. He hoped Mosca was home, but if not there was still time to pick him up at the Rathskellar or the club. No telephone on this.

Wolf opened the gate that cut the path from the sidewalk. He went up the stairs, knocked on the door, and Mosca opened it. He was dressed only in sun-tan trousers and a T shirt, his feet were bare. In his hand he held a can of PX beer.

"Come on in, Wolf," Mosca said. They went through the hall and through the door to the living room. Frau Saunders was sitting in one corner of the sofa reading a magazine. Hella was rocking the cream-colored carriage serving now as a crib. The baby was crying.

Wolf said hello to the women, and though he was impatient, looked at the baby and complimented Hella on its beauty. Then he said to Mosca, "Can I see you for a minute alone, Walter?"

"Sure," Mosca said. Still holding the can of beer he led Wolf into the bedroom.

"Listen, Walter," Wolf said excitedly, "it's finally come through, the contact on that scrip deal. I've got to meet the guy now and settle details. I want you to come with me just in case everything goes quick. O.K.?"

Mosca took a sip of beer. In the other room he could hear the murmur of voices as Frau Saunders and Hella spoke to each other and spaced in between, the tentative, discontented wailing of the baby. He was surprised and the shock was unpleasant. He had written the whole deal off and now he found he had no taste for it.

"I don't go for that any more, Wolf," Mosca said. "You'll have to get a new partner."

Wolf had already started toward the door of the bedroom. Now, stunned, he turned back again to Mosca, his white face angry and full of disbelief.

"What the hell kind of crap is that, Walter?" he said. "We knock our balls off all winter and now, everything all set, you back out? That's no good, Walter. That doesn't go."

Mosca grinned at Wolf's anger and excitement. It was an excuse not to feel ashamed of backing out. He knew he was giving Wolf a dirty deal. But he was glad the pasty-faced bastard was getting tough.

"What the hell, Wolf," he said, "we're not gangsters. It was an idea. Maybe I would have gone through with it six months ago. Now I've got a dame and kid to think about. If something screws up, what happens to them? Besides my marriage papers are coming through in a few months. I won't need all that money."

Wolf restrained his outraged anger. "Look, Walter," he said in a friendly, reasonable voice, "you're going back to the States in three or four months. Maybe you saved a thousand bucks while you've been here, maybe you made another thousand on the black market. That thousand I helped you make, Walter. In the States you have to set up a home, look for a job, a lot of other crap. You'll need dough." And then letting a hurt tone come into his voice he said earnestly. "And you're not treating me right, Walter. I lose out, too. I can't go running around for another partner. I need a guy I can trust. Come on, Walter, it'll be easy, you don't have to worry about cops, they can't turn us in. And since when have you been afraid of a couple of lousy krauts?"

"No dice," Mosca said, and took another sip from the can of beer. With his free hand he flapped out his T shirt and said, "Boy, is it hot."

"Christ." Wolf slammed the door with his hand. "Goddamn it, hangin' out with that yellow Jew and that gash hound Eddie made you lose all your guts? I thought you were a better guy than that, Walter."

Mosca put his beer can down on the dresser. "Listen, Wolf, keep my friends out. Don't talk about them any more. Now about this business. Wolf, you shrewd prick, I know you got your marriage papers; so now you can just pull off this deal and take off for the States. Meanwhile I sit here three or four months. I'm not afraid of krauts but I'm not walking around Bremen after I pull a stunt like that. If we do this it's either get out of Bremen afterwards or knock the guys off when we take the money. Right now I can't do either. And I'm not going to keep looking behind me the rest of the summer, not even for a million bucks." He paused and then said sincerely, "No shit, Wolf, I'm sorry."

Wolf stared at the floor shaking his head up and down as if pondering on something he already knew, and then, remembering the scene at the officers' club when the Adjutant had made Mosca back down, he said, "You know, Walter, I can bust this whole thing up, you and Hella. All I have to do is turn in a report at the base and at the Military Police. You're breaking a Military Government law living in a German billet. And there are a couple of other things I could really go to town on."

To his amazement and anger, Mosca burst out laughing and then said, "Wolf, for Christ's sake, have a can of beer or get the hell out. I don't mind playing gangster with you but don't for Christ's sake pull that line. I'm not one of those kraut prisoners you used to scare the shit out of."

Wolf tried to bring his head up to stare balefully at Mosca, but there was such evident power in the lightly covered body, so much force and confidence in the lean face and thin mouth, the dark serious eyes, that he could only sigh and smile weakly.

"Ah, you son of a bitch," Wolf said resignedly, "give me a beer." Adding ruefully, shaking his head. "A five-grand can of beer." But as he drank he thought of some way to pay Mosca back for the desertion. He saw there was really nothing he could do. If he turned Mosca in to the M.P.'s and then left for the States, that would not help this deal any, there would be no gain and there was always the possibility of retaliation. No, he was well off. He had a small fortune in diamonds and quite a bit of cash. Why invite any remote chance of disaster?

He sighed, sipped at his beer. It was hard to let such a fine opportunity go by. He knew he would never have the nerve to do it alone. Well, he thought, he would scrape together all the cigarettes possible, bargain around the base, buy .cheaply and sell high. He might clear a thousand bucks.

Wolf held out his hand to Mosca. "No hard feelings," he said. He was a little worried now that Mosca might take his former threat seriously, and he didn't want to keep looking around his last few weeks in Germany. "I'm sorry about trying to get tough, but losing all that dough . . . Forget what I said." They shook hands.

"It's O.K.," Mosca said. He walked Wolf to the door and said to him, "Maybe you can do something on your own."

When Mosca went into the living room, both women looked up inquiringly; they had heard the anger in Wolf's loud voice. The baby was no longer crying, was sleeping in his carriage.

"Your friend left so quickly," Frau Saunders said.

"He just wanted to tell me something," Mosca said. Then to Hella who was knitting and reading at the same time. "Wolf is getting married soon, he has the papers."

Hella looked up from her book and said absently, "Yes?"

Her thin pale face went back to the book as she murmured, "I hope ours come soon."

Mosca went into the bedroom for another can of beer and a tin of peanuts. He brought them into the living room and offered the opened can to the two women. They both took a handful. "Sure you don't need a beer?" They both shook their heads and kept reading.

They all sat, eating peanuts, Mosca drinking beer, the two women reading and Hella knitting. Hella's hair was cut very short for the summer, and the fragile bones of her face were scarcely veiled by the thin curtain of flesh and skin; a tiny blue vein coursed down her cheek to her lips. The room was filled with the warm, peaceful quietness of a summer evening, a slight cooling breeze came through the open window, ruffling the flowered curtain.

Mosca studied both women. One could be his mother, the other was actually the mother of his child, and the child in the carriage was his. He sorted all this out in his mind, making it very simple because the beer had made him sleepy. But everything jumbled together.

One day, long ago, he had put on his steel helmet, taken up his rifle, and on ships, in trucks, on the back of tanks had traveled through North Africa, England, France, Belgium, the Netherlands, to search out the enemy and put him to death. And even now this did not seem wrong, or stupid, or even ironical. It just seemed queer. A hell of a thing, he thought, a hell of a thing. He was amazed now that he thought of it. He took another handful of peanuts and almost missed his mouth, some of the nuts trickling to the floor. He felt very sleepy and went to stand by the window, letting the little breeze come through the porous cotton of his T shirt and onto his warm body. He walked unsteadily over to the carriage and stared down at the baby and said solemnly and out loud, "A hell of a thing."

Both of the women smiled. "I think I'll have to put you to bed," Hella said to Mosca. Then to Frau Saunders. "This is the first time he ever really looked at the baby. Don't you believe it, Walter, that you are a father?"

"He'll be better with the second one," Frau Saunders said.

Mosca kept staring down at the child. It was not ugly now, the wrinkles of the face had been filled out to a clean, white mask. The women were reading again. Mosca went back to the window.

"Don't be so restless," Hella said, not looking up from her book.

"I'm not restless," Mosca said. And it was true. He felt more as if he were exploring the room, really looking at it for the first time. He walked over to the carriage again and watched the baby sleeping. It was getting to look almost human, he thought. Then he said to Hella, "How about us going to the country club tomorrow? We can sit on the lawn with the carriage and I'll bring you hot dogs and ice cream from the PX snack bar. We can hear the band out there, too."

Hella nodded her head, still reading. Mosca said to Frau Saunders. "How would you like to come with us?"

Frau Saunders looked up and said, "Oh, no, I have some people coming."

Hella smiled at her. "He really meant it, he wouldn't ask you otherwise. You can eat yourself sick on ice cream."

"No, really," Frau Saunders said. She went back to her reading. Mosca realized that she wouldn't go because she was too shy, that she really thought he had asked out of politeness.

"No kidding," he said.

Frau Saunders smiled. "Bring me back some ice cream," she said.

Mosca took another beer can from the bedroom; everything was O.K., he thought.

"While you're feeling so friendly," Hella said, "I have a favor to ask you. Frau Saunders has an uncle in America and she wants you to send a letter for her through your Army mail."

"Sure," Mosca said. It was standard. All the Germans were writing to their relatives in the States hinting for packages. Frau Saunders said, "Thank you." And with a wry smile, "We are all very much concerned these days for our dear uncles in America." Hella and Mosca laughed, Mosca couldn't stop and choked on a mouthful of beer he had been ready to swallow.

The women had gone back to their reading so Mosca glanced at the copy of *Stars and Stripes* that lay on the table, then said, "Maybe Leo will be back from Hamburg tomorrow and come out to the club with us."

Hella looked up. "He has been a long time this trip. I hope nothing has happened to him."

Mosca went for a fresh can of beer. "You sure you two don't want some?" They both shook their heads. He stood by the window. "I guess Leo figured he'd spend the week end there, see what's doing. Otherwise he should have been back yesterday."

Hella put her book on the table and said to Frau Saunders, "Finished. It was fine."

Frau Saunders said, "I have others in the bedroom you haven't read. Go look at them."

"Not tonight," Hella said. She went to the window and stood beside Mosca, slipping her arm around his waist, under his T shirt. They both stared out into the darkness, letting the tree-scented breeze blow against them. They could smell the vegetable gardens and the river which flowed beyond; the summer night air had only the slightest acrid taint of ruins. The full moon was screened by clouds and all around him in the quiet darkness Mosca could hear German voices and laughter from nearby houses. A radio tuned to a Bremen station was playing soft string music. He had a sudden longing to go to the Rathskellar or the club, to shoot dice or drink with Eddie and Wolf.

"Oh, you are drinking so much beer," Hella said. "I hope you can walk to bed."

Mosca stroked her hair and said, "Don't worry about me, I'm all right."

She leaned against him. "I feel good tonight," she said. "You know what I'd like?" She said this softly so that Frau Saunders could not hear.

"What?" Mosca asked, and she smiled at him and reached up to kiss his mouth.

"You're sure it's all right?" he asked, speaking as softly as she. "It's only been a month." Eddie Cassin had told him he should wait at least two months.

"I'm all right now," she said, "don't worry about me. I feel wonderful tonight, like an old family woman, as if we were together, oh, so many years."

They stood there for a few moments longer, listening to the murmurings of the city and the night and then Mosca turned and said to Frau Saunders, "Good night." He held the door of the living room open so that Hella could wheel the carriage into the bedroom. When he followed her he checked the hall door to the apartment to make sure that it was locked.

# 18

MOSCA SAT in the shade thrown by a great, white-painted house, the requisitioned country club. Before him stretched the archery course with its blue- and red-circled targets, beside him Hella sat in a low, comfortable chair. On the wide lawn sat G.I.'s, their wives and baby carriages.

Over everything hung the peace of late Sunday afternoon. The evening had begun to fall a little quicker than usual, Mosca thought, autumn near, coming earlier this year. Scattered through the green of the lawn were patches of brown, and there was a reddish tinge in the leaves of the great elms that screened the golf course.

He saw Eddie Cassin coming toward them, skirting the archers. Eddie sat on the grass, tapped Hella's foot and said, "Hello baby." Hella smiled down at him and kept reading *Stars and Stripes*, forming the words silently with her lips.

"I got a letter from my wife," Eddie Cassin said. "She's not coming over." He was silent for a few moments. "The final word," he said, and smiled gravely, the delicate mouth twisting. "She's going to marry her boss. I told you she was screwing for him, Walter. I didn't even know anything then. Just pure intuition. How's that for intuition, Walter?"

Mosca could see that Eddie was well on his way to a big drunk. "What the hell, Eddie, you're not a family man."

"I could be," Eddie Cassin said. "I could try." He pointed to the cream-colored carriage which sat so prettily on its green carpet of grass, the blue woolen blanket peeping out of it. "You're not a family man but you're trying."

Mosca laughed. "I'm learning," he said.

They sat in silence for a time. "How about coming to the Rathskellar tonight?" Eddie asked.

"No," Mosca said. "We got some stuff in the house. Why don't you come over?"

"I have to keep moving." Eddie got up. "I can't sit around your place all night." He wandered away, moving between the archers and their targets.

Mosca lay back against Hella's legs, raised his face to the weak rays of a dying sun. He had forgotten to ask Eddie about the marriage papers. They were due now.

He thought about going home, about coming into his mother's house with a wife and child. Gloria was married (he smiled at that) so no worry there. But it would be queer going back for good though easier now than before.

Watching the archers bend the bowstrings awkwardly and the flight of the freed arrows, he remembered an older G.I. in a farmhouse behind the lines, the farm being used to show a movie for troops in reserve. Kindling wood packed high served for seats, and this old G.I., he must have been close to forty, Mosca thought, had held one of three French kids, a six-year-old boy, between his knees and carefully combed the unruly tangled hair, parting it neatly on the side, fluffing up the front into a wave. Then he had combed the hair of the other two children, one girl and another boy, holding them in turn between his knees, combing carefully with gentle and expert strokes, turning them around to get the part right. When the old G.I. had finished he gave each of the children a bar of chocolate, picked up his rifle where it rested against the wall and held it between his knees.

Feeling it important, sitting now in green grass spotted with baby carriages, he forced his mind to go back and remember the colored G.I. who had thrown great cans of pineapple juice out of his truck as he sped by the weary troops toiling from the beach toward the sound of heavy guns, a reminder to prepare, as the sound of church bells on Sunday stirs the soul to readiness, growing louder and louder as they approached, acquiring resonance, the sound of guns becoming denser, the crack of small arms like minor chords; and before the final entry, the final act of entry when they went into a ritual of mind and body almost as if entering a church—and then his mind stopped and went back to the sweet tinny coolness of the pineapple juice, the pause in the road, the passing of the can from mouth to mouth. And from this road to a road bathed in moonlight, a French village of small stone houses, blacked out, but against which were parked clearly visible trucks, jeeps and monstrous gun carriers. At the end of the street a tank was covered with the newly washed clothing, spread to dry by moonlight.

The twang of a bowstring and its arrow's thud seemed to awaken and stir a chilly evening breeze. Hella looked up from her book and Mosca pushed himself to his feet. "Do you want something before we go?" Mosca asked.

"No," Hella said, "I'm so full. And I'm afraid my tooth is beginning to hurt again." Mosca saw a small blue lump along her jaw.

"I'll tell Eddie to get you to the dentist at the air base." They gathered their things together from the chair and grass, piled them into the carriage. The baby was still asleep. They walked off the grounds to the streetcar stop. When the car came Mosca stretched his long arms and lifted the small carriage onto the rear platform.

The baby began to cry and Hella picked him up and held him. The conductor waited for fare and Mosca said in German, "We are Americans." The conductor looked Mosca up and down but did not protest.

After a few stops two WAC's climbed aboard. One of them noticed the child in Hella's arms and said to the other, "Isn't that a cute German baby?"

The other WAC leaned over to look and said several times, loudly, "Oh, it's a lovely baby," and looking up to Hella's face to see if she understood, said, *"Schön, schön."*

Hella smiled and looked at Mosca, but he made no sign. One of the WAC's took a bar of chocolate out of her purse and as they came to a stop she quickly put it on the baby's body. Before Hella could protest they were both out of the car and walking away.

Mosca had been amused at first, but for some reason he was angry now. He took the bar of chocolate and flung it into the street.

When they had left the *Strassenbahn* and were walking home, Hella said, "Don't be so upset because they took us for Germans."

But it was more than that. He had been frightened, as if they were really Germans, and had to accept charity, humiliation as one of the conquered. "We'll be out of here soon," he said. "I'll talk to Eddie tomorrow about speeding up the papers." He felt for the first time a sense of urgency.

Eddie Cassin left the country club with no idea of where he could go. The sight of Mosca sitting on the grass, his head resting against Hella's knees, one hand on the wheel of the cream-colored carriage, the sight of this was painful to him. He caught a *Strassenbahn* and thought, "I'll go see the gorilla." This cheered him up enough to watch the girls walking their way to the center of town. At the far end of the city he walked down to the river, crossed the bridge over the Weser and caught another *Strassenbahn* that continued on through the Neustadt. He got off at the last stop before the streetcar went out to the air base.

The row of buildings here was intact. He entered one and climbed up three flights of stairs and knocked. He heard Elfreida's voice say, "One moment." Then the door opened.

Eddie Cassin was shocked each time he saw her. The soft figure, full but really fuller than it looked, the trim ankles and hips and then that monstrosity of a head with its delicate violet eyes, red rimmed like rabbit eyes.

Eddie Cassin went in and sat down on the couch against the wall. "Get me a drink, baby," he said. He kept a supply of liquor here; he felt safe doing so. He knew Elfreida never touched the stuff unless he was present. As she mixed the drink he watched with fascination the movements of her head.

It was a little too large for its body and the hair was like mounds of brassy wire spikes. The skin was old and looked like chicken skin, with the yellow, fatty sheen and huge pores. The nose was splayed as if smashed by many vicious blows and her lips, until she made them up as she always did when Eddie came, were two puffy welts the color of veal. She had a great sagging chin and jaw. But as she moved around the room and spoke to him, her voice was soft and musical and somewhere in it the trill of a long-passed adolescence. She spoke English very well, was adept at languages and made her living as a translator and interpreter. Sometimes she gave Eddie lessons in German.

Eddie felt comfortable and safe here. She always lighted

the room with candles and Eddie thought, chuckling, that probably they had other uses. On the opposite wall was a bed and near it, against the wall which faced the window was a bureau on which stood a picture of her husband, a handsome-looking fellow whose uneven teeth showed in a good-natured smile.

"I didn't expect you tonight," Elfreida said. She gave him his drink and sat away from him on the couch. She had learned that if she made any gesture of affection or desire he would leave, but that if she waited until he had drunk enough he would put out the candles and drag her violently to the bed, and she knew then she had to pretend unwillingness.

Eddie lay back on the couch drinking, staring at the picture. The dead husband had fallen before Stalingrad and Elfreida had often told him how, with her fellow countrywomen, she had donned her widow black on the special day of mourning decreed for German men who had died there, so many that now the very name Stalingrad had a terrible sound in their hearts.

"I still think he was a fairy," Eddie Cassin said. "How come he ever married you?" He watched her agitation and distress which he always caused her on his bad nights.

"Tell me, did he ever make love to you?" Eddie Cassin asked.

"Yes," Elfreida said in a low voice.

"How often?"

She didn't answer.

"Once a week?"

"More," she said.

"Well, maybe he wasn't a complete fairy," Eddie said with a judicial air. "But I'll tell you one thing, he was unfaithful to you."

"No," she said, and he noted with satisfaction that she was already crying.

Eddie stood up. "If you're going to act that way, not even talking to me, I might as well leave." He was play-acting, she knew but she knew what her response must be. She fell to her knees and clasped his legs in her arms.

"Please, Eddie, don't go. Please don't go."

"Say your husband was a fairy, tell me the truth."

"No," she said, rising to her feet and crying with anger. "Don't say that word again. He was a poet."

Eddie took another drink and said solemnly. "You see, I knew all the time. All poets are fairies. See? Besides I can tell by his teeth." He gave her a sly grin.

She was weeping hysterically now with rage and grief. "You can go," she cried out, "leave here, you beast, you dirty, filthy beast." And when he swung and hit her in the face and dragged and knocked her on the bed she knew she had fallen into a trap; that he had deliberately made her angry to excite himself. When he threw his body upon her she tried not to respond but she sank under his frenzy, and as always, succumbed to a similar frenzy of her own. But tonight was worse than it had ever been. They sank further in their bed and their passion. He made her take long drinks from the whiskey bottle and humiliated her in every way. He made her crawl on hands and knees and beg with her mouth open. He made her gallop around the room in the darkness, changing pace with his commands. Finally he took pity on her and said, "Whoa," and she stopped. Then he let her come into the bed and into his arms.

"Now say your husband was a fairy." He got ready to push her out of bed again.

With a childlike drunkenness she repeated after him,

"My husband was a fairy." She was silent after this and lay supinely on the bed. He made her sit up so that he could see the shadow of her long, cone-shaped breasts. Like footballs, almost exactly like footballs. Eddie marveled. Dressed she seemed ordinary. He had experienced a thrill of delight the first time he had discovered that treasure.

"I feel sick, Eddie," she said. "I have to go to the bathroom." He helped her there and sat her naked on the toilet bowl. Then he fixed himself a drink and lay back on the bed.

"Poor Elfreida," Eddie Cassin thought, "poor Elfreida. Do anything for a stiff dick." When he had spotted her on the *Strassenbahn* the first time, he had known everything about her from the quick look she had given him. Now, sated, void of passion and hate, he wondered at his cruelty to her, a wonder without regret, and his willful destruction of the memory of her husband. And what kind of a guy was he to marry a woman with a head like that? From what Elfreida had told him at the beginning the guy was really crazy about her, and with a body like hers you could forgive a lot of other things. But not that head, Eddie thought.

He made another drink and went back to bed. So she had the luck to find the one guy in the world who would marry her, the one person who had the eyes to see her soul beneath the mask nature had given her, and from what she said and what the picture told you, a real hell of a guy. And he was corrupting that memory.

He could hear Elfreida throwing up in the bathroom. He felt sorry for her, knowing that he had terrorized her to quell his own panic. Now, finally, irrevocably, the last roots of his life had been torn away. He couldn't blame his wife. He had never been able to hide his disgust when she was sick. And carrying the kid she had been ugly, always throwing up like Elfreida now. He had never touched her then.

Eddie took another drink. His mind became hazy but he kept thinking of his wife as if she were standing beside him, legs spread apart; and into his mind came a picture of the old ice box his mother used to have, how he went down every day to the cellar of the coal man and brought up in a heavy wooden bucket the frosty block of ice, and then emptied the great hollow basin underneath the ice box which caught the water as it melted and dripped out. And when he emptied that great basin every morning, in that murky water floated bits of decayed food, shreds of newspapers, wet clotted wads of dirt and dead cockroaches, ten, sometimes thirty, floating on their hard brown shells, their thin threadlike feelers flattened into the water like innumerable streaks of watery blood. In his mind now his wife was standing with legs thrust apart, the gray enameled basin resting on the floor between her ankles. And falling slowly down from her body were decayed bits of food, the clotted dirt and the dead, brown-shelled cockroaches, falling end over end.

He raised himself up and called out, "Elfreida." There was no answer. He went into the bathroom and found her lying on the floor, her heavy breast pressed against the tile. He lifted her and brought her back to the bed and then saw she was crying silently, weakly. Suddenly it seemed as if he were standing far away, looking down at her and Eddie Cassin. He could see his own face reflected in the candles and the summer night and a great swift spear of terror went through his body. In his mind he cried out "God. God, help me. Please help me." He kissed her face, the great mouth and nose and yellow cheeks. "Stop crying," he said, "please stop crying. Your husband was a fine man, he wasn't a fairy. I was teasing."

And into his mind from long ago, he as a boy was listening to some one read the faintly remembered fairy tales. The word so beautiful then, the fairy tales, and like everything else once innocent, corrupted now. The voice reading, "Lost lost lost in the forest. Pity the lost princess." And into his mind came now as it had come then into his boy's mind, the picture of a virginal maiden with a crown and veil of white lace, the delicate features of an angel, the slight body of an undeveloped girl with no rotundity of hip or breast, no hint of nubility to mar the purity of her form. And then (was it in school or the bedroom of his home?) looking out the window, tear-blurred eyes sweeping over a forest of stone, he had wept silently and weakly, the imploring voice behind him softly saying, "Pity the lost beauty," and going on and on and on.

That night Hella and Mosca left the baby with Frau Saunders and strolled down to Metzer Strasse where Mosca still had his official billet. Mosca carried the blue gym bag in which were towels and clean underclothing.

They were both hot and dusty and looked forward to a leisurely bath. There was no heating boiler in Frau Saunders' house.

In front of the building stood Frau Meyer. She wore white slacks and a white blouse, presents from Eddie Cassin. She was smoking an American cigarette and looking curiously smug. "Hello, you two," she said, "You haven't been to see us for a long time."

"Don't tell me you're lonely," Mosca said.

Frau Meyer laughed, the buck teeth showing from the

pulled back mouth. "No, I'm never lonely. Not with such a house full of men."

Hella asked, "Frau Meyer, do you know if Leo has returned from Hamburg?"

Frau Meyer gave them a look of surprise. "Why, he returned Friday. Hasn't he been to see you?"

"No," Mosca said, "and I haven't seen him eating at the Rathskellar or the club."

The smug look was back on Frau Meyer's face. "He's in his room now with a wonderful black eye. I teased him about it but I could see he was angry so I left him alone."

"I hope he's not sick," Hella said. They went up the stairs and knocked on the door of Leo's room. Mosca knocked louder but there was no answer. He tried the door. It was locked.

"Old Meyer missed something for once," Mosca said, "he probably went out."

They went into Mosca's room and Mosca undressed and went to the bathroom at the end of the hall. He soaked in the tub for the time to smoke one cigarette, then washed quickly. When he came back to the room Hella was resting on the bed, cradling one side of her face in her hands.

"What's the matter?" Mosca asked.

"My tooth hurts," Hella said, "all that candy and ice cream I ate today."

"I'll take you to the dentist tomorrow," Mosca said.

"No, it will go away," Hella said. "I've had it before." She undressed as Mosca was dressing, put on the damp bathrobe and went down the hall.

Mosca was tying his shoelaces when he heard someone moving around in Leo's room. For one moment he thought it might be a German domestic looting and he called out sharply, "Leo?" He waited, then he heard Leo say through the wall, "It's me."

Mosca went out of his room and Leo had unlocked the door. When he entered Leo was already walking away from him and toward the bed.

"How come you didn't drop over?" Mosca asked.

Leo got onto the bed and when he turned to lay on his back Mosca saw his face. There was a dark-blue stain under one eye and a lump on the forehead. His face looked puffy and swollen.

Mosca stared at him for a moment then walked over to the table and sat by it. He lit a cigar. He had a good idea of what had happened, the headlines he had seen in *Stars and Stripes* last night. It hadn't registered then through all the beer.

There had been a picture of a ship sailing into the harbor of Hamburg. The ship was black with people. Underneath the picture was the story of how this ship had tried to make its way to Palestine carrying former inmates of concentration camps. The British had intercepted the ship and brought it to Hamburg. The people in it had refused to disembark and had been forced to do so by armed troops.

Mosca asked quietly. "You see that business up in Hamburg, is that it?"

Leo nodded. Mosca thought for a while, smoking, putting things together, the fact that Leo hadn't come to see them, hadn't answered their knock on the door.

"You want me to beat it?" he asked Leo.

Leo shook his head. "No," he said. "Stay a bit."

"Who hit you, the Limeys?"

Leo nodded. "I tried to keep them from beating a man they had taken off the boat. I got this." He pointed to his face. Mosca noticed there was no sign of the twitch, as if the muscles had been paralyzed with shock.

"How was it?"

Leo said evasively, "Didn't you read the paper?"

Mosca made an impatient gesture. "What happened?"

Leo sat on the bed, not speaking, and suddenly the tears were rolling down his face. The tic jerked the side of his face up and down and he put his hand to hold the flesh still. He burst out, "My father was wrong. My father was wrong."

Mosca didn't say anything and after a few moments Leo dropped his hands from his face. The tic had stopped. Leo said, "I saw them beating this man they had dragged down the gangplank. I said 'Don't do that,' I was really surprised and just pushed one of them away. The other said, 'Awright you Jew bawsted, you take some of his.' " Leo imitated the cockney accent perfectly. "When I was on the ground I saw the German dockworkers laughing at me, at all of us. I thought about my father then. I didn't think he was wrong, I just thought about him, what if he should see his son like this. What would he think then?"

Mosca said slowly. "I kept telling you, this is no place. Look, I'm going back to the States when the marriage papers go through. There's a rumor the air base is closing up so I'll be out of a job anyway. Why don't you come with us?"

Leo bowed his head in his hands. The proposal aroused no emotion in him, no desire to accept, no affection for Mosca, no feeling of kinship.

"The Jews are perfectly safe in America?" Leo asked bitterly.

"I think so," Mosca said.

"You just think so?"

"Nothing's sure," Mosca said.

Leo didn't say anything. He thought about the English soldiers in their rough woolen uniforms, the same men who had wept when they had liberated him and his fellow inmates, had stripped off their own clothes, emptied their trucks of food, and he had believed his father, human beings are good, man is moved easily to pity and more to love than to hate.

"No," he said to Mosca. "I can't go with you. I've arranged to go to Palestine. I leave in a few weeks." And then feeling he owed Mosca some explanation he said. "I don't feel safe any more except with my own people." And as he said this he realized that he was reproaching Mosca, that Mosca's affection for him was personal, that Mosca in a time of danger would defend him, Leo, but would not defend a Jew he did not know or did not care for. And this affection was no longer enough, could never give him real security. He would never feel safe, even in America, no matter what kind of material success he achieved. In the back of his mind would always be the fear that all security could be destroyed in a manner he could not fight against or control, and that even friends like Mosca would not fight against that force. The face of the liberator and torturer were one face, blended, friend and enemy only the enemy. He remembered a girl he had lived with shortly after coming out of Buchenwald, a thin and merry German girl with a gleeful and almost malicious grin. He had gone into the country and come back with a goose and a brace of chickens. And when he had told her of the low amount he had given she had looked up at him and said with a disturbing intonation and smile, "So, you are a good businessman." And yet now he realized or made himself realize the attitude of mind behind what she had said, he felt only a vague bitterness against her with the others. She had been tender and loving, she had cared about him, she had treated him with every consideration and fairness except for that one time. And yet, she and the many others like her had burned the blue numerals in his arm he would carry to his grave. And where could he escape these people? Not in America, certainly not in Germany. Where could he go?

Father—Father, he cried in his mind, you never told me that every human being carries his own barbed wire, his ovens, his canes of torture, wherever they go; you never taught me to hate, to destroy, and now when I'm humiliated, jeered at, I feel only shame not even anger, as if I deserved every blow, every insult and now where can I go? In Palestine I'll find barbed wire as surely as you found it in Heaven or in Hell. And then quite simply, clearly, as if really he had known it secretly for a long time, he thought, Father too was the enemy.

There was nothing more to think about. He saw Mosca still silent, still smoking his cigar.

"I leave in two weeks, I think, for Palestine, but I leave Bremen in a few days."

Mosca said slowly, "I guess you're right, Come over to the house before you leave."

"No," Leo said, "it's nothing personal. I don't want to see anybody."

Mosca understood. He rose and held out his hand. "O.K., Leo, here's luck." They shook hands. They could hear Hella opening the door of the other room.

"I don't want to see her," Leo said.

"O.K.," Mosca said and went out.

Hella had begun to dress. "Where were you?" she asked.

"With Leo, he's back."

"Good," she said, "call him in."

Mosca thought for a moment. "He doesn't want to see anybody right now. He had a little accident and hurt his face. I guess he doesn't want you to see him."

"That's silly," Hella said. When she had finished dressing she went out of the room and knocked on Leo's door. Mosca stayed in his own room, resting on the bed. He heard Leo open the door for Hella and listened as they spoke, their voices indistinct murmurs. He didn't want to go in, there was nothing he could do.

Mosca dozed off and when he woke he felt that it was very late, it was pitch dark in the room. He could still hear Leo and Hella talking in the other room. He waited for a few minutes and then he called out, "Hey, how about getting something to eat before the Red Cross closes up?" The voices broke off and started again. Then he heard Leo's door open and a moment later Hella came into the room and snapped on the light.

"I'm ready," she said, "let's go." He saw that she was biting her lips to keep from crying.

Mosca picked up the blue gym bag into which he had stuffed the wet towels and dirty underclothing. They went down the steps and out of the building. Frau Meyer was still standing on the steps. "Did you see our friend?" she asked. There was a slightly patronizing and amused tone in her voice.

"Yes," Hella said curtly.

On the way down the Kurfürsten Allee, Mosca asked, "He tell you everything?"

"Yes," Hella said.

"What the hell did you talk about so long in there?"

She didn't say anything for a time. "About when we

were children. He grew up in the city, and I was raised on the land but a lot of the same things happened to both of us. When we were children Germany was a nice country to live in."

"Everybody is leaving," Mosca said. "First Middleton, now Leo and pretty soon Wolf. That leaves just us and Eddie. I'll have to keep an eye on you and Eddie."

Hella looked at him without smiling. Her face was tired, the eyes a very pale gray. The blue lump had spread to a long welt the length of her jaw. "I want to leave now as soon as we can," she said. "I don't like Eddie, I don't like you to be with him. I know he is a good friend, he does things for us. But I'm afraid of him. Not about me but about you."

"Don't worry," Mosca said. "Our marriage papers will get here soon. We'll leave Germany in October."

When they were nearly home, Hella said tiredly, "Walter, do you think the world will get better for helpless people?"

"I don't know," he said, "but don't worry, we're not helpless."

Then to cheer her up he said, "I wrote my mother about the whole deal. She's real happy, especially that I'm going home. She just hopes I picked a good girl." They smiled at each other.

"I think I'm good," Hella said a little sadly. "I wonder about my father and mother, what they would think of me if they were alive. They wouldn't be happy." She paused for a moment. "I'm afraid they wouldn't think me a good girl."

"We're trying, baby," Mosca said, "we're trying like hell. It's a different world."

They turned into the little path that led to their home,

following a stream of moonlight to the door. Through the walls of the stone house they could hear the baby crying, not desperately, but in perfunctory protest. Hella smiled at Mosca. "That little stinker," she said, but she ran up the steps ahead of him.

# 19

IT WAS the first time Hella had ever come out to the air base, and Mosca went outside the wire fence to meet her and bring her past the guards. She was very slim and chic in a suit made from officer's pink. He had bought the material with Ann Middleton's Army store card. With the suit she wore a white silk blouse and white hat and veil. The veil screened her swollen cheek. She held onto Mosca's arm as they entered the gate of the air base.

In the Civilian Personnel Office, Inge left her desk and stood up to greet Hella. They shook hands and murmured their names. Herr Topp, the chief clerk, came in from the outer office with some papers for Eddie Cassin to sign. He was all smiles and pleasantness. "We have a great dentist on the air base, American dentists are the finest," Herr Topp assured Hella.

"Did you fix it with Captain Adlock sure?" Mosca asked Eddie.

Eddie nodded, then said to Hella gently, "How do you feel?"

"It hurts a bit," Hella said. She could feel the power that Eddie and Mosca held over the people here, how respectful Herr Topp and the girl Inge were, here the role of conqueror and conquered clean-cut, not blurred by sex or personal service. It made her shy of Eddie, and Mosca too, so that she said almost defensively to Eddie, "The German dentists couldn't help."

"We have the medicines they can't get," Eddie said reassuringly. "Captain Adlock will fix you up fine." He turned to Mosca. "You can take her over there now."

Hella and Mosca left the Civilian Personnel Office. In the outer room the German clerks stopped work, as if in interested surprise, to see that the ugly American with his curt manner and cruel face had chosen a seemingly shy, sweet girl, slender and tall, directly opposite to what they had thought his choice would be.

They penetrated to the interior of the air base, crossing the many walks that radiated to the hangars, the flying fields, the Administration Building, until finally they came to the long low barrack that served as the medical dispensary and base hospital.

The dental chair of black leather was empty as was the white-walled room. Then a German doctor in white smock came in. He said, "Captain Adlock asked me to attend you. He is busy at the moment. Please." He motioned Hella toward the dental chair.

She took off her hat and veil and gave them to Mosca. She put her hand to the swollen cheek as if to hide it, then sat in the dental chair. Mosca stood near her and she reached out her hand to hold his arm. The German dentist's eyes narrowed as he saw her swollen cheek. He helped her open her mouth wide, forcing the jaws apart gently but firmly. He took one long look. Then he turned to Mosca and said. "We can do nothing until the infection is cleared up. It goes all the way down to the root, the bone. She needs penicillin and hot compresses. When the swelling goes down I can take out the root."

Mosca said, "Can you give her the shots?"

The German dentist shrugged. "I cannot do it. The penicillin is locked up and only the American doctors have the authority to use it. Shall I call Captain Adlock?" Mosca nodded. The German left the room.

Hella raised her head to smile at Mosca, as if to apologize for the trouble she was causing. Only one side of her face twisted. Mosca smiled back and said, "It's O.K." He put the hat and veil on a chair.

They waited a long time. Finally Captain Adlock came in. He was a stout, young, kind-looking man who wore his uniform with a recruit's sloppiness, the tie loosely knotted and pulled down from the unbuttoned collar, his blouse open.

"Ah, let's see now," he said cheerfully and stuck his fingers impersonally into Hella's mouth to separate her teeth. "Yes, I'm afraid my boy is right." He nodded toward the elderly German dentist who had re-entered the room. "She has to get penicillin shots and compresses. When the swelling goes down we can fix her up with no trouble at all."

Mosca knew what the answer would be but he had to ask. "Can you give her the penicillin?" He realized that his voice sounded angry, surly, that he had worded the question the wrong way. He felt Hella's hand pressing on his arm.

"I'm sorry," Captain Adlock shook his head. "You know how it is. I don't mind breaking the regulations but if I did it for you every G.I. would bring his girl here. And the penicillin has to be strictly accounted for."

"I've got my marriage papers in," Mosca said. "Does that make any difference?"

"I'm sorry," Captain Adlock said. Mosca saw the genuine regret. The Captain was thoughtful. "Look, as soon as your papers come back from Frankfort approved let me know and I'll give her full treatment. We won't have to wait for you to actually get married. I wouldn't want to wait and fool around with an infection like that."

Hella put on her hat and veil. She murmured her thanks to the Captain, who patted her shoulder and said, "Now keep putting compresses on her cheek. Possibly the swelling will go down with just that. If it gets worse take her to the German hospital." As they went out the door, Mosca saw a look of doubt on the face of the elderly German dentist, as if it were all being taken too lightly.

Back in the Personnel Office, he told Eddie what had happened. Hella sat in the chair at Mosca's desk, seemingly calm, undistressed.

Eddie clucked with sympathy. He said, "Why don't you go up to the Adjutant's office and see if he can make Frankfort rush those papers through."

Mosca said to Hella, "Can you wait here a little while, or do you want to go home now?"

"I'll wait," she said, "but don't take so long." She squeeze his hand and her palm was wet with perspiration.

"You sure you're all right," he asked.

She nodded. Mosca left.

The Adjutant was speaking over the phone, his voice polite, the bland, ingenuous face courteous with attention to the dead instrument. He raised his eyebrow to show Mosca he would be through in a moment. When he hung up he said briskly, "What can I do for you?"

Mosca stumbled over the words, feeling defensive and overawed. Then he said. "I wonder if anything came through on my marriage papers?"

"No, nothing yet," the Adjutant said politely and began

leafing through a bound volume of Army regulations.

Mosca hesitated again and then said. "Is there any way of rushing them through?"

The Adjutant didn't look up. "No," he said.

Mosca resisted the impulse to turn away and leave. "Do you think if I went down to Frankfort it would help? Maybe you could tell me who to see?"

The Adjutant closed the thick, heavily bound book and looked up at Mosca for the first time. His voice was impersonal but curt. "Look, Mosca," he said, "you lived with this girl for a year, you didn't file an application for marriage until six months after the ban was lifted. Now all of a sudden there's a big rush. I can't stop you from going to Frankfort, but I guarantee it won't help. You know how I feel about working outside the channels."

Mosca felt no anger, only embarrassment and a sense of shame. The Adjutant went on in a softer tone. "As soon as they come in I'll let you know, O.K.?" And with this dismissal, Mosca left.

Walking back to the Personnel Office he tried not to feel depressed or anxious, knowing that Hella would see it in his face. But Hella and Inge were drinking coffee together and talking. Hella had her hat and veil off and she could only take little sips of coffee but he could see from her bright eyes that she had been telling Inge all about the baby. Eddie was leaning back in his chair, listening, smiling and when he saw Mosca he asked, "How did it go?"

Mosca said, "Fine, he'll do what he can," and smiled at Hella. He would tell Eddie the truth later.

Hella put on her hat and veil and shook hands with Inge. She shook hands with Eddie and then took Mosca's arm. When they were out of the office and had gone through the gate of the air base, Mosca said, "I'm sorry, baby." She turned her veiled face to him, squeezed his arm. He turned his head away as if he could not bear her gaze without flinching.

In the early morning hours before dawn Mosca came out of sleep and heard Hella crying softly, sobbing into her pillow. He pulled her to him so she could bury her head in his naked shoulder. "Is it that bad?" he whispered. And she said, "Walter, I feel so sick, I feel so sick." Saying the words seemed to frighten her and her crying became unrestrained like the weeping of a terrified child.

In the darkness the pain swept over her, took control of her blood and the organs of her body. The memory of Mosca at the air base powerless to help her gave her a sense of terror, made her helpless to restrain her tears. She said again, "I feel so sick," and Mosca could barely make out the words, there was a curious distortion in her speech. "I'll make you some more compresses," he said and turned on the night lamp beside the bed.

He was shocked when he saw her. In the dim yellow light the side of her face was distended, the eye almost closed. There was a strange contour of her facial bones, giving her a mongoloid look. She put her hands up over her face and he went out into the kitchen to get some water for the compresses.

The ruins of the city rode on two morning sunbeams straight into the stunned eyes of Yergen's daughter. She sat on a great stone dipping her fingers into an open tin of *mirabelle* plums. The smell of rubble was just beginning to rise from the earth. The little girl serenely fished out the yellow, waxlike globes of fruit and then licked the sticky juice from her fingers. Yergen sat on a stone beside her.

He had taken her to this secluded valley of ruins so that she could eat the rare delicacy without sharing it with the German woman who cared for her during the day.

Yergen watched his daughter's face with love and sadness. The eyes showed clearly the slow fragmentation and splintering of her childish brain. The doctor had told him that there was one hope, to get her out of Germany or the continent. Yergen shook his head. All the money he made in the black market went to build a wall between his child and the suffering, the misery of the world around her. But the doctor had made him understand that this was not enough. That it all seeped through somehow.

Now at this moment he made his decision. He would buy false papers and settle in Switzerland. It would take months to prepare and a great deal of money. She would be cured, she would grow and live to happiness.

She held up a gleaming *mirabelle*, shiny pale yellow in its coat of syrup and to please her he opened his mouth to receive it. She smiled at him and the smile made him put his hand on her face, in love and protection, for in this valley of ruins his daughter seemed like a plant growing, inhuman, her eyes blank, the smile a muscular spasm.

The morning air was cold, autumn had weakened the strength of the rising sun and changed the color of the earth, turned the rubble gray and patched it with dead brown grass.

Yergen said gently, "Giselle, come now, I must take you home, I must go to work." The child let the can of *mirabelles* slip from her hand, the heavy syrup spilled out, clotted over bits of stone and brick. She began to cry.

Yergen lifted her up from the great stone she sat on and held her, pressed her head against his neck. "I'll be home early tonight, don't fret. And I'll have a present, something to wear." But he knew she would continue to cry until he carried her up the church steps to their apartment in the steeple.

Framed against the pale sky, Yergen saw a man coming over a hill of ruins and then disappear and then come over another little hill, always coming toward him, coming out of the sun's light. Yergen put the girl down and she clung to his legs. The figure came over the last little rolling hill. Yergen was surprised to see that the man was Mosca.

He was wearing his officer greens with the white civilian patch. In the morning sunlight his dark skin had a grayish tinge and lines of tiredness in his face that cut the features away from each other, making each distinct in its own right.

"I been looking all over for you," Mosca said.

Yergen stroked his daughter's head. Neither looked directly at Mosca. Yergen felt a little strange that they could be found so easily. Mosca seemed to sense this. "Your housekeeper, she told me you usually come over this way mornings."

Daylight was now at full strength, Yergen could hear the clanging of the *Strassenbahn*. He asked slowly, mistrustfully, "Why do you want to see me?"

On one of the slopes surrounding them there was a shifting and falling of rubble, a tiny landslide that sent a small cloud of dust toward the sky. Mosca shifted his feet, he could feel them sinking in the treacherous ground. He said, "I need some morphine or codeine and some penicillin for Hella. You know about that tooth. She's become really ill." He paused awkwardly. "I need it today, the morphine, she's in very bad pain. I'll pay anything you say."

Yergen picked up his daughter and began to walk over the ruins. Mosca walked beside him. "That will be very hard to do," Yergen said, but everything had already clicked together in his mind. At one stroke he would come three months closer to Switzerland. "The price will be terribly high."

Mosca stopped, and though the morning sun had no fire Yergen saw that the sweat was pouring off his face, and Yergen saw in that face an enormous relief.

"Christ," Mosca said, "I was scared you couldn't swing it. I don't care what I pay, you can steal me blind. Just get the stuff tonight."

They were standing now on the last hill and before them was that part of the city not completely destroyed, with the church Yergen lived in. "Come to me at midnight," Yergen said. "Don't come in the evening, my daughter will be alone and she is very ill, she must not be frightened." He waited for Mosca to make an expression of sympathy and felt an angry bitterness when none came. This American so concerned about his mistress, why didn't he take her to America and safety? And the fact that Mosca could do for someone he loved what he could not do for his daughter increased the bitterness in Yergen. He said almost spitefully, "If you come before midnight, I won't help you."

Mosca stood on top of the hill and watched Yergen sliding down it, the child cradled in his arms. He called after him. "Don't forget, pay anything to get the stuff." Yergen turned and nodded, the child's face in his arms staring directly upward to the autumn sky.

# 20

EDDIE CASSIN and Mosca left the Civilian Personnel Building, walked through the gray autumn twilight toward the hangars and the take-off strip.

"Another guy leaving the old gang," Eddie Cassin said. "First Middleton, Leo, now Wolf. I guess you'll be next, Walter."

Mosca didn't answer. They were walking against the stream of workers leaving the base, German laborers and mechanics moving toward the guarded exits. Suddenly the ground began to shake and they could hear the roar of powerful engines. Rounding a corner of the Administration Building, they came upon the great, silvery plane.

The late afternoon sun was far away across the sky. Mosca and Eddie waited, smoking cigarettes. Finally they saw the jeep come past the hangars and onto the field. They started down the ramp toward the plane and reached it the moment the jeep swung around its finned tail and came to a stop.

Wolf, Ursula and Ursula's father got out of the jeep, the father unloading the heavy Val-packs at once. Wolf gave his friends a huge, joyful grin.

"It's damn nice of you guys to see me off," he said and shook their hands, then introduced them to the father. They knew Ursula.

The propellers blasted great gusts of air that almost blew

the words away. The father went close to the airplane, ran his hands over the gray skin, then prowled around it like a hungry animal.

Eddie Cassin said jokingly to Wolf, "He going to stow away?" And Wolf laughed and said, "He couldn't stow away on the *Queen Elizabeth*."

Ursula had not understood. She watched with quick darting eyes the luggage being carried aboard the plane, then put her hand on Wolf's arm.

Wolf extended his hand again to Mosca and Eddie and said, "Well, so long you guys. It's been a pleasure, no kidding. When you get to the States, look me up. Eddie, you got my address."

"Sure thing," Eddie said coolly.

Wolf looked into Mosca's eyes and said, "Good luck, Walter. I'm sorry that deal didn't go through, but now maybe I think you're right."

Mosca smiled and said, "Good luck, Wolf."

Wolf hesitated. Then he said. "One last piece of advice. Don't wait too long to get out of here, Walter. Get back to the States as soon as you can. That's all I can say."

Mosca smiled again and said, "Thanks, Wolf, I will."

The father came waddling around the nose of the plane. He came close to Wolf, arms extended. "Wolfgang, Wolfgang," he cried out emotionally, "you will not forget me here, Wolfgang?" He was close to tears. Wolf patted his shoulder and the fat old man embraced him. "You are like a son to me," the old man said, "I will miss you."

Mosca could see that Wolf was annoyed, bored and anxious to be off. The father took Ursula into his arms. He was sobbing now. "Ursula, my daughter, my little daughter, you're the only one I have, you won't forget your old father, you won't leave him all alone in this terrible land, eh? My little Ursula would not do such a thing?"

His daughter kissed him and murmured comfortingly, "Papa, don't take on so, you will come too as soon as I can make the papers. Please don't take on so."

Wolf had a tight little smile on his face. He touched Ursula on the shoulder and said in German, "It is time."

The fat old man let out a wail, "Ursula, Ursula." But now the girl, herself overwrought, with guilty anger at this unseemly grief for her good fortune, tore herself away and ran up the steps into the plane.

Wolf took the old man's hand. "You've upset her. Now I promise. You will leave here. You will spend the rest of your days in America with your daughter and your grandchildren. Here is my hand on it."

The old man nodded his head. "You are good, Wolfgang, you are very good."

Wolf gave Eddie and Mosca an embarrassed half-salute, then quickly went up the steps into the plane.

Through one of the windows Ursula's face appeared grimacing a farewell through dirt-streaked glass to her father. He burst into tears again and waved a great white handkerchief to her in return. The engines roared into sound again. Ground-crew men wheeled the mobile stairs away. The great silvery plane began to move slowly, pushing itself along the ground. It made a slow, seemingly wing-dragging turn and rolled away faster and faster until reluctantly, as if fighting some malignant power, it parted itself from the earth and flew toward the dark autumn sky.

Mosca watched the plane until it disappeared. Then he heard Eddie saying, "Mission accomplished, a successful man leaves Europe." There was only a faint note of bitterness in his voice.

The three of them stood silently staring at the sky, their

shadows blending into one great shadow as the sun escaped the autumn clouds before it fell below the horizon. Mosca looked at the old fat man who would never see his daughter again, who would never leave this continent. That great meat-creased face stared dumbly into the empty sky, as if searching for some hope or promise and then the small slitted eyes rested on Mosca, the voice thick with hate and despair, said, "Ach, my friends, it is gone from us."

Mosca dipped the linen rag into the hot pan of water and after wringing it out, applied the steaming cloth to Hella's face. She lay on the sofa, tears of pain in her eyes, the swollen flesh pulling the nose out of line and twisting the side of her mouth, making a grotesque distortion of the left eye. In the armchair near the foot of the sofa Frau Saunders held the baby, tilting the nippled bottle so that the infant could feed more easily.

As he kept changing compresses, Mosca spoke to Hella softly, soothingly. "We'll keep this up a couple of days and everything will be O.K., just hold still now." They had been sitting so all afternoon and the swelling had gone down a little. The baby in Frau Saunders' arms began to cry and Hella sat up on the sofa and reached for him. She pushed the compress away and said to Mosca, "I can't any more." She took the baby from Frau Saunders. She put the good side of her face against the infant's head and crooned softly, "Poor little baby, your mother can't look after you." And then with fumbling hands she began to change the wet diapers, Frau Saunders helping her.

Mosca watched. He saw that the continual pain and lack of sleep for the last week had drained her of strength. The German hospital doctors had said her case was not serious enough to warrant penicillin. His only hope was that Yergen would have the drugs for him at midnight, to-night. The last two nights Yergen had disappointed him.

Hella finished dressing the baby and Mosca took the child from her. He cradled the infant in his arms and watched Hella try to smile at him as she lay back on the sofa. As he watched he saw the tears of pain start to her eyes, and she turned her head away from him. He could hear the small, uncontrollable whimpers.

Mosca stood it as long as he could then he put the child back in the carriage. "I'm going to see if Yergen has the medicine," he said. It was a long way to midnight but the hell with it. He might catch Yergen home. It was near eight, the German supper time. He leaned over to kiss Hella and she put up her hand to touch his face. "I'll be back as soon as I can."

The Kurfürsten Allee was chilled with the first cold of winter and in the darkness he could hear the falling leaves sifting along the ground to become lost in the ruins of the city. He caught a *Strassenbahn* to the church in which Yergen lived. The side entrance was open, and he ran up the steps to the steeple. Standing a step below the door which was cut into the wall he knocked as hard as he could. He waited, there was no answer, no sound behind the door. He tried a variation of knocks, hoping that by some chance he would hit on Yergen's signal and the child would open the door and he could question her. But for some reason he did not call out. He waited again for some moments and then he heard a curious animal-like sound, monotonous, on one level shrilling tone and realized that the child behind the door was crying and would in her terror never open the door. He went down the stairs and waited outside the church for Yergen.

He waited for a long time. The wind became colder and

the night darker, the rustling of the trees and falling leaves louder and more sibilant. As he stood there waiting there grew in him a sense of certain and terrible disaster. He tried to remain still but suddenly was walking away from the church and down Kurfürsten Allee.

As soon as he had left the church and walked a few minutes the fear left him. Then the thought of watching helplessly the tears and pain he would be sure to see made him stop. All the strain and tension, the humiliations and refusals of the past week, the turning away by Dr. Adlock, the rebuke by the Adjutant, the dismissal by the German hospital doctors, and his inability to fight back in any way against them—all this overwhelmed him. He wanted a drink, three or four drinks, so bad that he was surprised. He had never needed liquor. But now, without hesitating any longer, he turned and started walking toward the avenue that led to the Officers' Club. He felt for one moment a sense of shame that he was not going home.

It was a quiet night at the club. There were some officers at the bar, but no music or dancing and only a few women. Mosca had three shots of whiskey very quick. It worked like magic. He could feel the tension flow out of his body, the fear, and he saw everything in correct proportion, that Hella had only a bad tooth and that the people who seemed such implacable enemies were only obeying laws imposed by others.

One of the officers at the bar said to him, "Your friend Eddie is upstairs shooting crap." Mosca nodded acknowledgment and another officer said with a grin, "Your other buddy is up there too, the Adjutant. He's celebrating making Major."

"I gotta have a drink on that," Mosca said and they laughed. Mosca unbuttoned his jacket and lit a cigar and had a few more drinks. He felt warm and sure that things would turn out all right. Hell, it was only a toothache, and he knew Hella was extra-sensitive to pain. It was funny how she had courage in everything except physical pain, he thought. She was a real coward about that. Not coward; he felt a sudden rush of anger at himself that he thought of such a word in connection with her. But she cried easy. And now some of the warmness left him. In the inside pocket of his open jacket he caught a flash of white and remembered that a few days ago Hella had written her first letter to his mother and he had forgotten to mail it. His mother had written asking for a letter and pictures of the baby. Mosca left the bar and dropped the letter in the mail box in the hall. He hesitated for a moment, somewhere in his mind was a faint warning not to go up, but the whiskey clouded over it. He went upstairs to the game room.

Eddie was at a corner of the table, in one hand a small sheaf of dollar scrip bills. The Adjutant was opposite him and there was something strange about the Adjutant. The ingenuous face was flushed and twisted into an expression of slyness. Mosca felt a sense of shock. Christ, the guy was loaded. For one moment he thought of turning and going out. But then curiosity made him go to the dice table. He thought, let's see if the bastard gets human on a drunk.

Eddie asked, "How's your girl?" Mosca said, "All right." A waiter came upstairs and into the room with a tray of drinks.

The game was slow—relaxation, not gambling. Mosca liked it that way tonight. He made small bets, talking casually to Eddie.

The Adjutant was the only one playing with gusto. He tried everything to goad the players into higher action. When his turn came to shoot he laid down thirty dollars.

Only ten was faded. He offered bets in various fashions, but the players, seemingly out of perversity, refused to become excited and continued to bet in one- or five-dollar amounts.

Mosca felt a little guilty. He thought, "I could leave and go home and see how Hella is and then go to Yergen." But in another hour the club would close for the night. He decided to stay.

The Adjutant, looking now for any kind of excitement and giving up hope of finding it in the game, said to Mosca. "I hear you had your *Fräulein* out to the base for some free medical treatment. You should know better than that, Walter." It was the first time he had ever used Mosca's given name.

One of the officers said, "For Christ sake, relax, don't talk shop in the club."

And in that moment Mosca knew why he had stayed, why he had come to the club. He tried to make himself leave now, tried to make his body move away from the table, tried to take his hands off the green felt. But the cruel satisfaction rose in his body and flooded over his mind and reason. All the humiliations and defeats of the past week poisoned his blood, the vessels of his brain. He thought, "All right you son of a bitch, all right, all right." But he kept his voice casual, saying, "I just thought the Doc might help." Making it sound a little nervous. He'd eaten shit all week, just this little more won't hurt.

"Things like that don't happen where I'm running things," the Adjutant said. "And when it does, and I find out, it's usually somebody's ass. And I usually find out."

"I'm not a prick," the Adjutant went on in a serious tone. "I believe in fair play. But if he treated your *Fräulein* all the G.I.'s would start bringing their clapped-up *Fräuleins* to the base for shots. Can't have that." The Adjutant's ingenuous face had a boyish, happy smile. He raised his glass and took a long drink.

Mosca stared at the dice, at the green cloth on the table. Eddie was saying something but the words were jumbled up. He made an effort and looked up. He said quietly, "I'll shoot the two bucks there."

The Adjutant put his glass on the window sill behind him, then threw a ten-dollar bill on the table. "I got you," he said.

Mosca picked up the bill and threw it back at the Adjutant. "Don't you fade me." He said it in a cold, deliberate voice. One of the other officers threw some money down and Mosca rolled the dice.

"You're pretty touchy about that *Fräulein,*" the Adjutant said. He was in a good humor, did not sense any of the tension around him. "Maybe you think those *Fräuleins* have a pure, disinterested love for your homely mugs. If it were up to me I wouldn't let any of you chumps marry here."

Mosca let the dice drop on to the table. In an almost indifferent, casual voice he asked. "That why you held up my papers, you sneaky bastard?"

The Adjutant smiled with real delight. "I'll have to deny that and ask where you got your information." He said this with his coldly formal, official manner, in it a note of menace and command.

Mosca picked up the dice. He had stopped thinking or caring. He was just waiting for the Adjutant to pass him.

"Where did you get that information?" the Adjutant asked. His bland face was serious, had its familiar look of youthful sternness. "Where did you get that information?" he repeated.

Mosca rattled the dice and threw them out carelessly. He said to the Adjutant, "You stupid prick, go scare some krauts."

Eddie Cassin broke in, "I told him and if the Colonel wants to know, I'll tell him the story. That you let the papers lay for two weeks before you sent them to Frankfort." He turned to Mosca, "Come on, Walter, let's get out of here."

The Adjutant was on that side of the table hemmed by the wall and window. Mosca wanted him to come out, to squeeze by the corner. He thought for a moment, then said, "You think this fuck gets away with it tonight?"

There was a split second before the Adjutant recognized the threat. Then, he shouted angrily, "Let's see what you'll do about it," and started to come around the table. Mosca waited until the corner would pin his arms. Then he swung as hard as he could at the profiled face. The blow glanced off the Adjutant's cheekbone and skull not hurting him, but making him fall. Mosca kicked viciously underneath the table. He felt the heel meet with a solid shock against bone. Then an officer and Eddie were pulling him away. The Adjutant, really hurt now, was put on his feet. Submissively Mosca let the officer and Eddie push him toward the door. Suddenly Mosca whirled and ran across the room. The Adjutant was standing straight up. Running he swung as hard as he could into the Adjutant's side and they both fell on the floor. The Adjutant screamed with pain. The look on Mosca's face and his attack on the defenseless man so horrified the other men that for one second they were frozen motionless. Then three of the officers swarmed over Mosca as he put his fingers inside the Adjutant's ear and tried to tear the side of his face off. One of them hit Mosca a stunning blow on the temple and then they were hustling him down the stairs and out of the club. There was no thought of retaliation in this, Eddie was helping them. The cold night air cleared Mosca's brain.

He and Eddie were alone. "That last shot queered everything," Eddie said. "Why the hell couldn't you be satisfied?"

Mosca said, "I wanted to kill the bastard, that's why." But the reaction had set in. He couldn't keep his hands from shaking when he lit his cigarette and he felt a chilly sweat over his body. Christ, he thought, over a lousy fist fight, trying to keep his hands still.

They stood together in the dark street. "I'll try to fix it," Eddie said, "but you're washed up with the Army. You know that? Don't wait, shoot down to Frankfort tomorrow and try to get those marriage papers. I'll cover you here. Don't worry about anything but the papers."

Mosca thought for a moment. "I guess that's it. Thanks Eddie." For some reason he shook hands with Cassin, awkwardly, knowing that Eddie would do everything he could to help.

"You going home now?" Eddie asked.

"No," Mosca said. "I have to see Yergen." He turned and walked away from Eddie, then called back over his shoulder, "I'll phone you from Frankfort."

A cold, autumn moon lit his way to the church. He ran up the steps and before he could knock Yergen had opened the door.

"Be very still," Yergen said, "my daughter has just fallen asleep after much trouble." They went into the room. Behind the wooden partition came the sound of the child's heavy breathing. Mosca could hear a curiously halting stitch in it. He saw that Yergen was angry and almost belligerent.

"Were you here earlier this evening?" Yergen asked.

"No," Mosca lied. But he had hesitated a fraction of a second and Yergen knew.

"I have the drugs for you," Yergen said. He was glad that Mosca had frightened his child and given him the angry courage to do what he must do. "I have the penicillin vials and the codeine tablets, but they cost a great deal." He took out of his pocket a small cardboard box, uncovered it to show Mosca the four dark-brown vials and the square box of large, red-shelled codeine tablets. Even now his instinct was to tell Mosca that the penicillin had only cost a fraction of the usual black-market price and therefore might be useless; to charge him a reasonable price for the drugs. But in that wavering moment there was a great stitching gasp in his daughter's breathing, the room was completely still. He could see Mosca looking at the wooden partition, then before either of them could move, the breathing started again, regularly, in the heavy rhythm of sleep. Yergen relaxed. "The cost will be fifty cartons of cigarettes." He saw the tiny black lights in Mosca's eyes focusing on him with a sudden cruel insight and understanding.

"All right," Mosca said. "I don't care what I pay. You sure it's good stuff?"

In time Yergen paused only for a moment but many thoughts flashed through his mind.

He needed as many cigarettes as possible, then he could swing a big deal he had planned and be out of Germany in a month. Hella probably did not really need penicillin, the Bremen doctors when they knew a girl had an American friend always asked for penicillin so that they could keep some for themselves. And he thought of his daughter again, she came before everything.

"You can be certain. I guarantee it," Yergen said. "This source has never betrayed me." He touched his breast with his hand. "I take the responsibility."

"All right," Mosca said. "Now listen. I have twenty cartons, maybe I can get some more. If I can't I'll pay you at the rate of five dollars a carton in scrip or American Express checks. Is that O.K.?" He knew that he was being fair and that Yergen was making a real steal, but the reaction of his encounter with the Adjutant still affected him. He felt an immense weariness, hopelessness and isolation. In his mind he bowed before the little German, asked for pity, for mercy. And Yergen, sensing this, became cautiously arrogant.

"I have to pay in cigarettes," Yergen said, "I think you will have to give me cigarettes."

Behind the wooden partition the little girl moaned in her sleep. Mosca remembered Hella whimpering with pain, she had expected him home long ago.

He made a last try. "I need this stuff tonight."

Yergen said, "I must have the cigarettes tonight." This time there was a malicious note of triumph in his voice, unconsciously, not knowing that he had spoken so, that he had always hated this American.

Mosca made himself not feel anything, not do anything. He was ashamed now and fearful of what would happen because of the fight in the club. He had to be careful not to make any mistakes. Gravely, without anger or menace, he picked up the cardboard box and slipped it into his jacket. He said politely, reasonably, "Come to the house with me and I'll give you the twenty cartons tonight and the money. I'll try to get you the rest of the cigarettes in the next few days and then you give the mcney back."

Yergen saw that nothing could keep Mosca from leaving with the drugs. He felt a moment of fear, a weakness of blood. He was no coward but was always afraid that his daughter would be left alone in the ruined land. He went behind the partition to arrange the blankets over his sleeping child and then went through the doorway of the other partition for his hat and coat. They walked to Mosca's house without exchanging a word.

Mosca let Yergen wait for his pay until he had given Hella a codeine tablet. She was still awake and he could see in the dark the white outline of the swollen jaw.

"How is it?" he asked softly, speaking almost in a whisper so as not to awaken the baby in the carriage.

She whispered to him, "It hurts very much."

"Here's something for the pain." He gave her one of the large, red-shelled codeine tablets and he could see her pushing it down her throat with her finger and then drinking the water from the glass he held to her lips. "I'll be right back," he said.

He made a package, bulky and untidy, of the cigarette cartons. He brought it to the door and gave it to Yergen, then took from his wallet the American Express checks, signed them, and put the blue thin paper in Yergen's pocket. Out of politeness and some remorse, he asked, "Will you have trouble because of curfew? Shall I take you back?"

"No, I have a curfew pass," Yergen said, and then with a soft laugh, the bulky cigarettes under his arm cheering him up, "an essential businessman."

Mosca let him out, locked the door and returned to the

bedroom. Hella was still awake. He lay down beside her, not undressing. He told her what had happened at the club and that he had to go to Frankfort the next day.

"I'll get those papers and in a month we'll be out of here, on a plane to the States," he whispered to her. He told her stories about his mother and Alf and how glad they would both be to see her. He made it all sound sure and easy, inevitable. He could feel her getting warm and sleepy and then suddenly she asked, "Can I have another tablet?" He got up to give it to her and held the water to her lips again. Then before she fell asleep he told her about the penicillin and to go to a doctor the next day to get some shots. "I'll call up every night from Frankfort," he said. "I won't be away three days even." When she fell into a sleep in which she did not even breathe he smoked a few cigarettes in a chair by the window, watching the ruins of the city fresh and clear in the autumn moonlight. Then he put on the light in the kitchen and packed his blue gym bag with the few things he would need for the trip. He made himself some eggs and tea, hoping the food would help him sleep. He lay beside Hella again and waited for dawn.

# 21

THROUGH THE CURTAIN of heavy, exhausted slumber and codeine Hella heard the short angry wails of hunger. Fully awake it gave her a feeling of pleasant anxiety, knowing how easily she could still the infant; she listened, then left her bed to prepare the bottle.

She felt weak though she had slept well the last two nights. The constant use of codeine had taken effect and the pain in her head and mouth was numbed. She reached up and felt surprised and shocked that her fingers and cheek met so quickly. Her face had swollen even more during the night but she had felt no pain. Waiting for the baby's milk to heat she took another codeine tablet, shoving it down her throat with her finger. It was hard now to swallow saliva. Then she brought the child his bottle and absolute quiet descended on the room.

She was very tired and she stretched out on the bed again. In the other rooms she could hear Frau Saunders moving about, cleaning her own two rooms and the living room they shared. They had been lucky with Frau Saunders, Hella thought. And Walter liked her. She hoped he would bring the marriage papers so they could leave Germany. Now she was always afraid, more about the child than anything. That if the child became ill they could not get any American medicines. They couldn't take chances on the black market where the baby was concerned.

When she felt a little stronger Hella rose from the bed and cleaned her own rooms. Then she went into the living room. Frau Saunders was already sitting by the iron stove and drinking coffee. There was a filled cup waiting for Hella.

"When is your man coming back?" Frau Saunders asked. "Wasn't he supposed to have come this morning?"

"He has to stay a few days longer," Hella said. "He will have definite news when he calls tonight on the telephone. You know what documents are."

"Have you told him about the penicillin?" Frau Saunders asked.

Hella shook her head.

"I thought this Yergen was really a friend of yours," Frau Saunders said. "How could he possibly do such a thing?"

"I don't think it was his fault," Hella said. "The doctor told me it was impossible to use because it hadn't been properly cared for. It was really penicillin. Yergen would have no way of knowing."

"He must have known," Frau Saunders said. Then dryly, "He will find his profit small when Herr Mosca goes to visit him."

In the other room the baby began to cry and Hella went to bring him out. Frau Saunders said, "Let me hold him." Hella gave her the baby and went for some clean diapers.

When she brought the fresh linen into the room Frau Saunders said, "Here, let me change him." It was a ritual they went through in the morning. Hella took the empty iron pail beside the stove and said, "I'll go down for some briquets."

"You're not strong enough yet for that," Frau Saunders said. But she was tickling the baby and spoke automatically.

The morning air was iced with autumn, dying summer sunlit trees and fallen leaves with dark-brown and reddish fire. From somewhere Hella could smell a deep, cidery tang of fallen apples; beyond the rising, gardened hills she could smell the freshness of the Weser River newly washed by autumn rains. On the other side of the Kurfürsten Allee she saw a young, pretty girl with four small children playing underneath the trees, kicking dead brown leaves piled high as snowdrifts. Then she felt very cold and went inside.

She went down the cellar stairs and unlocked the wire-mesh door which enclosed her portion of the basement. She filled the pail with oblong coal briquets. She tried to pick up the pail and to her surprise found that she could not. She made a great effort. The strength drained out of her body and she felt faint. For one moment she was frightened. She held onto the wire screen and the faintness faded away. She took three of the briquets and put them in her apron, holding the ends of it to form a basket. She snapped the lock of the wire door with her one free hand and then began to climb the stairs.

Halfway up the last flight her legs refused to move. She stood for a moment in surprise, unaware. A terrible chill struck her body. A great vessel burst and pain stabbed through her brain like an iron pike so that she did not hear the coal slip out of her apron and crash down the stairs. As in terror she began to fall, she saw Frau Saunders' veiled face leaning over the bannister, the baby in her arms, seeing them hazily but very close. She raised her arms to them and began to scream and then began to fall away from Frau Saunders' horrified face and the white swaddled baby, and still screaming, fell away from her own screams so that she never heard them.

# 22

EDDIE CASSIN paced up and down the Civilian Personnel Office. Inge was patiently explaining to someone at the other end that she must have the information. Then she would be switched to someone else and begin the same explanation over again.

She motioned to Eddie to come to the phone. "Yes," Eddie said into the phone.

The voice of a man, speaking almost perfect English, heavy with authority, said, "I am sorry, we cannot give information over the phone."

Eddie knew it would be hopeless to argue with that voice. He recognized the tone. The confidence of a man complying strictly with laws and regulations which governed his own little but complete world. He said, "Let me ask one thing. The woman you have in your hospital, her husband or her lover, what you will, is in Frankfort. Now. Is it serious enough that I should tell him to return immediately to see her?"

The heavy voice said, "I would advise that you do so."

Eddie Cassin said, "He is there on important business. He would not wish to return, unless it is absolutely necessary."

There was a short silence. Then the heavy voice with a surprising gentleness, said, "I think you should tell him that he must come."

Eddie hung up. He saw Inge was watching him, wide-eyed. He said, "Get me a clean glass." When she went out he picked up the phone and asked the Army operator to get him the line to Frankfort. He was still waiting when Inge came back with the glass. He let her hold the phone and made himself a strong drink from the bottle of gin and tin of grapefruit juice in his desk. Then he took back the phone.

When he got through to Frankfort, he asked for the Adjutant Section of the headquarters. He talked to three officers before he learned that Mosca had been there the day before and was now probably in the Legal Section. When he got through to the Legal Section they told him that Mosca had left an hour before. They didn't have any idea where he would be now. Eddie hung up the phone and finished his drink. He made another and picked up the phone again. He thought a moment, then when he got the Frankfort line, he asked for the message center in the I. G. Farben Building. A Sergeant answered and he explained briefly why he had to locate Mosca and asked him if he would broadcast a message over the loudspeaker for Mosca to come to the phone. The Sergeant told him to wait. Then he came back to say that the announcement would go on and that he should hold on.

Eddie waited for a long time. He had finished the second drink. Suddenly Mosca's voice came over the phone, saying, "Hello, who is this?" There was only surprise in the voice, no anxiety.

Eddie couldn't speak for a moment. Then he said, "Walter, it's Eddie. How are you making out?"

Mosca said, "I don't know yet, they just chase me from one office to another. Is anything wrong up there?"

Eddie cleared his throat. He spoke casually. "I guess

you'll have to let that deal go, Walter. Your landlady sent a messenger to Meyer that Hella was taken to the hospital. Meyer sent the messenger out to the base and I called the hospital. They wouldn't give any information over the phone but it sounds serious."

There was a pause and then Mosca's voice came over the wire, haltingly, as if he were searching for the words. "You really don't know anything else?"

"I swear to Christ," Eddie said. "But you better come back."

There was a still longer pause. Then Mosca said, "I'll catch the night train at six o'clock. Meet me at the station, Eddie. I think we get in about four in the morning."

"Sure," Eddie said. "I'm going down to the hospital as soon as I hang up. O.K.?"

"O.K. Thanks, Eddie." There was a click on the other end and Eddie Cassin hung up.

He made himself another quick drink. He said to Inge, "I won't be back today." He put the bottle and juice in his brief case and left the air base.

The city of Bremen was dark when Mosca got off the train from Frankfort. It was not quite four in the morning. In the square outside the station an olive-drab Army bus waited, barely visible. The square was illuminated only by a few weak lampposts which scattered tiny scars of light through its corners and down the streets away from the station.

Mosca looked in the waiting room, but there was no sign of Eddie Cassin. He looked up and down the street but there was no jeep waiting.

He stood uncertainly for a few moments, then followed the streetcar tracks down the Schwachhauser Heer

Strasse, swinging off into the long, curving Kurfürsten Allee, not conscious of the blue gym bag he was carrying, carefully picking his way through the ruins of the ghostly city. He never knew afterward why he did not go directly to the hospital.

As Mosca approached his home he saw in the darkness of the city one single light burning and knew it was the light in his apartment. He turned into the little gravel path. As he ran up the steps he could hear the baby crying.

He opened the door of the living room and saw Frau Saunders seated on the sofa, facing him, watching the door, pushing the baby carriage back and forth across the rug. The infant's cries were patient, hopeless, as if nothing could ease or still it. Mosca saw that Frau Saunders' face was white and strained with fatigue, the usually neat, tightly drawn-back hair now loose and straggly around her head.

He stood in the door waiting for her to speak but saw that she was frightened and would not do so.

He asked, "How is she?"

"She is in the hospital," Frau Saunders said.

"I know. How is she?"

Frau Saunders didn't answer. She stopped pushing the baby carriage and put her hands over her face. The baby's wails became louder. Frau Saunders' body began to rock back and forth. "Oh, how she screamed," she said, "oh, how she screamed." Mosca waited. "She fell down the stairs and screamed," Frau Saunders said, weeping.

She let her hands fall away from her face as if she could no longer hide her grief. She began to push the carriage back and forth again. The baby was still. Frau Saunders looked at Mosca waiting patiently in the doorway. "She is dead, she died in the evening. I waited for you." She saw Mosca still waiting there patiently, as if she had not said anything, as if he were still waiting for her to speak.

He felt only a numbness, like a tight fragile shell to keep out pain and light. He heard Frau Saunders say, "She died in the evening," again, and he believed her but could not accept it as truth. He went out of the house and through the dark streets. When he came to the hospital he followed the arc of the great iron fence until he came to the main gate.

Mosca went into the Administration Office. Behind the night-duty desk was a nun in the great white hat of her religious medical order. Then on a bench against the wall he saw Eddie Cassin.

Eddie rose and stood awkwardly. He nodded to the nun. She motioned Mosca to come with her.

Mosca followed the great white hat down the long silent corridors. He heard in the stillness, the exhausted sleeping breath of the sick. At the end of the corridor they weaved through black-clad charwomen who knelt and scrubbed the tiled floors white.

They turned into another corridor. The nun opened the door of a small room and he entered behind her. She stepped off to one side and closed the door.

Mosca took a step into the room and in the corner, framed in the white pillow, he saw Hella's face, her body covered with a white sheet to the neck. He could not see clearly and took another step into the room.

Her eyes were closed and the side of her face was no longer swollen, as if the poison and life had fled her body together. The mouth was colorless, almost white. There was no spot of red anywhere. There were no lines in her face and she looked younger than he had ever remembered; but the face was vacant, the great hollows of her closed eyes giving it the effect of blindness.

Mosca went nearer and stood beside the bed and on the sill of the draped window he could not see there stood a great vase filled with white flowers. He looked down at Hella, feeling confused, knowing now he must accept the fact of her death but not knowing what to do, not able to think or feel. Death not being strange to him in its violent form, but now seeing it as it came disguised, seeing for the first time someone he had kissed and loved physically no longer possible to contact, feeling a revulsion to the dead form here, having seen what a body became after death. He reached down to touch the blind eyes and touched her cold face and put his hand on the white sheet which covered her body. He heard a curiously crackling sound and drew down the sheet a little further.

Her body was enclosed in a shroud of heavy brown wrapping paper and he could see that underneath there were no clothes. Behind him the nun whispered, "Many wish it so, they need the clothing."

He had drawn the sheet with arrogant certainty, with faith in the armor he had grown against grief, trusting his memory of the terrible years to shield him now. But he thought, she has enough clothes to be buried in, I can do that for her. And suddenly a thousand enemies came coursing through his blood, the bile rose in his throat, a giant hand cramped the beat of his heart, drowned all light. Then without knowing how, he found himself outside the room, leaning against the wall of the corridor.

The nun waited patiently for him. Finally Mosca said to her, "I'll bring some proper clothes, will you dress her for me?" The nun made a motion of assent.

He left the hospital and began to walk. He followed the perimeter of the fence. Though it was not yet light he became conscious of the *Strassenbahn* going by and people passing him in the streets. The curfew had ended. He kept turning into deserted streets but as he entered them people seemed to spring out of the rubbled earth and buried apartments. Then there was a cold wintry sun and a pale light over the earth and he found himself on the edge of the town, walking into the countryside. The air was very cold. Mosca made himself stop.

He accepted it all now and was not surprised that everything had turned out badly. There was left only a tired hopelessness, and far down in his being a shameful guilt.

He thought of what he must do; bring a dark-colored dress to the hospital for Hella to be buried in, make arrangements for the funeral. Eddie could help him, would arrange everything. He turned back and felt something at his arm. He looked down and saw that he was still carrying the blue gym bag. He was very tired and had a long walk before him so he let it drop in the deep wet grass. He lifted his eyes to the light of the frozen morning sun and started to walk back into the city.

# 23

A TINY CARAVAN passed through the huge central gate of black iron, left the hospital grounds and entered the surrounding city. Gray, early morning light shrouded the ruins with ghostly sheets of vapor.

The ambulance carrying Hella's coffin led the way. The jeep, open to the wind, followed slowly behind, Eddie and Mosca hunched down to escape the cold. Frau Saunders, alone in the seat behind them, was wrapped in a brown Army blanket that hid her mourning from the world. Following the jeep came a little Opel car with its wood-burning motor and small smokestack. In it was the minister to whose church Frau Saunders belonged.

The caravan rode against the tide of the world coming to the center of the city, clanging *Strassenbahns* crammed with workers, olive-drab Army buses; people whose life-rhythm had been broken only by rest and sleep and dreams. The bitter cold of late autumn, the early cold unprepared for and unforeseen, more bitter than the cold of deepest winter, iced the metal jeep and froze the body and mind. Mosca leaned toward Eddie, "You know where the cemetery is?" Eddie nodded. Mosca said emotionlessly, "Let's get there." Eddie swung the jeep to the left and it shot forward, raced down the broad avenue winding in a slow curve through and out of the city. Then on to a little side road and through an open wooden gate and finally rolling slowly to rest on a small lawn before the long deep rows of tombstones.

They sat in the jeep, waiting. Frau Saunders put the blanket aside. She was dressed in a black coat and veiled hat and wore black stockings. Her face was gray as the winter light filtered from the descending sky. Eddie and Mosca were in dark officer greens.

The ambulance came slowly along the rutted road and entered the cemetery gate. It stopped and the driver and his helper got out. Eddie and Mosca went to help them. Mosca saw that they were the two men who had brought Hella to the hospital for childbirth. They had the two rear doors of the ambulance open and as they shoved out the black box, Mosca and Eddie gripped the handles of the end near them.

It was rough wood stained watery black, the handles dull rough iron, the color of the sky. The two ambulance men faced Mosca over the coffin but pretended not to know him. They swung the coffin around so that they would lead. It was very light. They took a path through the scarred and broken tombstones until finally they came to an open pit. Two little round-shouldered Germans in caps and dark jackets rested on their black, heart-shaped spades and watched the coffin being set down near the hole they had made. Behind them was a great pile of raw brown earth.

The little Opel car came through the gate, its smoke-stack pouring a rope of mourning to the sky. The minister came out. He was tall and thin and his craggy face was stern. He walked slowly, slightly bent, dragging his long black robe against the damp earth. He spoke a few words to Frau Saunders and then to Mosca. Mosca kept his eyes on the ground. He could not understand the heavy Bavarian accent.

The stillness of the air was broken by the even, guttural prayer of the minister. He heard the words love and pray and the German word pray was like the word beg, he heard the voice saying forgive forgive and accept accept accept and something of the wisdom and mercy and love of God. Someone gave him a handful of earth, and he threw it before him, heard it strike wood, then heard other little pats of earth. Then he heard great chunks striking like great slow steady heartbeats, growing softer and softer until there was just the inaudible sighing of earth falling on earth, and above the blood pounding in his head, Mosca could hear Frau Saunders weeping.

Finally there were no more sounds. He could hear them moving. He heard the roar of a motor, then another, then the jeep.

Mosca looked up. The mist from the city they had left behind had stolen through the graves and stones. He raised his eyes to the opaque and sunless sky as men raise their eyes to pray. In his heart he cried out, with hatred, impotent anger, "I believe, I believe." Crying out that he believed in the true God, that his vision was clear, that he saw the true tyrannical Father, merciless, pitiless, bathed in blood, drowning in terror and pain and guilt, devoured and consumed by His insane hatred for mankind. In his heart and mind great fissures opened to receive the God he saw and then a pale-gold sun appeared before the curtained sky and forced his eyes to earth.

Across the plain that lay before the city he could see the empty ambulance and the Opel car rising and falling on the bumpy road. The two black spaded men had disappeared. Frau Saunders and Eddie sat in the jeep waiting for him. Frau Saunders had the blanket wrapped around her, hiding her mourning. It was very cold. He motioned that they should leave and watched the olive-drab jeep move slowly through the gate. Frau Saunders turned for a last look, but he could not see her face. Her black veil, heavy threaded and covered with mist, shielded her eyes.

And now alone for the first time Mosca could look at Hella's grave, the mounded earth, the raw brown dirt her body had displaced. He felt no sorrow, only a bewildered sense of loss, as if there was nothing he could ever want to do and no place in all the world he could go. He looked across the open field to where the city began and under whose ruins more bones were buried than would ever fill this prepared and holy ground. The dead winter sun, shrouded in clouds, shed its pale yellow light and Mosca tried to see across the field to his own life and everything he had felt and known. He tried to reach back over a great continent of graves to the games he had played as a child, the streets he had walked in boyhood, the love his mother gave and the face of his father long dead, his first farewell. He remembered his mother always saying, "You have no father but God is your father." And saying, "You have to be extra good because you have no father and God is your father." He tried to reach back and find the love he had felt then, the streams of pity and mercy that hollowed wells for tears.

Seeking pain he thought of Hella, of her face so delicately fragile it exposed blue veins defenseless, without a veil of flesh to death and the world. He thought of her unconscious love springing like magic out of her heart and how fatal it had been, a weakness, in this world a sickness terrible and mortal as unclotting blood.

He walked down the narrow path, past the chipped, scarred tottering tombstones wounded by war. He went out the cemetery gate. Walking toward the city his mind filled with images of Hella, how she had looked when he came back and the love she gave him that he needed to stay alive, the overwhelming relief at finding her so, but now it seemed that even then he had known he would bring her to death and to this grave.

He shook his head. Bad luck, just bad luck, he thought. He remembered the many evenings he had returned for supper and found her asleep on the couch and he would put her to bed and leave and return to find her still asleep, a great deep sleep in which she was safe till morning. Bad luck, he thought again to save himself, but without hope, remembering the cruelty that had taken her away when she was completely alone, without warning, without letting her see or touch the few people she loved.

In the moment before he entered the city he tried to reach the other God, to summon him from the other world, the world his mother lived in, the upright homes, the happy, well-fed children, the virtuous women securely fastened to life with kind men and golden wedding rings. He tried to reach the world rich in drugs to soften nearly every agony, to call forth those great deep shadows of painless memories that might save him now.

And if he could have seen the city beneath him untouched, its skin of stone unlacerated, its flesh firm; and if the sun had shone and the iron sky had bled with light, and if he could have felt some love for the people groping through the shrouded winter ruins, he might have summoned that masked God who shielded his known true face with patient mercy.

Mosca descended the rolling hill to where the paved street began. Now he could not focus his mind on any real image of Hella. Just once in the misted street he thought clearly and nakedly, "It's come to an end." But that too escaped him before he could think of what it meant.

# 24

HE GAVE Frau Saunders money to look after the child and moved back to the billet in Metzer Strasse. In the nights that followed he went to bed early. The parties would be just starting, music and laughter in the rooms around and below him. And he would sleep through it all. But in the night, after the merriment had died and the billet was still and dark, he would come fully awake. He would look at his watch on the night table and it always read one or two o'clock. Then he would lie still, afraid to turn on the lamp because of its depressing, weak yellow light. A little before dawn he would fall asleep again and sleep through the bustle of men preparing and leaving for work. Every night it would be the same. When he woke he would lift up the watch and holding the tiny circle of yellow eyes near his face hoping it would tell him an hour near morning and light. And always he would have to smoke a cigarette and sit against the wooden headboard and prepare himself for the long dark hours he must remain awake. He would listen to the gurgling of pipes, the breathing of the couple in the next room, their drowsy moans and gurgles like death rattles and the muted cries of their somnambulist passion and then the drip of water in the bathroom. There would be little clicks and scraping of floors against walls as if they too were settling for rest. There would be a murmur of a faraway radio sometimes, and then someone alive speaking and footsteps along the hall, and in the street below his window the muted laughter of women as they left the billet. And then as dawn came Mosca would fall asleep and wake in the quiet noon of an empty house, the walls of his room painted pale lemon by winter sunlight.

On one of these afternoons, two weeks after the burial, Mosca heard the quiet broken by footsteps in the hall and then there was a knock. He got out of bed and put on his trousers. He went to the door, unlocked it and pulled it open.

Before him was the face he had seen only once but would never forget. Honny, with his skullcap of yellow hair, his fleshy nose and heavy freckles. Honny smiled and asked, "May I come in?"

Mosca stepped aside, then closed the door. Honny rested his brief case on the table and looked around the room, then said pleasantly to Mosca, "I'm sorry if I woke you."

"I was just getting up," Mosca said.

The little blond man said slowly, "I was sorry, very sorry to hear about your wife." He smiled uncertainly.

Mosca turned and walked to the bed. "We weren't married," Mosca said.

"Ah, so." Honny nervously passed his hand over the bald front of his head until he could feel the reassuring silkiness of the hair further back. "I came to tell you something very important."

Mosca cut in, "I have no cigarettes."

Honny said gravely, "I know you have no cigarettes, that you are not a PX manager, that I know since Wolfgang went back to America."

Mosca smiled at him, "So what."

"No, you misunderstand," Honny said quickly. "I came

to tell you about Yergen. That penicillin he gave you he bought through me. I was the intermediary." He stopped for a moment. "Yergen knew it was defective, he only paid a fraction of the usual price to the contact I gave him. You see?"

Mosca had to sit on the bed. He put his hand on the scar, his stomach hurt. Suddenly he had a great throbbing headache. Yergen, Yergen, he thought, Yergen who had done so much for them, made Hella happy, whose daughter Hella loved. He felt a sick humiliation that Yergen could trick him so and into such sorrow. He bowed his face into his hands.

Honny was speaking again, gently. "I learned you refused to go on with Wolf's scheme. I am not stupid. That means you spared my life. Believe me if I had known that Yergen meant his goods for you I would have stopped him. I learned too late. Yergen was willing to sacrifice me, and he was willing to sacrifice your woman." He saw that Mosca still sat on the bed with his face in his hands and so he said even more softly. "I have good news. Yergen is back in Bremen, in his old place. Your landlady, Frau Meyer sent word to him that all was in order, that he need have no fear."

Mosca stood up from the bed. He said quietly, "You're not lying?"

"No, I do not lie," Honny said. His face had gone dead white and the freckles stood out on his skin like spots of grease. "If you think back, you will know I do not lie."

Mosca went to the wardrobe and unlocked it. He felt himself moving quickly and though his head was aching he felt almost happy. From the wardrobe he took a book of blue American Express checks, signed five of them. They were each for a hundred dollars. He showed them to Honny. "Get Yergen to come here tonight and these belong to you."

Honny backed away. "No, no," he said, "I cannot do that. What made you think I can do that?"

Mosca held out the blue checks and took a step toward him. Honny backed away, murmuring, "No, no I cannot do it." Mosca saw that he would not. He took the man's brief case from the table and gave it to him. "Thanks for telling me, anyway," he said.

Alone, he stood in the center of the room. His head pounded as if a great vein was filling and emptying itself with each giant blood stroke of his heart. He felt a little faint, as if his lungs could not swallow the close air of the room. He finished dressing and left the billet.

Out in the street he was surprised by the warmth of the sun. The early winter that had invaded autumn seemed to have died away. He turned into the Kurfürsten Allee, toward what had been his home, skirting the frail shadows cast by almost bare trees. Except for the headache he felt better than he had felt in a long time. He thought, tonight I'll be able to sleep right through.

He let himself into the apartment very quietly and stood outside the door of the living room. He heard the squeak of a baby carriage, and when he went in he saw Frau Saunders pushing it back and forth. She sat on the sofa, in her left hand a book, her right on the creamy wood of the carriage. She sat straight and calm, a grave acceptance of sorrow upon her strongly lined face. The child in his carriage was asleep. Light blue veins ran through his pink forehead, and tinier veins laced one trembling eyelid into a delicate membrane leaf.

"Is he all right?" Mosca asked.

Frau Saunders nodded. "Everything is well." She freed her hands from the book and the carriage and locked her fingers together.

"Did you get the package I sent?" The week before he had sent her a great carton of food.

She nodded her head again. She looked much older. Mosca recognized something familiar in the way she sat and in the way she answered.

He didn't look at her when he asked, "Can you keep the child indefinitely? I'll pay you well, anything you say." His head felt as if it were swelling with pain, and he wondered if she would have aspirin.

Frau Saunders picked up her book again, held it unopened. The severe face had no touch of the wry humor he always remembered. "Herr Mosca," she said formally, "if you give your consent I will try to adopt your child as my son. That would solve your problem." She said this very coldly, but suddenly the tears streamed down her face. She let the book fall away to the floor and used her hands to hide and stop her tears. And Mosca recognized what he had thought familiar, she was acting like his mother when he gave her pain.

Because she was not his mother and could not really touch him, he walked over to the sofa and rested his hand on her arm for a moment. "What is it, what have I done?" His voice was calm, reasonable.

Her hands had stopped the tears and dried them. She said quietly, "You don't care for the baby, you didn't come once all this time. What if she knew you would be like this? How terrible, how terrible, she loved you both so much. She always said you were good, and when she fell down the stairs she stretched out her arms for the baby. She was in such pain and she screamed, but she thought of the baby. And now you think nothing of what she loved so much." She paused for breath, went on hysterically, "Oh, you are a terrible man, you tricked her, you are not a good man." She leaned away from him and put her two hands on the carriage.

Mosca stepped back and away from her. To help her he said, "What do you think I should do?"

"I know what she would wish. That you take the child to America, give him a safe and happy life so that he will grow old."

Mosca said simply, "We weren't married and therefore the child is German. It would take a long time."

"So," she said eagerly, "I can take care of him until then. You will do it?"

"I don't think I can," he said. And suddenly he was impatient to leave. He was conscious of his headache again.

Frau Saunders was saying in her cold voice, "Do you want me to adopt him?"

He looked at the sleeping baby. He felt nothing. He took the Express checks he had signed from his pocket and left them on the table. "I don't know what will happen," he said. He went to the door.

"When will you come to see your son again?" Frau Saunders' voice was angry. There was contempt in her face. Mosca turned back toward her.

The pain in his head was a great heavy beat, and he wanted to leave, but that look was more than he could bear. "Why don't you speak the truth, why don't you speak what is in your mind?" Not knowing his voice was rising he said, "You think it's my fault, you think she died because I didn't do enough to save her. Tell me the truth. That's why you are so angry, you look at me as if I'm an animal. You believe, 'That American, another German he killed.' Don't pretend you're angry about the child, don't pretend, don't act that lie. I know what you believe."

For the first time Frau Saunders looked at him carefully, directly into his eyes. He looked very ill, his skin was yellow and his eyes were very black, there were angry red splotches forming on his mouth. "No, no," she said. "I never thought so badly." And as she said the words she realized for the first time that he spoke some truth.

But he was under control now. He said quietly, "I'll show you it's not true." He turned and left, she could hear him running down the stairs.

Out in the street he lit a cigarette and looked up at the cloud-filled sky and then down the Kurfürsten Allee. He had nearly smoked the cigarette away before he started walking back to his billet in the Metzer Strasse. The ache in his head was hurting his eyes and the veins in his neck. He looked at his watch. It was only three o'clock. There was still a long time to wait before he could do anything about Yergen.

# 25

HIS ROOM was filled with afternoon shadows. He took some aspirin and lay on the bed. He was surprised at the tiredness he felt. He closed his eyes, it seemed only for a moment, and then he heard a knocking on the door, and opening his eyes he found himself in darkness. He switched on the table light and looked at his watch. It was only six o'clock. There was another knock and then the door was opened, and Eddie Cassin was in the room. He was neatly dressed, shaved and smelled of talcum.

"Christ, you should lock the door when you sleep," he said. Then casually, "How you feeling, wake you up?"

Mosca rubbed his face. "It's O.K.," he said. His headache was gone but his face felt very hot, his lips dry.

Eddie Cassin threw some letters on the table. "Picked up your mail. You got a drink?"

Mosca went to the wardrobe and took out a bottle of gin, then two glasses.

"Big party tonight," Eddie said. "Come on down."

Mosca shook his head, handed him a glass. They both drank. Then Eddie said, "Your orders come in a week. The Adjutant tried to stop it, said it was his fault. The Colonel said no good." He leaned toward Mosca. "Give the word and I'll lose some papers, give you an extra couple of weeks."

"It doesn't matter," Mosca said. He got up from the bed

and looked out the window. There was still some twilight in the streets and he could see a group of children, waiting with unlit lanterns for complete darkness. He remembered hearing their song the last few nights, its softness not shattering the light film of sleep that shielded his brain, not waking him, but seeping through somehow.

Eddie Cassin behind him said, "What about the kid?"

Mosca said, "Frau Saunders, she's keeping him."

Eddie's voice was low. "I'll go see her. Don't worry." He paused. "It's tough, Walter. Guys like you and me are jinxed. Just take it easy."

The children in the street formed two files and marched down the Metzer Strasse and out of sight, their lamps still dark. Eddie said, "Those letters are from your mother. I cabled her. I figured you not to write."

Mosca turned around to face him. "You've been a good friend," he said. "Could you do me one last favor?"

"Sure," Eddie said.

"You never told me Yergen was back in town. I want to see him. Can you get him over here?"

Eddie took another drink and watched Mosca move around the room. There was something wrong, he thought. Mosca had his voice under control, but his eyes were like black mirrors and ever so often a spasm twisted his face into what seemed a second of rage and hatred.

Eddie said slowly, "I hope you're not figuring anything stupid, Walter. The guy made a mistake. It wasn't his fault. Hell, you know Yergen went out of his way for Hella all the time."

Mosca smiled, "Hell, I just want to get back the cigarettes and money I paid for that stuff. Why should I pay?"

Eddie was so surprised and then so relieved that he let out a yelp of relief and joy. "Christ, boy, now you're back to normal. Why the hell should you pay for it?" Back in his mind flashed the thought that this was like Mosca to think of not being cheated, even in his grief. But his relief was genuine. He was glad to see that Mosca had finally come back to normal.

He was struck by an idea. He grabbed Mosca by the arm. "Look," he said, "listen to me. I'm going with Frau Meyer for a week, up to the mountains around Marburg. You come along. I'll get you a girl, a real sweet girl. We'll have lots of laughs, farmer food, liquor. C'mon, say, yes, for a buddy."

Mosca smiled at him. "Sure, O.K.," he said.

Eddie laughed out loud. "That's it, Walter. That's fine. Fine." He slapped Mosca on the shoulder. "We'll leave tomorrow night. Wait till you see those mountains. Beautiful, really beautiful." He paused for a moment and with real affection, almost fatherly, he said, "Maybe we can figure a way to get your kid back to the States with you. That's the thing you know she'd want, Walter. More than anything else." Then with an embarrassed smile, "Come on down. Just for one drink."

Mosca said, "You getting Yergen here for me?"

Eddie looked at him thoughtfully. Mosca said, "The truth is I'm broke, Eddie. I have to leave money with Frau Saunders for the kid. I need dough to go with you to Marburg." He laughed. "Unless you're treating for the whole week." He made his voice quietly sincere. "And I need the money for the trip to the States. That's all there is to it. I paid the guy a small fortune for that stuff."

Eddie was convinced. "Sure, I'll get him," he said. "I'll go right now. And then after you come down to the party. O.K.?"

"Sure," Mosca said.

When Eddie left Mosca looked round the empty room. He saw the letters on the bed, picked one up, and sat down on the bed to read it. When he finished he realized he had not understood a sentence. He went over it again. He tried to connect the words so they would mean something. They wavered through his unfocused mind, filtered through the noises of the billet.

"Please come," his mother wrote, "don't think about anything, please come home. I'll take care of the baby. You can go back to school, you're only twenty-three, I always forget how young you are and for six years you've been away. If you feel bitter now, pray to God, that is the only thing that helps. Your life is beginning . . ."

He threw the letter on the floor and stretched out on the bed. Below him he could hear the parties starting, the soft music and the laughing voices. His headache was beginning again. He switched out the light. The tiny yellow eyes of his watch told him it was six-thirty. He had plenty of time. He closed his eyes.

He thought of how it would be, the return home, seeing his mother and child every day, finding another girl and settling down. Buried inside himself he would carry this other life, his hatred for everything they believed. His life would be a stone over the grave of everything he had ever seen or done or felt. He thought with surprise of what he had shouted at Frau Saunders. It had sprung out of him. He had never even thought such a thing. But now he could see all the mistakes he had made, he forced his mind on to something else.

Drowsily the images formed into Hella carrying the child off the boat and meeting his mother. Then all of them in the living room together, and then every morning, every night, seeing each other's face. He fell asleep.

He dreamed, or thought, a fraction of his brain awake, that he was on his way home, that the sign on the door read, "Welcome Home, Walter," that he had left Hella alive in Germany and on his way home had dreamed a year away. That he had never returned to Hella, that she had not held the gray bread in her hands and let it fall to the floor, that he had opened that other door and Gloria and his mother and Alf were waiting for him, and he had come out of a nightmare to them, and they were in a great flood of light. But then his mother had a bundle of pictures in her hand, and he could see a crib in the corner and the curled back of a sleeping child and he was afraid, and then they were all sitting down and passing photos and mother said Oh what's this and he looked and saw his combat jacket and his blanket skirt and smiling over a mounded grave, That's my third victim he said and laughed and laughed, but Alf was angry and stood on one great tall leg and shouted, That's going too far, Walter, that's going too far. Everybody was standing up and his mother was wringing her hands, and he saw his face saying Good-bye Good-bye and then everything was very dark. But Wolf came with a candle and he was in the cellar with Wolf, and Wolf held his candle high in the air and said, She's not here, Walter, she's not here, and he felt the shifting rubbled floor pulling him down down below the candlelight, and he began to scream.

He was awake and knew he had made no sound. The room was completely dark, the windows painted black by night. Great shrieks of laughter filled the billet. Undulating waves of sound, music, loud male voices, many feet running up and down the stairs. In the room next to his he heard a couple making love. Then the girl saying, "Now, let's go down to the party. I want to dance." The man grumbling, angry. And the girl's voice, "Please, please I want to dance." The sighing of the bed as they rose, then the girl laughing in the hall, and he was in silence and darkness.

Eddie Cassin couldn't help dropping in on the party before he went to Yergen, but he was only a little drunk when he spotted the two young girls. They were not more than sixteen. Dressed exactly alike, in little blue hats, little blue tailored jackets, white parachute-silk blouses, they delighted his eye. Their skin and hair set off their clothes with delicate pinks, creamy whites and there were ringlets like golden coins across their foreheads. They danced with some of the men but refused all drinks and always came together when the music stopped as if they found a virtuous strength in each other.

Eddie watched them for a time, smiling, planning the attack. Then he went to the prettier one and asked her to dance. One of the men said protestingly, "Hey, Eddie, I brought her up here." Eddie said, "Don't worry, I'll fix it."

While dancing he asked her, "Is that your sister?"

The girl nodded. She had a pert little face and on it was the look of frightened haughtiness he understood so well.

"Does she always follow you around?" Eddie asked and his voice was a compliment to her, an invitation to disparage her sister in a gentle way.

The girl smiled with an innocent fatuousness he found charming. She said, "Oh, my sister is a little too shy."

The record ended and he asked, "Would you and your sister like a little supper in my room?" She was immediately frightened and shook her head. Eddie gave her his paternally sweet smile, his delicate face had an almost fatherly understanding. "Oh, I know what you think." He led her to where Frau Meyer was drinking with two men.

"Meyer," he said, "this little girl is frightened of me. She refused my invitation to supper. But if you come and chaperon, I think she will say yes."

Frau Meyer put her arm around the girl's waist, "Oh, you don't worry about him. He is the one good man in the house. I'll come with you. And he has the finest food, food you girls haven't tasted since you were in diapers." The girl blushed and went to call her sister.

Eddie went over to the man who had brought the girl. "It's all fixed," he said. "Go with Meyer to my room. Say I'll be there later." Eddie went to the door. "Save me some," he said laughing, "I'll be back in an hour."

Mosca watched the city from his window. Far away across the plateau of ruins, the heart of the city, he saw a long rope of green and yellow light, an arrow pointing as if drawn, to the blazing windows of the Metzer Strasse. He knew it was the children with their lanterns. But the shouts of laughter, the party noises of music and uneven tread of dancing feet, the small coy shrieks of drunken women, all these drowned what he listened for, the song they sang.

He left the window open and took his shaving kit and towel and went to the bathroom. He left the bathroom door open so that he would hear anyone going to his room.

He washed thoroughly, the water cool on his hot face. Then he shaved, studying the smooth and quiet features, the long thin nose, the long thin mouth with almost color-less lips, the hollow black eyes and dark bronzed skin, gray now with fatigue and splotched with fever sores.

He rinsed the soap off his face and then kept looking at it. He was surprised at how strange it seemed to him, as if he had never really seen it. He turned his head to look at each profile and how the deep eye socket cast shadows over his jaw. He saw the cruelty and evil, the black glints in the dark eyes, the firm and brutal chin. He stepped back, his hand out to cover that mirror face, but surprised, let his hand drop before it touched glass. For a moment he smiled.

In his room it was cold. There was a strange hum in the air. He went to the window and closed it. The hum ceased. The green and yellow lights crossing the ruins were much nearer. He looked at his watch. It was nearly eight o'clock. He felt suddenly weak and feverish, nausea made him sit on the bed. The ache that had been buried by aspirin broke into its steady beat, and with a terrible despair, as if he had lost final hope for salvation, he was sure that Yergen would not come. He felt very cold and went to the wardrobe and put on his old green combat jacket. From an empty cigarette carton he took the Hungarian pistol and slipped it into his pocket. He put all his cigarettes in a small suitcase, then the shaving kit and the nearly full bottle of gin. Then he sat on the bed to wait.

Eddie Cassin parked the jeep in front of the church. He went around the side entrance and up the steps to the steeple. He knocked on the door, there was no answer. He waited, then knocked again. On the other side of the door, Yergen's voice came, unexpectedly clear, "Who is there?"

Eddie said, "It is Mr. Cassin."

Yergen's voice said, "What do you want?"

Eddie Cassin said, "Frau Meyer sent me with a message."

The bolt slid back and the door opened. Yergen stood by it, waiting for him to enter.

The room was dark, except for one little table lamp in the corner, and beneath this lamp, on a small sofa, Yergen's daughter held a book of fairy tales. She rested against great cushions piled against the wall.

"Yes, what is it?" Yergen said. He looked much older, his slight figure was thinner, but his face was still sure, still proud.

Eddie put out his hand. Yergen shook it. Eddie said with a smile, "Come, we've known each other a long time, we've had many a drink together. Is this a way to act with me?"

Yergen smiled reluctantly, "Ah, Mr. Cassin, when I worked in the Metzer Strasse I was a different man. Now—"

Eddie said slowly, sincerely. "You know me, I wouldn't trick you. I've come for your benefit. My friend, Mosca, wants his money and cigarettes back. What he paid for the defective drugs."

Yergen was watching him intently, then said, "Of course, I will do that. But tell him not immediately. I cannot."

Eddie said, "He wants you to come see him tonight."

"Oh, no, oh, no," Yergen said. "I will not go to see him."

Eddie looked at Yergen's daughter lying on the sofa. She had opened her eyes into a wide, blank stare. It made him uncomfortable.

"Yergen," he said, "Mosca and I are leaving tomorrow for Marburg. When we come back he leaves for the States. Now if you don't come to see him tonight, he will come here. If he becomes angry, he will frighten the little girl when he quarrels with you."

As he had known it would, this last argument took effect. Yergen shrugged, then went to get his coat. Then he went to his daughter.

Eddie watched them. Yergen with his heavy fur-collared overcoat and neatly combed brown hair, his look of quiet dignity and seriousness, knelt humbly, sadly, to whisper into his daughter's ear. Eddie knew he was giving her the signal, so that when he returned and knocked on the door, the little girl would slide back the iron bolt. He could see the little girl's blank eyes watching him over her father's shoulder and he thought, what if she forgot the signal, what if she never answered her father's knocking on the door.

Yergen rose, took his brief case and they went out. Yergen paused, waited until he heard on the other side of the door the sound of iron sliding over wood, until he knew that his daughter was locked away from the world.

They got into Eddie's jeep. Once during the ride through the dark streets, Yergen said, "You will stay with me when we meet?" And Eddie said, "Sure, don't worry."

But now in Eddie Cassin rose a vague uneasiness. They drove into the light of the Metzer Strasse and the billet. Eddie parked the jeep and they got out. Eddie looked up. There was no light in Mosca's room. "Maybe he's at the party," Eddie said.

They went into the billet. On the first landing, Eddie said to Yergen, "Wait here." He went into the party but saw no sign of Mosca. When he went out into the hall, Yergen was waiting for him. He could see that Yergen's face was pale, and suddenly Eddie Cassin felt a terrible sense of danger. Through his mind flashed everything Mosca had said and he felt it was all false. He said to Yergen, "Come on, I'll take you home, he's not here. Come on."

Yergen said, "No, let us finish this. I am not afraid. No more—" But Eddie Cassin started to push Yergen down the steps. He was certain, almost overwhelmed with suspicious terror, and then suddenly he heard Mosca's voice above them, cold and with controlled fury say, "You fuckin' Eddie, let him go." Yergen and Eddie looked up.

He stood on the landing above them and in the weak hall light his face was sickly yellow. Two great red fever sores blistered his thin mouth. He stood very still. The green combat jacket seemed to make him bulkier than he really was. "Come on up, Yergen," he said. One hand was hidden behind his back.

"No," Yergen said in an unsteady voice. "I am leaving with Mr. Cassin."

Mosca said, "Eddie, get out of the way. Come up here." Yergen held on to Eddie's arm. "Don't leave me," he said. "Stay here." Eddie held up his hand to Mosca and said, "Walter, for Christ sake, Walter, don't do it." Mosca took two steps down. Eddie tried to pull free from Yergen, but Yergen clutched his arm and cried out, "Don't let me stand alone—Don't, Don't—" Mosca took another step down. His eyes were black, opaque, the red fever sores on his mouth burned in the hall light. Suddenly the pistol was in his hand. Eddie flung himself away from Yergen, and Yergen alone, with a despairing cry tried to turn, tried to run down the stairs. Mosca fired. In his first step Yergen fell to his knees. He raised his head, the faded blue eyes staring upward, and Mosca fired again. Eddie Cassin ran up the steps past Mosca and kept running to the attic.

Mosca put the gun back in his pocket. The body rested flat on the landing, the head dangling over to the descending steps.

From the rooms below came a great wave of laughter, the phonograph began a loud waltz, there began a great stamping of feet and loud yodeling cries. Mosca ran up the stairs quickly to his room. Dark shadows stretched through the window. He waited and listened. He went to the window.

There was no alarm, but the ruins of the city, the great hills of rubble crawled with a mass of brilliantly hued caterpillars, bobbing lanterns that lit the coming winter night with long tracers of green fire. A great rash of sweat poured over his face and body. He began to tremble, a great circling blackness sickened him and he pushed the window open and waited.

Now, in the street below, he could hear the children singing. The lanterns he could not see swung in his mind and heart, and as the choral died away, he felt an extraordinary release from fear and tension. The cold air rushed over him and the sickness and blackness left his body.

He picked up the packed suitcase and ran down the stairs, over Yergen's body, past the party noises. Nothing had changed. Out of the billet he started walking across the black plateau of ruins, then turned for one last look.

Four great stages of light cast a burning shield against the darkness of the city and the night and from each tier came a long rolling wave of music and laughter. He stood outside that shield of light feeling no remorse, only thinking that he would never see his child or Eddie Cassin, his country or his family again. He would never see the mountains around Marburg. Finally he had become the enemy.

Far across the ruins, toiling upward toward the black and falling winter sky he could see the green and red of the children's lanterns, but he could no longer hear their song. He turned away from them and walked toward the *Strassenbahn* that would take him to the railroad station.

It was all familiar to him, the farewells to time and place and memory, and he felt no sorrow, no desolation, that finally there was no one, no human being to speed him on his way, only the wind which swept across the ruined continent he could never leave. Before him he saw the round bright glare that was the headlight of the *Strassenbahn* and heard the cold crystal clanging of its bell. Out of habit he began to run to catch it, the suitcase bumping against his leg, but after a few steps halted, knowing it made no difference whether he caught this one or the next.

# Omertà

## Mario Puzo

Omertà, the Sicilian code of silence, has been the cornerstone of the Mafia's sense of honour for centuries. Born in the Sicilian hills, omertà carried the Mafia through a century of change, but now at the century's end it is becoming a relic from a bygone age. Honour may be silent – but money talks.

New York – a mob boss is assassinated. His nephew and the head of the city's FBI both launch investigations into the murder. But silence spreads like a contagion: the silence of rival gangs, the silence of crooked bankers, even the silence of the courts. However, the world of the Mafia is one without integrity, and driven with greed. And when the money starts to talk . . .

'Hugely effective fiction . . . [Puzo] keeps his pact with readers to unfailingly deliver the goods'
*Literary Review*

'Here is all the classic material of Mafia mythology . . . Spins a spell all of its own'
*The Times*

'Puzo's genius was to create a world so thick with personality and acknowledged rules of behaviour, along with its crime and violence, that reading his books becomes a seriously guilty pleasure'
*New York Post*

arrow books

# *Fools Die*

## Mario Puzo

Within the interconnecting worlds of bigtime gambling, publishing and the film industry, the power of corruption and the corruption of power are nowhere better explored. From New York to Las Vegas, Merlyn and his brother Artie obey their own code of honour in the ferment of contemporary America, where law and organised crime are one and the same . . .

'Fame and wealth, skulduggery and cheating and pimping, love affairs and carnal arrangements, one scene following another pell-mell, all written with unflagging vitality . . . bawdy, comic, highly coloured, hypnotic. It would be a very cool reader indeed who did not devour the whole mixture greedily'
*New York Times*

'Curruptly compulsive'
*Daily Express*

'Unforgettable . . . will rivet your attention'
*Cosmopolitan*

arrow books

# *The Family*

## Mario Puzo

'We are a family,' Alexander told his children. 'And the loyalty of the family must come before everything and everyone else. We must learn from each other, protect each other, and be bound first and foremost to each other. For if we honour that commitment, we will never be vanquished – but if we falter in that loyalty, we will all be condemned . . .'

What is a family? Mario Puzo first answered that question, unforgettably, in his landmark bestseller *The Godfather*; with the creation of the Corleones he forever redefined the concept of blood loyalty. Now, thirty years later, Puzo enriches us all with his ultimate vision of the subject, in a masterpiece that crowns his remarkable career: the story of the greatest crime family in Italian history – the Borgias.

'Head-long entertainment, bubbling over with corruption, betrayal, assassinations, Richter-scale romance, and, of course, family values'
*Time*

'Dazzling, passionate, a masterwork that ranks with Puzo's best.'
Nicholas Pileggi

'Pure Puzo'
*New York Daily News*

arrow books